PREACHER RAISES
THE DEAD

PRAISE FOR THE EVAN WYCLIFF MYSTERY SERIES
MULTIPLE-AWARD-WINNING NOVELS

This is literature masquerading as a mystery. Carefully yet powerfully, Gerald Jones creates a small, stunning world in a tiny midwestern town, infusing each character with not just life but wit, charm, and occasionally menace. This is the kind of writing one expects from John Irving or Jane Smiley.

— MARVIN J. WOLF, AUTHOR OF THE RABBI BEN MYSTERIES, INCLUDING *A SCRIBE DIES IN BROOKLYN*

This is an excellent read. Such an engaging storyteller! It really sucked me in. That last page did cause a triple-take, quadruple-take, and whatever comes after, up to about eight. Jones is definitely one of my favorite authors.

— JOHN RACHEL, AUTHOR OF *BLINDERS KEEPERS* AND *THE MAN WHO LOVED TOO MUCH*

Preacher Finds a Corpse is an absolute pleasure to read. Reminiscent of Charlaine Harris's mysteries and Barbara Kingsolver's early novels like *Animal Dreams* and *The Bean Trees*, it's full of quirky characters who animate the small town in which they live. Evan Wycliff is a complex and compelling protagonist, conflicted and lost in his own life but nevertheless fiercely dedicated to uncovering the truth about his friend Bob Taggart's death.

Jones manages to infuse a deceptively simple story with suspense, angst, and whimsy, as well as surprise. His command of setting, history, and behavior is beyond exceptional. I can't wait for the next book in the series.

— PAULA BERINSTEIN, AUTHOR OF THE AMANDA LESTER DETECTIVE SERIES AND HOST OF "THE WRITING SHOW" PODCAST

As anyone who's spent time in a small town the American Midwest knows, there's a lot more going on behind the scenes than you'd expect. Or suspect. And there are plenty of suspects in the latest Evan Wycliff mystery by Gerald Everett Jones. *Preacher Fakes a Miracle* haunted my dreams as I read it, in the way that a good story about a bad situation should. I'm looking forward to reading the next installment of the Evan Wycliff mystery series.

— PAMELA JAYE SMITH, *MYTHWORKS,* AWARD-WINNING WRITER-DIRECTOR-PRODUCER

A fast-moving mystery with twists and surprises that take you in unexpected directions. Jones is adept at creating unique and fascinating characters. His mystery sleuth is a part-timer with lots of heart who splits his time between religion, skip tracing and sometimes the metaphysical. The hero's search for a missing girl and his interactions with various eccentric individuals in the small town make him both sympathetic and compelling. A bit of a shock to learn what's really going on with the abducted young unwed mother... and amazing how it relates to real stories in the news today.

— M.J. RICHARDS, COAUTHOR OF *DISHONOR THY FATHER*

PREACHER RAISES THE DEAD

AN EVAN WYCLIFF MYSTERY

GERALD EVERETT JONES

LaPuerta Books and Media www.lapuerta.tv Email: bookstore@lapuerta.tv

The novel in this book is a work of fiction. Names, characters, places, and incidents either are products of the author's imagination or are used fictitiously. Any resemblance to actual events or locales or persons, living or dead, is entirely coincidental.

Throughout this book, the author has attempted to distinguish proprietary trademarks from descriptive terms by following the capitalization style used for the brand by the mark owner.

Trade paperback ISBN: 978-1-7359502-5-9

Ebook ISBN: 978-1-7359502-6-6 / Kindle ASIN: B09PH1BWSM

Library of Congress Control Number: 2022900099

LaPuerta is an imprint of La Puerta Productions www.lapuerta.tv

Design by La Puerta Productions

Editor: Jason Letts

Author photo: Gabriella Muttone Photography, Hollywood

"The Sea Hath Its Pearls" poem by Heinrich Heine (1799-1856), translated by Henry Wadsworth Longfellow (1807-1882) [PD]

"Orpheus and Eurydice" poem by Edward Burrough Brownlow (1857-1895) [PD]

Aquarian Gospel 178:43, *The Aquarian Gospel of Jesus the Christ,* Leo W. Dowling (aka Levi, 1844-1911), 1907 [PD]

For Pearl

PART I

Appleton City, Missouri,

eight months into the pandemic…

1

___

Evan Wycliff didn't consider Stuart Shackleton his personal adversary, but the investment banker certainly was his nemesis. Every time the fellow made a request of Evan, it led the preacher into a nest of snakes. And now, as a result of Evan's curious meddling into matters that needn't concern him, Shackleton was behind bars pending trial on a charge of first-degree murder. If this unscrupulous man were convicted, perhaps the unhappy consequences of his schemes would soon be at an end.

It was the height of the pandemic. The balmy spring weather in southern Missouri at least offered more opportunities for holed-up families to venture outside and greet their neighbors. Here in the courtroom, fewer than half the participants were wearing masks. State government hadn't mandated wearing them, and Evan well knew that whether on or off was pretty much a badge of political affiliation. Predictably, the defendant wasn't masked. He had friends and connections in Jeffersonville. Evan had one on, and his reputation as science apologist to his church congregation required him to set an example. Now that he was pastor, those pressures were wearing him down.

Despite what I think and advise, if all of the folks were wearing masks, it would look like a convocation of the Klan in here.

The alleged murder of Father Michael Coyle of Flat Bank Catholic Charities had occurred more than a year ago. As the pretrial of the case had dragged on, Shackleton was in jail because he was a flight risk. A guy with all that money and access to private jets would have to be.

So it was ironic in the extreme when last evening Shackleton's attorney Bertram Harrison phoned Evan and urged him to pay a compassionate visit to Ann Shackleton because her husband was in lockup.

"She's in a bad way," Harrison had told him, perhaps saying all he knew about it.

Evan had never visited the assisted-living wing of the Myerson Clinic. He'd certainly had enough to do with the adolescent treatment and rehab programs when he'd counseled Shackleton's teenage son Luke. He was struck by the signage on the building: *Myerson Memory Center.* True, many if not all of its patients were challenged with dementia, but he doubted whether the focus of treatment was improving or even recapturing their memories. Now he was here to see Ann because presumably her husband was worried about her, but the reasons were still unclear. Before erstwhile pastor Rev. Marcus Thurston had retired, regular compassionate visits had been part of his routine. Now Evan realized making those rounds would fall to him.

Thurston had served as the first black minister of a predominantly white congregation in this farmland community. Evan could only imagine how difficult it had been for him, especially in the early days of his service. And as long as Evan had known him, the old pastor had been wise about knowing when to keep his mouth shut. And perhaps fortunately for his sanity, he'd retired before the onset of Covid. On public health policies since that time, he'd expressed no opinions, while agreeing privately with the deacons when they decided worship services should be suspended.

Amid governmental confusion over pandemic policies, local medical facilities and assisted-living centers in this state were still permitting compassionate visits, counseling family members to come less often and to distance themselves when they did. As a member of the clergy, Evan was permitted everywhere except inside an ICU, but he had to wear both a mask and a plastic face shield as well as answer a checklist of health questions to gain admission to each facility.

Before she'd slipped into dementia in recent years, Ann Shackleton had been a devout Catholic. She might not know or care about Evan's denomination, but it baffled him why Stuart Shackleton should be so eager to enlist a Baptist minister — especially Evan — for this personal mission.

What about her home church? Do they even know I'm involved?

When he asked after Ann Shackleton at the desk, Lucille, the receptionist, looked puzzled. The petite girl was so young she might be an intern. Her head was a mass of carrot-colored hair and blue-paper mask, with her eyes just peeking out, so her confusion was a perceptible squint. Rather than waving Evan through, she advised him to go back to Urgent Care and take a seat in the waiting room. After what seemed a long delay there, a registered nurse came out to greet him. Her badge identified her as Ornette Wheeler. She was middle-aged and slender, with a gaunt face the color of cocoa and more than a lifetime's share of worry lines. She'd been sweating so much the perspiration was fogging her face shield.

When he introduced himself, she also looked puzzled, asking, "Reverend, may I ask the purpose of your visit? The priest has only just left, and I must tell you it's been a difficult few hours."

"The priest?"

"Father Vasquez from All Saints," she sighed, adding in a subdued tone, "he'd come to give her the last rites at two this morning, but she went too quick."

"Oh, my," Evan said, regretting right away he hadn't asked more questions of Harrison. "I assume someone has informed her husband."

"The contact information we have at the nursing station is for his lawyer. Last night I let Mr. Harrison know she was having arrhythmia, but she's had those episodes before. Then early in the morning, as I say, she got very much worse, very fast. There's always a priest on-call, but by then all we got for the lawyer at that hour was voicemail."

I doubt you know I'm her son's guardian, but did his mother even know the boy exists?

The situation with Luke would be too complicated to explain just now. All Evan could think to say was, "I wasn't aware of the urgency. I should have come earlier. I've come too late."

"No," Nurse Wheeler assured him, "I wouldn't say that. I wouldn't say that at all."

"I don't follow."

"You see, we thought we'd lost her. Actually, we *did* lose her. She'd been in a-fib through the evening. We medicated — but suddenly, arrest. She coded, the team tried to resuscitate her, but she stayed flat-line. The doctor called it, and the team left the room. I sent a pickup order to the morgue. But evidently miracles do happen. I don't know how, but when they came to get her, she was back! Sitting up and chattering like a jaybird!" The nurse shook her head as if wondering whether she'd imagined it all.

"How is she now?"

"That's the thing. Before this, she was withdrawn. She has hardly said a word to anyone for months. Listless, low appetite. After a serious episode like this, we'd expect to keep her in ICU for a while. But today she's sitting up and running on like a motor mouth! She's not making much sense, which is her way, but she's acting like she's got a new lease on life!" This usually stoic nurse seemed close to grateful tears.

Evan asked cautiously, "May I see her? This may not be the time…"

"She's negative for Covid, so this cardiac episode is unrelated. The night-shift attending has gone home. The resident is here, but he wasn't on the floor when she coded. Me, my shift was over an hour ago, but I really want to be sure she's stabilized. You shouldn't stay long, especially if it makes her more agitated. We'd give her a sedative, but all that adrenalin right now might actually be what's sustaining her. So I'm thinking, if seeing you might help her calm down, it could be just the thing. If it's all right, I can stay in the room — I'll give you a nod if it's not working."

"Actually, she doesn't know me at all, so I don't expect she'll be telling me anything you shouldn't hear. I'm a friend of the family. Her husband is indisposed, which is why you had to go through Mr. Harrison. I want to give Stuart a report, but if this is not the time, I won't stay."

IT WAS JUST past eight in the morning. Ann Shackleton was indeed sitting up in bed in a private room. There were oxygen tubes in her nostrils, and she was hooked up to a heart monitor, which was displaying a steady sinus rhythm.

"Doctor!" she declared as Evan entered the room with Ornette. The patient's cheeks were rosy, her eyes were sparkling blue, and her hair was a mass of white curls. Evan calculated she should be in her mid-fifties, but because of the effects of her long-term illness, he'd always thought she looked much older. Today she seemed vital and didn't look at all like an invalid who had been anywhere near death's door.

"Doctor of Divinity, actually," Evan muttered as he sat. "I'm Reverend Wycliff from Evangel Baptist. Stuart asked me to call on you." Nurse Wheeler stood next to the bed and gently took Ann's arm by the wrist with her gloved hand as if taking her pulse. The monitor's electronics were already doing that, but Evan guessed the nurse thought her touch might be comforting to the patient, and it was her excuse to linger by the bed.

"Stuart. Stuart. Stuart. Stuart," Ann tsked, with a pronounced lisp. "That man will be the death of me. But not yet!"

And of how many others? Wait — innocent until proven guilty!

"He's had some life challenges of his own recently," Evan offered. "I'm sure he'll want to see you as soon as he can put things in order."

"You know, doctor," the woman insisted, "my left arm was hurting s-s-something awful. And pressure on my ches-s-st! But now I'm breathing easier. What did you give me? Must be good s-s-s-tuff!"

Evan realized her hissing lisp was because several of her upper teeth were missing.

Ornette interjected, "We gave you medicine to keep your heart beating steadily. You're doing fine now. But you need your rest. The Reverend can't stay long."

Evan thought to ask Ornette, "Does Mrs. Shackleton perhaps have a denture? She might be more comfortable talking if she can have it."

"Oh, I'm so sorry!" Ornette exclaimed. "In all the excitement last night I forgot where I put it."

She started to open the drawer to the bedside table when Mrs. Shackleton shouted, "Not in there. You put it in my slippers, dear."

Evan looked where Ann was pointing to see a pair of fuzzy pink slippers near his elbow, perched on the radiator. The slippers were monogrammed with the patient's initials, AKS, except the S was larger and in the middle, spelling *ASK*.

Now, there's an omen.

Evan was startled to hear Nurse Wheeler gasp as she rushed over to grab the slippers. She shoved her hand inside to retrieve Ann's dental bridge, removed it from its clear plastic bag, and quickly handed it over. Ann shoved the denture in, and her face lit up in a broad smile. Having all her teeth certainly made her prettier. Also tucked inside one of the slippers was gold jewelry, which Ann clutched at eagerly, perhaps not realizing her watch and wedding rings had also been missing.

"And put those slippers back on me," Ann commanded, this time with no lisp. "My feet are cold."

The nurse turned the covers down, replaced the slippers, and tucked the patient in. Then she turned to Evan and whispered, "Could we have a word outside?"

Ornette looked solemn, and she was shaking. Evan couldn't imagine what had transpired in the last few moments to upset her so.

As Evan got up to follow the nurse out, he said to Ann, "We'll have a longer visit when you're feeling better. Is there anything you'd like me to bring you?"

She flashed him a girlish grin and replied, "You always tell me I already have all that I need, Father."

First I'm the doctor, now I'm the priest. Yet she seems to know her husband's name.

"Wise words," Evan agreed.

She must think I'm her parish priest. I wonder whether he was the one who came to give her the rites.

In the hallway just outside Mrs. Shackleton's room, Nurse Wheeler grabbed Evan's arm as if clutching him for support.

"What's the matter?" he asked her. "Are *you* feeling okay? I suppose it's been an ordeal."

She responded breathlessly, "I removed her slippers, then I removed her denture. And her watch and her rings. I was gathering her personal effects. Procedure is to bag them before they come to take her to the morgue. But I didn't have a bag handy, so I just set them aside."

"What are you trying to tell me?"

"She couldn't have seen me do it! She'd been clinically dead for fourteen minutes!"

2

E van had wanted to march right back into Ann Shackleton's room and ask her to tell him about her near-death experience, but Nurse Wheeler advised him to make it another time, explaining that asking the patient to relive the event now might stir emotions and jeopardize her recovery. He'd read about out-of-body consciousness, but he'd never known anyone who'd experienced it. Encountering it this morning didn't shake Evan's faith. If anything, it could confirm it. Life after death? Sure. Granted Ann in her demented state would almost certainly be an unreliable narrator, but the nurse — however stressed she might have been from these events — seemed to have a firm grip on reality.

Was it a lucky guess? But Ann insisted she saw *where Ornette put it.*

Evan had no current phone number for Shackleton, who wasn't allowed to have one while he was in jail. So he called Harrison to give him the surprising news but had to leave voicemail. Evan was aware that Shackleton's arraignment hearing was scheduled for this morning at 11 a.m. He fully intended to be there.

~

EVAN'S WORKDAY was just beginning, and he'd had no breakfast. He'd just managed a quick cup of coffee, but there was no one to help him eat a stack of his favorite banana sweetcakes, even if he was willing to take the time to whip them up. Stores were open for patrons who took precautions, and Loretta had set out in their big black Lincoln Navigator at first light, saying she had shopping errands to run for the Loving Embrace committee. Luke had already made himself his obligatory bowl of oatmeal, walnuts, banana, and soy milk, hunching over his laptop as he readied himself for a session with his math tutor, the geek-for-hire Walter Engstrom. For now, Luke had to be home-schooled not only because of the pandemic but also because the high school offered no advance-placement courses in either calculus or physics. Even so, the administration wasn't yet sure they were ready to admit a student who depended regularly on a cocktail of psychoactive drugs to "maintain," as his caregivers put it.

Evan drifted back to his habitual hangout, the C'mon Inn on Main Street, where he expected regulars would always be welcomed unless they had the sniffles. Even though he'd promised Zip Zed he'd trade in the thing, Evan persisted in driving the robin's-egg-blue Cinquecento that the car dealer had loaned him "because no one else in these parts will ever want it." As Evan took his usual place at the counter, his wise confidante and counselor Coralie Angelides was ready, immediately pouring from her Pyrex pot of Farmer Brothers, which seemed permanently attached to her hand.

"Where you been?" she quipped as she poured.

"Why, laboring in the fields of the Lord," Evan shot back.

She giggled. "Gimme a break! What's the matter? That cocktail waitress of yours don't know how to make them pancakes you like so much?"

"Those are healthy, aren't they?"

Cora scoffed. "Just Satan's way of getting you to eat white flour, sugar, and butter. They say the good die young, but you're lookin' mighty fit, Rev!"

Coralie, you never believed in Satan. I even wonder whether angels have to believe in God. Maybe they just take orders, as you do, no questions asked.

Evan had the build of a football player, although one who in his retirement had never met a meal he didn't like. He'd promised Loretta he'd be more careful about his diet, but he regarded the C'mon as a retreat and a throwback to his old ways. As for Cora's teasing, Loretta's rapid transition from a career in hospitality at a casino to being a pastor's wife was a topic of amused conversation around town. It wasn't that anyone judged his lovely bride unsuitable for the role. If anything, in Evan's opinion, she was far too conscientious about both looking and acting the part. Loretta now preferred simple jersey dresses in either plain black or navy, with prim, white-lace collars. Hem length past the knees with black hose and "sensible" pumps. Evan feared that look had gone out of style even before there was a Walmart to sell it. And then wearing her long hair drawn back in a bun with a pair of rimless granny glasses (which she only needed for reading) completed the ultraconservative outfit.

If I see her carrying one of those Bibles with a zippered leather cover, I'll tell her she's gone too far.

Cora liked to tease because, if it hadn't been for Loretta, she might have broken it off with Clint Everly and made an all-out play for the preacher. Which at the time he might not have resisted.

"In truth, Loretta's off doing I-don't-know-what-all, and I've just come from Myerson, where I checked in on Ann Shackleton. She had a heart attack last night, but they brought her around."

Cora leaned forward and said in a hushed, conspiratorial tone, "You mean you raised that woman from the dead."

Oh, this is already getting way out of hand!

"I did nothing of the kind. They must've used the paddles on her, and she was alive and kicking before I even got there, before I even knew she was in danger." Then Evan grew suspicious, "And, by the way, how would you know all this?"

"Clint phoned me. Not much goes on over there he don't know — and don't tell me."

Cora's boyfriend Clint gave the appearance of a bald-headed wrestler. He was an orderly in the adolescent-treatment wing at Myerson. He brought both muscle and a cool head to the job. When Luke Shackleton was in treatment there for what the physicians theorized was schizophrenia, Clint was just about the only member of staff who cut the boy a break now and then.

"Yes, I'll have those pancakes," Evan said, hoping he could change the subject.

"With sausage?"

"No. You've told me to cut out the grease."

She grinned in triumph, asking playfully, "Well, then, how about margarine and sugar-free syrup to go with?"

"Don't push it, Cora," Evan teased back. Then he insisted, "And don't advertise that rumor. This isn't the first time you've repeated the rumor I'm a faith healer."

As she scribbled on her order pad, she tossed back, "And it's not the first time trouble has been followin' you around."

A RAP of the gavel changes a life, changes in an instant a whole network of life paths. Creates, as the quantum math suggests, a branching of myriad alternative realities. Rev. Evan Wycliff understood the math as theory but didn't grant the possibility of alternatives. To him and this little farm community, there was only one — the here and now. And at times it seemed more than a modest cleric could bear.

This morning in the St. Clair County courthouse, the murder charge against Stuart Shackleton was summarily dismissed. Insufficient evidence. The arguments of his high-priced defenders had ensured that the case would never go to trial.

Shackleton's attorneys had delayed and delayed, and pretrial discovery had failed to turn up conclusive evidence. During that time, daytime skip tracer and part-time preacher Evan Wycliff had succeeded Rev. Marcus Thurston as pastor of Appleton City's Baptist church. Never mind that he hadn't yet been ordained. Thurston informed him that, under the rules of the Southern Baptist Convention, the sitting pastor had the authority to confer an ordination as long as the board of deacons concurred.

However, a sizable faction of the church's membership did not welcome Evan as their new pastor. Many disapproved of his occasionally agnostic-sounding sermons, his insistence that science and theology could coexist, his urging them during the pandemic to get vaccinated as soon as the shots were available, to wear masks indoors, and — not least — his choice of a presumably fallen woman in matrimony. Some persisted in circulating the rumor that he could work miracles, which connoted *faith healer* and therefore *charlatan*. And the fact that Loretta's unlucky sister Melissa suffered from epilepsy could be, according to some spiteful gossips, evidence of demonic possession.

Perhaps another reason for the defection was that Evan had begun holding Sunday worship services online. As a rule, members of the congregation who had school-age children had access to their kids' computers. Many more at least had a smartphone. The defectors tended to lack digital devices and also to be highly suspicious of the internet.

Soon after Thurston ordained Evan, the objecting faction broke away from the church and formed a new congregation, Calvary Baptist, in a former one-room schoolhouse in Rockville. Followers of Marcus and Evan renamed their church *Evangel Baptist* — over Evan's objection. He wasn't confident enough in his own faith to see his mission as evangelical, and he disliked the implication that the new community had somehow been named after him. But it was certainly a sneering message to the Calvary folks whose side Evan's loyalists were on.

And since Evan had, also over his own objections, won a reputation as the preacher who could work miracles, his loyalists were steadfast in their support. (This was even before rumors began circulating about Ann Shackleton's resurrection.) Evan wasn't at all sure he wanted or was ready to take the job, but his new responsibilities as husband and child guardian required him to have a more reliable income.

Seated among the attendees at what should have been the first day of the investment banker's trial, Evan lamented to himself that so many of the recent major challenges in his life and ministry had begun and ended with Stuart Shackleton.

Except, after this judge's abrupt ruling, Evan feared the most recent chain of pain wouldn't be over.

I should've known I wasn't done with him.

As various interested parties cleared out of the courtroom amid hushed buzzings of amazement, Evan saw Shackleton's attorney Bertram Harrison striding toward him. The tall, silver-haired gentleman in the obligatory three-piece suit looked less like a country lawyer, more like a distinguished advocate who was ready to argue a case before the Supreme Court — which indeed he had done with success on other occasions. He was the senior partner of an old-line firm in St. Louis, and Evan had every reason to worry this wasn't the last he'd be seeing of this dapper fellow and his Ivy-League charm.

Shackleton, who had been seated at the defendant's table, had already disappeared through the door by the jury box. As Harrison drew near Evan, the lawyer gently laid a hand on his forearm and said quietly, "Reverend, Stuart would like a private word with you."

It might not be only about Ann. Maybe he wants custody of Luke — while he's up to his old tricks trying to steal the Emmett farm. And what about little Buzz? Surely he can't manage care of his grandson on his own.

Wondering whether he was about to be rebuked or challenged, Evan followed Harrison out the same door Shackleton had taken and into a paneled conference room that adjoined the judge's chambers.

Perhaps because he was accustomed to chairing board meetings at

Bates Bank and convocations of his brethren at the Masonic lodge in Osceola, Shackleton sat calmly at the head of the long table.

He'd already managed to change from prison jumpsuit into his habitual aristo business attire. He was fondling his new phone, another privilege of his new freedom.

Evan took a seat at acceptable social distance on Shackleton's left side. Harrison was about to seat himself on the right, but the banker waved him away, saying to the lawyer, "Don't worry, Bert. I won't say anything to incriminate myself." And the fellow left the room.

How can he be so sure? Should I be recording this?

In the awkward pause that followed, Shackleton stared frankly into Evan's eyes as if trying to read whether the preacher were friend or foe. Evan was at a loss, the emotions of the morning having encompassed revivals of the just and the unjust. Evan removed his mask, hoping exposing his face wouldn't telegraph his contempt for the man.

I won't be the one to speak first, no matter how embarrassing the silence.

Finally, Shackleton announced, "I need you to know I didn't kill Father Coyle."

Amazing and stunning and hardly believable.

Evan was shocked that the banker wasn't more concerned about his ailing wife. "What about Ann? I assume by now you've heard she's out of the woods. But what more do you want me to do? And so far I haven't told Luke. Should I take him to see her? I know all of this has come on you so suddenly, but…"

Shackleton drew a long breath, then explained, "Ann has not been herself for a very long time. It's crass to say she's already dead to me, but I must be honest. Especially with you. As for Luke, as his condition got worse, I wouldn't allow him to see her. She didn't recognize him — she can't really identify anyone anymore — and it would infuriate him. The last time — this was before he was admitted to the clinic — he raged at her. He was red-faced, in tears. And of course his anger upset her terribly. She didn't understand why this strange kid was screaming at her. So, you see, there was nothing to be done."

Evan said, "But when I saw her this morning, she seemed calm, even knew your name. She said you'd be the death of her, which I believe she meant as something of a joke. Sorry to be the messenger, but you should know."

"Dementia can have its own sense of humor," Shackleton said dryly. "But thank you for looking in on her."

No mention of Luke? Or his grandson? I'm not going to push it.

"I believe Ann had what's called a near-death experience," Evan told him. "Medically, she'd been pronounced dead, and then she revived unexplainably. They say her heart had stopped for fourteen minutes, which is twice the estimated safe revival time without brain damage. And yet she seems to be alert, maybe even more than before. If you don't mind, I'd like to speak more with her about it, also ask her care-givers what else they can tell me."

"Would you say your visit upset her? Who did she think you were?"

"First she must have thought I was one of her doctors, then she addressed me as a priest. Nurse Wheeler told me Father Vasquez had been summoned to give Ann the last rites, but I don't think he was able to go through with it."

"We don't know him. If you're not upsetting her, she might enjoy your visits. I can assure you I won't be going over there," Shackleton said tersely, frowning before he went on. "You ministered to my son when I asked you. And you've helped him heal, whether you say it was a miracle or not. You've befriended him, and now you've taken him and my grandson into your own home, into your family. If things had gone the other way in there this morning, they might've been living with you indefinitely."

Will he want them to live with him now? Luke won't want that.

Toddler Robert was Luke's son — Stuart Shackleton's grandson. To everyone he was Baby Buzz and perhaps would be into his teens.

Melissa was the mother, but she couldn't care for him while she was in treatment for outrages that had been visited upon her — not by Shackleton but almost certainly by his partners in crime.

"Luke and Buzz are both doing very well," Evan had to admit. "But what happens now? Are you saying you want custody?"

"I'm not saying that at all," Shackleton said soberly. "I can't think that far ahead. All I know is, you're a much better influence on Luke than I could ever be. And I believe he trusts you. Frankly, I haven't earned the right. Can we give it some time? I know it's asking a lot."

"I'm not disparaging you as a father, but Luke and Buzz are family now, and Loretta and I will continue to do whatever we can for them. There are decisions to be made when Melissa can come home, of course. I can imagine you need to put your own house in order. Please, as far as we're concerned, things are fine as they are."

I'm making it sound like an offer, but it's more of a request. A demand, actually.

"You're right," Shackleton said, seeming relieved. "I'll be retiring from the bank, perhaps from my leadership of the Lodge as well. I plan to manage my personal investments. Nothing more to do with those Russians, of course." He sighed and added, "I don't know where I stand with Edie. She seemed willing to take the risk I could go to jail for some slick real-estate deal, but when she suspected I had dealings with Churpov, the possibility we might both be shot in our beds was a bit much. Last I heard, she was back with her sister in Scottsdale."

Edith Taggart had been wife to Evan's best friend Bob, who had killed himself two years ago. Evan doubted Bob had known about the affair. Evan's informal investigation of the tragedy had uncovered that Bob had other reasons for ending his life.

Evan hesitated before offering, "We could pray you'll be wise about what to do next."

Shackleton chuckled, "I'm not sure I'm ready for that. Especially if it involves repentance." He paused carefully before he added, "But there is one more thing."

The banker reached into his coat pocket, pulled out a long envelope, and shoved it across the table to Evan.

What's this? It had better not be something for me to sign.

The envelope was unsealed. Opening it, Evan found Shackleton's signed power of attorney for matters involving the health and welfare of both his wife and his son and his grandson, along with a cashier's check for $50,000 made out to the church for "benefit of the building fund."

Evan had to look at the check twice to believe the number. He protested, "But we don't have plans to build. We're already at the limit on that lot, and the sanctuary is in good repair."

Shackleton smirked playfully and said, "I understand the parsonage is in need of substantial renovation."

3

I ndirectly, Reverend Wycliff had been Stuart Shackleton's principal accuser. Fr. Michael Coyle had been found dead in his office at the Sisters of Mercy children's home. He was known to have had a chronic heart condition, and a bottle of angina pills was found spilled in front of him where he had expired at his desk.

But on inspecting photos from the coroner's autopsy report as directed by Sheriff Chester Otis, Evan had pointed out an anomalous detail, offering its interpretation along with the inference that the priest had died — not of natural causes but "at the hands of another." Someone, presumably an attacker, had smudged an ashen cross on the forehead between and just above the eyebrows. And at the center of those marks was a wound that farm-boy Wycliff identified as burn marks from an electric cattle prod.

An inconvenient complication in the case was that the device, if it was indeed the murder weapon, had never been found. And the evidence that Shackleton had been the intruder — much less, the attacker — was circumstantial. The only witness was the elderly Sister Margaret, who was hard of hearing and had been stationed at the convent's reception desk that morning. The nun thought she'd heard a motorcycle pull up outside, then a rider dressed in black and wearing a helmet that covered his face had entered the administrator's office, emerging just minutes later and carrying the same briefcase he'd brought.

Sister Margaret hadn't been concerned about seeing this stranger because Father had previously informed her that he was expecting a courier.

It was Evan who later informed Sheriff Otis that he'd encountered Shackleton on that same day dressed in similar all-black riding attire as he showed off his new Ducati Superleggera motorcycle.

As EVAN SAT with Shackleton wondering what he should do with that check, the banker said with a shrug, "I admit I paid Coyle a visit. I was supposed to pick up the papers authorizing Churpov's guardian-ship of Melissa Benton. And Coyle was expecting a check for his placement fee. But the guy must have had a change of heart, so to speak, because he refused to give me the document. He pitched a fit, we argued, he gulped down some pills, and I walked out of there without giving him the check, which I'm sure pissed him off even more."

If that's not incriminating, it's at least suggestive, maybe not of murder, but of his role in Churpov's trafficking schemes.

"Are you saying he was alive when you left him?" Evan asked.

"Alive with his Irish full up," Shackleton replied with no sign of remorse.

"And what about the marks on his forehead?"

"Harrison had the medical examiner's photos in the case file, and I had a good look at them. There was nothing like that on him when I left."

Evan suggested, "I wondered whether wounding him in his third eye might be somehow symbolic. An occult message?"

Shackleton smirked. "Appropriate enough, I suppose. You might say he deserved what he got. But, as I say, I didn't do it, and I don't know who did."

"But can you guess?" Evan asked.

Shackleton shook his head. "Churpov needed those papers. How else do you leave the country legally with an underage girl? He didn't think the other charges against him would stick. Especially not after he was home and dry back in Armenia."

The sheriff told me the Feds let Churpov go. It must have been some kind of a plea deal. So, yes, he could be back across the water and feeling like he's outwitted us all. But at least he doesn't have Melissa.

Evan felt he could forgive the man but not the sins. Despite all the harm that Shackleton might have caused, the reverend didn't resent the fellow, didn't recoil at the thought of helping him further. There were too many innocent people involved. And certainly donations were welcome, but what was the source of those funds?

Is this some of his dirty money?

As Evan and his friend Leon Weiss had eventually figured out, orphaned young women from the Sisters of Mercy home were placed in work-study programs, including at Jack Nathan's fashion school. From there, talent-spotter Nathan would send the attractive ones to summer jobs in the laundry of the Twin Dragons Resort and Casino at Osceola. Some of the underage girls would train to work as massage therapists in the spa, then the cooperative and talented ones would get "promoted" upstairs as prostitutes who were provided on-demand and gratis to high-roller casino patrons.

We knew Shackleton's bank had a major stake in the resort development, but it's still an open question how much he knew about — or may have even benefitted from — the trafficking. Certainly he played a role in Churpov's attempt to adopt Melissa. Is it possible Shackleton was ignorant of the abuse and thought she'd be much better off as the trophy wife of a billionaire?

Evan's investigations had exposed a crime ring. Behind this operation — not only here but also at other resorts — was Russian mobster Dmitri Churpov, CEO of Armenian Consolidated Holdings, a seemingly legitimate entertainment and hospitality group out of Nashville.

One of the victimized girls was Melissa Benton. Churpov must have wanted her for himself, hence the kidnapping from Sisters of Mercy. She bore a striking resemblance to his estranged wife, Tatyana Bulganin.

Evan's most recent miracle had been to make Churpov believe that Melissa, who genuinely suffered from fits of epilepsy, was possessed of devils. Evan had reasoned that, although the mobster had long since turned his back on his Eastern Orthodox upbringing, his belief in and fear of Satan were still very much alive. As a result of Evan's ruse, Melissa had been rescued, and the unscrupulous Russian was now in federal custody. Since then, she had been in treatment, both for epilepsy as well as the stress of the kidnapping, and during that time she'd turned eighteen. If the doctors soon judged she was competent, she'd be deciding on her own where she wanted to live next. And that was sure to be with her soulmate Luke, their little son Buzz, and her sister Loretta, the new wife of the pastor of Evangel Baptist.

4

Whenever life threw Evan a breaking curveball, he'd seek the counsel of his mentor, Rev. Marcus Thurston. Driving straight to the old one-bedroom parsonage in Appleton City from the courthouse in Osceola, Evan hadn't phoned to announce his arrival. He didn't want to worry the man, and he wasn't at all sure he wanted to stay for long. But he needed a reality check — perhaps along with a spiritual transfusion.

It was early spring, this fine early-May morning was warming rapidly, and Evan expected to find Thurston laboring in his garden. But today when Evan let himself in the front door, he was surprised to see the former pastor seated comfortably in the parlor of his Depression-era clapboard home having coffee with Sheriff Chester Otis, who had brought a box of his favorite fresh-baked crullers.

Evan felt fortunate to have the trust and friendship of Reverend Thurston and Sheriff Otis, and it pleased him that these black men held positions of responsibility in the community. Like Thurston, Otis had been judicious in his career, knowing when to pick his battles. Evan knew the sheriff insisted on hearing any new rumors around town, but he rarely acted on them without hard evidence.

Thurston and Otis aren't wearing masks in here, as if disease wouldn't dare visit this house.

Before Evan even had a chance to sit, Thurston demanded, "What did you do to Ann Shackleton? I thought I told you to lay off the faith healing."

Evan knew the accusation was in jest, but he didn't enjoy being teased about it. "It was over before I got there," he muttered.

The other two simply nodded courteously to him and watched as he emptied three scoops of instant into a cup of boiled water, added three green packets of sweetener , and stirred. The coffee, also as expected at Thurston's, was instant Folgers. Evan always carried a few packets of it in his coat pocket so he could doctor the weak Farmers Brothers at the C'mon. He also used to keep several packets of sugar in his pocket, but now Loretta had him using stevia.

"Your wife's got you off the sugar," Thurston mused, spotting the green packets. "Is she having any luck with the alcohol?"

As Evan sat and sipped, he replied, "Oh, was this meeting all about me? I didn't get the memo."

"I saw you at the courthouse," Otis teased. "Then you disappeared into the back with that lawyer. Now that you bring it up, why *don't* we make this meeting all about you? What did Shackleton have to say for himself? Or would that be a secret of the confessional?"

"I'm not sure how that works," Evan said. "He is Catholic, true. Or at least his wife Ann is, they tell me. But in the first instance he wouldn't be offering a confession, and secondly I wouldn't be the one to hear it."

"So...?" Otis persisted.

Evan took a huge gulp of his syrupy coffee before he announced, "He swears he didn't kill Father Coyle. He admits he was the courier who came and left so quickly, but he says even though the guy got so upset he needed his angina pills, he was still breathing when Shackleton stomped out of there." Then Evan added, "*Without* the custody papers, mind you."

"Coyle was holding back?" Thurston asked.

Evan mused, "Crisis of conscience? Or holding the money back as leverage because he hadn't gotten his placement fee?"

Otis huffed, "We'd have Coyle up on charges now if a person or persons unknown hadn't shut him up. And I would have thought the diocese would have closed down that orphanage, considering how that work-study program was more like work-or-get-fucked."

"You know," Evan said, "crooked as Coyle was, we don't know whether he actually knew what those girls he'd placed over at the resort were doing. He'd gotten them paying jobs as interns, and if the hotel was kicking back a placement fee, let's guess he was using those funds to keep the orphanage going. From what Mother Bernadette told me, they've had trouble meeting their budget for a very long time."

"You're being awfully generous with that opinion of him," Otis grunted, as he scarfed down half a cruller in a bite. He swallowed, gulped more coffee, and went on, "Which leaves the question, if we're to believe Shackleton, who *did* kill Coyle?"

"Could be the cattle-prod wound and the ash smears were post-mortem," Evan said. "Coyle might've died of a heart attack after all. Then whoever found him administered the wound."

"But Sister Margaret didn't see anybody else go in there," Otis protested.

"She might not have," Evan offered, "if the old gal was asleep at her desk."

"Normally," Otis said, "that device wouldn't kill a person. But if an attacker knew the guy had a dicey heart, it might be just enough to put him down. Thing is, in these parts, it's not exactly an uncommon piece of equipment, and it's not traceable or distinctive, as a firearm would be. And if it was used with malicious intent, you can bet the weapon is at the bottom of the lake somewhere."

"That's all Shackleton told you?" Thurston asked Evan. "That he didn't do it? It's not like he has any more reason to tell the truth now that there won't be a trial."

"He doesn't want custody of Luke, at least not now," Evan said. "After all we've been through, he hands me this power of attorney and expects me to make his family decisions."

"He's got ice water for blood," Otis said with a mouthful of donut. "We all know that."

Shackleton and his envelopes! Should I have turned it down?

Evan informed Thurston, "He gave me a donation to the church. Said it was for our building fund. Fixing up the parsonage, which I'm guessing means *my* house?"

The old pastor laughed, "You know he doesn't mean this place. By all rights, it should be yours now. But then old Redwine gifted you that house, now you're stuck with that ramshackle place, and the deacons are saying I don't have to move." He laughed some more adding, "But I gotta pay rent!"

"Get outta here!" Otis scoffed.

"Twenty bucks a month. Not a dollar, not a thousand — *twenty!* That's our deacons for you. Not about to give me the place, not about to sell it. If they prayed for guidance in the matter, I have to wonder whether the answer didn't get scrambled. They must think after all those years I didn't save a dime. It's not like they couldn't use the money."

"But what am I supposed to do with Shackleton's check?" Evan asked. "It's fifty grand!"

Thurston shook his head, saying, "Amazing to me how well the rumor mill works in these parts. We were in everybody's business long before social media. Shackleton's in jail, and yet somehow he knows Arthur Redwine's gone to live at Knox Village and given you his house. What is it — pre-Civil War? Yeah, it needs fixing all right. A stick of dynamite might be a good first step. But then that check wouldn't go far."

But Evan wanted to know, "Do we accept it? We know he's been involved in shady dealings."

"We *don't* know," Otis corrected. "If we did, we'd still have him locked up. If not for murder, for money laundering or fraud or some other stinker's scheme. Evan, you gotta understand, as of this morning, Shackleton has to be ancient history to you. If anyone murdered the priest, most probably it was some Russian hood. The Feds have got Churpov, and unless anything relevant shakes out of that investigation, we've got nothing on Shackleton. You and I both know he had designs on the Emmett farm, and now that he's out he could be up to his old tricks. You've got the Taggart probate case in the courts, and it will all play out as it must. But if you and Loretta are going to keep providing a home for Luke and the kid — and maybe soon for Melissa as well — I'd agree with Marcus. That check isn't near enough."

"I'm no lawyer," Thurston sighed, "but churches and charities and political parties are all accountable to the penny for how they spend their budgets. But do they — or should we — ever ask where the donations come from? Are you kidding? Might as well ask whether the air you breathe has ever been in the lungs of some criminal. You look at it that way, be glad Shackleton's spending it on you and yours and not on some evil scheme."

You're an old pragmatist, Marcus. I worry I have so much to learn. But you were never rash enough to get so deeply involved in asking questions. Maybe that's how you've avoided trouble — and I walk right into it.

Evan said, "I'm going back to Myerson. Seems like Ann Shackleton had a near-death experience."

Thurston's eyebrows shot up. He looked over at Otis and winked, "You know, Sheriff, if it wasn't for Evan here's obsessively curious mind, life in Appleton City would be about as interesting as watching you eat."

5

Before Luke had been discharged from Myerson and come to live with them, Evan's returning home at midday to see the lovely Loretta would get him not only a sandwich but very probably a nooner. But not today.

He found her in the kitchen of the Redwine house, which was now theirs, making enough sandwiches for either a small army or a very long bridge game. In this phase of the pandemic, some activities still met at the church in small groups, especially when young people were involved. Some of the white-bread wedges Loretta was making held peanut butter, some a single slice of processed cheese with mayo, some only margarine. Evan knew she could do better, but the church outreach budget couldn't. Kissing her as she worked, he said, "I thought there were others on the committee who could help with this stuff. Don't you do enough?"

"There's a newly marrieds' counseling class tonight, and Vera Hartung took sick. Can't have her making the food."

"Not Covid, I hope."

"If it was, do you think she'd tell anybody? People in these parts believe in Satan, who they haven't seen unless they're tripping. His devils afflict my sister, or so they say. But Covid, which some see up close and personal, is a rumor started by communist politicians as a mind-control experiment."

"So you volunteered? Who's looking after Buzz?"

"Leslie has him chasing squirrels or stray cats or crows or some critters in the yard. Her plan is to keep him moving for an hour, tucker him out, and then put him down for a nap. Someone should tell her that might not be enough. *She* may want to nap. I'm sure he won't."

Leslie was a late-teens caregiver, a volunteer from church. She was scrawny and bookish, training to be a hairdresser. Evan guessed she had a crush on the Engstrom boy and coming over here was her excuse to see him. Walt and Luke would usually be staring at screens in the back room, and if either of them took notice of her, it would be a first. Still, keeping the young people at a safe distance from one another should be one of the pastor's responsibilities, particularly if they were kin of church members. He expected Melissa would soon be coming to live with them, and there was already talk about how it would look for a young, unmarried couple to be living in the parsonage.

As he grabbed a cheese sandwich, Loretta mock-slapped his hand. He took hold of hers, turned her around, nuzzled her neck, and muttered, "You know, we were both a lot more interesting people when we were living in sin."

"We're still sinners, as you well know," she said, kissing him back meaningfully this time. "It's just we're not allowed to enjoy it so much."

"Speak for yourself," he said as he pulled her closer.

She nudged him backward, saying, "I have to finish this," and resumed her work at the cutting board. She added thoughtlessly, "How was your morning?"

Evan wolfed down the tiny sandwich and grabbed another. "I paid a compassionate visit on Ann Shackleton. She died last night…"

Loretta gasped, turning around again. He laid a comforting hand on her and went on, "…but only for a short time, and now she's back in the land of the living."

"Evan Wycliff," she sighed. "Are people saying you had something to do with bringing her back?"

"It was all over before I got there. But I had breakfast in town, and, yes, Cora was teasing me about it."

As she went back to making sandwiches, Loretta muttered, "I'd be jealous if I didn't like her so much."

Evan persisted, "I'm curious to find out who or what Ann saw on the other side, but I'm not sure she'll be able to tell me. As for her husband, who apparently has no inclination to see her, in court this morning the charges against him were dropped for lack of evidence."

Loretta fretted, "Jesus, Evan! You sound so cool and calm, and you wait to bring me news like this? I'll just switch on the TV. Their news is always disgusting but nowhere near as upsetting. How did that scum manage to get off?"

"Now he swears to me he didn't do it."

"He *talked* to you?"

"He did."

"I hope you didn't promise him anything."

Evan tried to remain even-tempered as he explained, "Stuart says he knows nothing about nothing. Oh, and as for Luke and Buzz, he's perfectly happy for us to keep looking after them. And he handed me a generous-sized check, presumably to get this tumbledown residence up to code. If it's for that, it's generous. But if it's meant for support of his son and grandson, it's not nearly enough."

"Wow," she said, unimpressed. "That guy continues to fall short of the minimum definition of a human being." She frowned and asked again, "What did you promise him? What's the money really for?"

Evan shrugged, "I told him I'd visit Ann. Understand, he didn't let on it was urgent. I wish I'd been there last night. He wasn't allowed to have a phone until this morning, but the clinic must have phoned his lawyer that his wife had been moved into critical care. He did give me power of attorney so her doctors would speak to me — also so I could continue making decisions about Luke and Buzz. As for the money, he should have told me it was for their welfare, not for the house — although we need it either way. Stuart Shackleton never does anything without a carefully calculated reason. Yes, I'm a bit wary of his intentions. But if he's not going to put up a fight about custody, it's major good news no matter what he plans to do."

"And what about Melissa? Will he object if they say she can come to live with us? Is he going to accept that she and Luke want to be together?"

Evan hoped to sound reassuring when he replied, "As of now, she's still a ward of the state. I need to set up a meeting with Chuck Holloman from Child and Family Services. What happens next will be mostly up to some social worker, and Shackleton won't have anything to say about it."

"I want to see her! You gave her that phone, but she doesn't answer, and she won't call. I think the only person she talks to is Luke, and he won't tell me anything."

"I'll go see her, and soon," Evan insisted. "I'll find a way to bring her home, but for now I need to have a word with Luke about his mother."

"I saw him and Walt walking off toward the pond."

Evan sounded surprised, "Without their computers?"

"Yeah. No fishpoles either. Probably guy-talk. You know, somewhere we can't overhear."

~

Evan found Luke and Walt standing at the edge of the closest of the five fishponds on the property. They were throwing stones and watching them skip across the water.

"What's the matter?" Evan asked as he approached. "Are all the internet servers down?"

Luke focused on his toss as he answered, "We're deciding whether it's surface tension or hydroplaning."

"Yeah," Evan said. "I hope you know you're also scaring the fish."

Walt was likewise intent on his sidearm throwing but acknowledged, "Hello, sir."

Luke was suddenly serious when he turned to Evan to ask, "How do you know there are fish in here?"

Evan laughed. "Well, they told me when old Arthur Redwine owned the place, he made sure to stock the ponds. Catfish and bass, mostly. I caught a five-pound smallmouth myself. I had a bamboo pole with a footlong night-crawler on a hook. Of course, that was twenty years ago. If there are critters in here and no one has fished them out, they could be the size of sea monsters by now."

When we were boys and played on this farm, Bob taught me to fish that time. He had no luck that day. I wish he'd been the one to catch it. Not that it would have changed anything. We decided to throw it back.

"There are no freshwater sea monsters," Luke declared.

Walt had stopped throwing rocks and stood close enough to hear. Evan lowered his voice to ask Luke, "You and I need to talk. I visited your mother this morning. I also had a long talk with your father." He gestured toward a huge, sheltering weeping willow tree, far enough away from the soggy bank for the soil around it to be dry. "How about you and me sit under that tree for a while?"

Luke insisted, "Walt is my friend. He can hear anything you have to say to me."

"Okay," Evan said, "let's all sit down."

As they sat on the cool grass in the shade of the tree, Walt said, "The bright sun is intense. And its glare on the water makes you squint. Yes, this is a good place for a talk. I hope you don't mind me being here, sir. Luke is my only friend as well, you see."

But you wouldn't mind if Leslie offered her affection!

Evan told him, "I don't mind at all, if you'll stop with the *sir.* You're making me feel old."

"Roger that," Walt replied.

Where is this military jargon coming from? Some video game, no doubt.

"Luke," Evan said, focusing on what he came here for, "your mother had a major cardiac episode last night. They didn't think she'd pull through, but she did. I know you haven't seen her in a while, and I understand that you haven't wanted to. But I'd like you to consider going with me later today. Honestly, I'm not sure how much longer she'll be with us."

There was no visible reaction from Luke. All he said was, "Is she dying?"

Evan answered carefully, "At the moment, I think not. I left instructions for them to call me right away if her condition gets worse. But if you mean, is she in declining health, I'd say probably yes. You see, last night she actually expired. The doctors thought they'd lost her. But she came back. It was kind of miraculous. But next time, maybe not."

Walt blinked and his eyes widened. "Then she had a near-death experience! Did she tell you about it?"

"No," Evan said. "They wouldn't let me spend much time with her. And even if I did, I don't know how sharp she'll be. She's had memory issues for a long time now. She might not remember much about it at all. But, Luke, if you don't take this chance to say goodbye, I think you'll come to regret it. If not now, someday."

Luke gritted his teeth, then shouted, "She never knows who I am!"

Evan answered calmly, "I'm sure in her heart she must still love you very much. But she's confused about everything. She didn't know me either. She thought I was her doctor, then her priest. But she's aware of her surroundings. And I suspect seeing us will be a comfort to her — on some level."

Luke sat in silence and stared out at the silvery surface of the pond, the water shimmering in the wind.

Walt chimed in, "There's a lot being written in the medical literature these days about NDE. Serious studies, not just anecdotal. Patients claim religious experiences, but there are likely physiological explanations for their perceptions. For example, many reports include moving toward a bright, white light. But a perfectly plausible explanation is, as the brain dies, its last memory is the baby's journey through the birth canal and into the light of the OR, which would be blinding at first to a mind that's known only the darkness of the womb."

Wow, I don't want to get into this with him now. But I wouldn't mind hearing what else this wiz kid has to say about it. Still, I can't help but ask.

Evan asked Walt, "What about out-of-body visions and sensations?"

"The medical definition of death is rather crude," Walt replied. "Legally, a person is dead when their heart stops and it can't be restarted, but it actually takes the brain several minutes to cease to function completely, about seven. The duration may vary depending on how much oxygen and glucose are in the bloodstream at the time of the arrest."

From what I saw, he's got that right. There has to be a plausible explanation for how Ann came through it as though nothing had happened.

Evan asked, "So, Walt, do you believe in the afterlife?"

The boy answered, "When there is a testable scientific theory of consciousness, I may be able to form an opinion."

If I ever need a guest speaker for Sunday school, here he is.

Luke had been moping and broke his silence with, "What about Melissa? When can she come home? She's blue all the time now, you know."

Luke claimed to be permanently plugged into the girl's emotional state, and Evan wasn't about to disagree. But now that they both had phones and FaceTime, there was no mystery. He assumed they chatted at least daily.

"I'll be going to see her, too," Evan said. "But there's paperwork with social services. It's complicated, and I can't promise anything."

"I want to go!" Luke insisted.

All Evan could say was, "I have to find out whether that's possible."

Luke muttered, as though he was obliged to ask, "And what about my dad?"

Evan crossed his arms. He knew Luke wondered why his father had always kept his distance. "You know he was going to stand trial, but now that's all over. His case was dismissed for lack of evidence. I believe that means he will be able to see you soon. He told me he's okay with you living here."

"Did he kill that guy?"

"He says he didn't. No one knows the whole story."

"You can tell him I never want to see him either. After all, I'm eighteen now, and I can make my own decisions."

Yes, but we must be able to add 'and of sound mind.'

EVAN OFTEN THOUGHT how different his ways had become in just a few months since formally taking up the ministry. Not long ago, preaching was a part-time job, not always paid, when he wasn't working on commission for Zed Motors negotiating make-good deals on unpaid auto loans. He'd lived in a broken-down trailer and had no use for an alarm clock. He'd drunk as much whiskey as coffee — sometimes more — and his diet was motivated by his cravings for fat and sugar and salt, including when his meager budget drove him to last-minute convenience-store grabs of potato chips and beef jerky.

Now he was a community leader and a family man with responsibilities. Loretta had him on a diet, which she enforced by doing all the shopping and cooking for him most of the time. Backsliding at the C'mon might be his only vice these days. He had to come up with a sermon once a week, whether he was inspired or not. He officiated at ceremonies, many of which he had to lead in-person, where much of what he said had to be by rote, whether he agreed with the phrasing or not. He'd done weddings, funerals, Eucharists, and baptisms. With the deacons, he'd once presided over the laying on of hands. The church had a four-foot-deep, galvanized-metal-lined baptismal font behind the pulpit so there would be no wading into the river and the rite could be performed year-round. The Baptists performed complete immersion — a full dunking rather than a sprinkling — and only for faith-professed tweens, teens, and adults rather than newborns. The candidates donned white-cotton robes over their skivvies, but because Evan had to remain standing in the water the whole time, in addition to his gown he wore hip-length fishing boots.

The old Evan would have considered the procedure awkward and comical, but the new pastor appreciated the sincerity and inspiration the congregation gave to the practice. A clean slate. A new beginning. Never mind it was difficult for him to regard it as anything but a chore. His persistent fear was that these resolutions of repentance and righteousness wouldn't last longer than the next temptation.

Not that I think there's anything remarkable about sinning. It's what people do.

His essential problem came down how some days he simply didn't believe. Labels were difficult, but even in his darkest moments he didn't consider himself an agnostic. His guess at these times was like Voltaire's, who proposed that God created the universe as some marvelous mechanical clock, wound it up, then walked away.

Divinity school had soured Evan, no doubt. The history of Christianity, the bickering of factions for centuries after Christ and into the present, the perpetual wars with heathen and rival religions, and conflicting interpretations of scripture including literalism — none of those controversies seemed to have anything to do with spirituality or understanding the soul's journey.

Earning his degree didn't put a cap on his fretting. He undertook graduate work in astrophysics. He found many more questions than answers. During this time, he met Naomi Weiss. They were engaged, then not, then she was killed in a missile bombardment in Lebanon when she was on assignment doing unspecified work for a defense contractor.

Back in his trailer days, Naomi's apparition would visit him from time to time, especially when he was lonely or in crisis. He didn't believe in ghosts, much less that she was an angel. He didn't think she was an entity at all — just an external manifestation of his desire, an incredibly vivid hallucination. This theory was borne out by the discovery that the ephemeral Naomi had no more information than he did — although it amused her to insist she was smarter than most mortals, and especially him.

She had also kept urging him to find a living, breathing, human life partner. Cora was nominated, then Loretta. And when Naomi judged her powers weren't sufficient to help Evan cope with some criminals, she'd dispatched her brother Leon, who seemed on first appearance to be a ghost but turned out to be a bona fide if eccentric federal agent.

Now Leon was gone, although the fellow was presumably still breathing somewhere, and Evan had Loretta. No more visitations, no more crime-stopping helpers. Thurston was there to give advice, but he refused to take ownership of problems. Sheriff Otis was more or less an ally, although he refused to act on hearsay, speculation, or intuition — which was all Evan usually had to go on.

Evan hadn't anticipated that visitations would be taking up most of his time. Marcus should have warned him, but Evan suspected it was the part of the job his mentor enjoyed most. He probably didn't think of it as a chore.

I shouldn't either. Who is this new man I'm becoming? I used to be able to laugh at my flaws. But will I now wince at my hypocrisies?

Evan vowed he'd revisit Ann Shackleton this afternoon, and he'd try to cajole Luke into going. Although the preacher had known her not at all, his curiosity about her near-death was pulling him back, not to mention his promises to her husband. He was overdue to see Melissa Benton, but his visit would just frustrate her if he hadn't worked out the details with her social worker about her homecoming. That would be a chore and a negotiation, he was sure. Then he really should drive up to Knox and visit Arthur Redwine, at the very least to thank him for the gifts of the house as well as the well-appointed SUV Loretta was driving, which Evan had secretly named *The Midnight Monster.* When Zip Zed had informed Evan that Redwine wanted to buy him a new car, the dealer let him know the exterior paint on the Lincoln Navigator was Infinite Black. Asking after the other options, Evan learned there was also Pristine White Metallic, which he said he preferred.

Zed gave him what he had on the lot.

Another omen?

6

Loretta had the Lincoln loaded up with her sandwiches and was about to leave to deliver them when she got a call from Alice Olinger, the church secretary.

"I was just headed over to see you," Loretta told her. "I'm pretty sure I made enough. Nothing fancy, of course."

"Much appreciated." The woman's voice sounded shaky. Alice's was not an assertive personality, and she didn't cope well with stress. Her employment dated back to Thurston, who couldn't remember why he'd brought her on. Considering how grief could find its way into a church on a daily basis, Loretta had advised Evan perhaps he should hire someone else and either reassign her or suggest she retire.

"Mrs. Wycliff, that's not why I'm calling. I wasn't sure whether it was important, but a minute ago a man called here wanting your number. He wouldn't give his name. I was going to put him in touch with the pastor, but he insisted he wanted your personal phone. Then he says, all concerned like, it's a family matter. Could be it's one of those insurance salesmen, but I thought you have a right to know in case it really is something."

Yes, it could have been a salesperson or a scam call, but in Loretta's recent past there had been only one man who would need to be so cagey. She agreed with Alice it might be nothing but asked for the number.

She called it when she was on the road. She knew from "Loretta?" that the voice was Mick Heston's, her former employer at the Twin Dragons Casino. And at one time, her lover.

"Mick, I heard you took off for New Zealand. This is a new number, but it's local. Where are you?"

"Close by, darlin'. Very close."

"Please say you're not *stalking* me."

He replied with a stage laugh, saying, "No man would blame me in your case, but I'm no creep."

Mick had been a decent boss, and he'd even set her up with a place to live and the use of a company car. But it was only after the casino closed down that she suspected he was crooked. Evan informed her Heston must have been involved in the sex trafficking ring that had exploited Melissa. Assuming he'd be running from the law, she figured she'd never see him again.

So, yes, he was a creep.

"I have to see you. We need to talk," he said soberly.

"What about? I have no business with you. I'm the pastor's wife now, as you must know considering how you found me."

"That's just it," Heston said. "I need to tell you some things to keep him out of trouble."

"Spill it."

"Not on the phone. If you're headed into town, we can meet in the cemetery. Wouldn't be unusual for a preacher's wife to be consoling a friend."

Loretta debated with herself whether she should meet with him at all. In her new role as righteous wife, she was in fierce denial she'd ever cared for Mick. He'd helped her — more than enough to win her loyalty — but at the time she didn't think of herself as any more than his private side hustle. And she waited for the day he'd lose interest and move on.

But now? What could he possibly want from her?

MICK HAD AN ATHLETIC BUILD, dark features, and was movie-star handsome. Despite his recent misfortunes, he still walked with a swagger. His easy manner made it seem as though he'd never had to work hard to get anything he wanted.

He was wearing what had been his standard office uniform — designer sport coat, golf shirt, and slacks. With expensive slip-on loafers. The kind with tassels on them.

She was in faded jeans and a plain, loose-fitting T-shirt. She didn't need a bra. If that was immodest, so be it. She'd only planned to make a quick stop with the sandwiches.

He'd picked a gravesite that must have been adorned that morning with fresh flowers. She realized how smart that was. Recent burial, contrite relative.

He approached her, coming close as if nothing had happened between them and he expected a kiss. She pushed him away.

"Gorgeous as ever," he grinned.

"I have to get over to church, so if you don't mind, make it short."

"You probably know they dropped the murder charge against Stu Shackleton."

"Yes. Evan told me he thinks maybe the guy didn't do it after all."

"No matter. The point is, he's out and about. There's nobody to tell him he can't do whatever."

"And why should that concern me? Or Evan?"

"The reason I'm here walking free on the soil of the good old U-S-of-A is that I copped a plea and cooperated with the Feds. Shackleton was in on the casino development deal, partners with the Russians, and cozy with the politicians."

"Are you saying he was in on the prostitution?"

"If he was, it can't be proved. Or they'd have charged him long ago."

She gritted her teeth. "But you were. You must have been. You broke those girls, and you were going to sell my sister into slavery."

"None of them were in the trade who didn't want it. Melissa would have been a superstar, and believe me she wanted it. Designer clothes, private apartment, easy street. But then this boss Churpov decides he wants her for himself. If the Feds hadn't picked him up, she'd be living in his villa in Montenegro. As his wife? His daughter? Either way, she'd be living a life any celebrity would envy." He drew closer, unafraid to challenge the protective sister of a girl he'd abused — or allowed to be abused. And he insisted, "If the orphanage hadn't sent her to fashion school, and if the school hadn't offered her the work-study program in the spa, where would she have ended up? Sewing dresses in a sweat-shop? Waiting tables — as long as she didn't have one of her fits and drop the plates?"

Loretta wouldn't give him the satisfaction of getting angry. "Yes, Mick. No matter what you do or who you hurt, you'll always be the hero of your own story. That much is clear. I haven't forgiven you, maybe I never could, but the life I'm living now says I have to try. You still haven't told me why Evan has to worry about Shackleton."

He flashed another grin, asking, "You. Are you for real?"

"What are you suggesting? Look at me. We're barely getting by. I'm not trying to look plain. I won't spend money on makeup. Shackleton's son is living with us now, and his father helps with expenses. We've got this broken-down farmhouse rent-free. And a sweet man donated this car. We're not starving." She frowned. "Are you thinking I'm working some con?"

"Now that Shackleton is out of jail, he won't be diving back into his old schemes. There are too many eyes on him. He was careful before, without a doubt. But I'm going to guess he'll come to Jesus. It's been done before. Ex-cons and crooked politicians get washed clean. He'll be helping your hubby some way, you watch."

"What are you trying to tell me?"

"You were always a practical girl. You watched out for your sister, you showed up, you worked your job. You took what I offered, and you knew the deal. I treated you fair, you know that. I'm guessing you suspected more than you let on about the operation, but you were careful not to ask questions. Am I wrong?"

"I thought you were a decent guy. Now I know different. Like I said, I have no more business with you."

"I won't be sticking around. I'm just in the country to spill my guts, sign the paperwork, and I'm gone. You won't be seeing me, don't worry. But what I want to tell you is, if you're careful around Shackleton, money will come your way. And I'm going to bet you'll find a way to take it."

"You're disgusting."

He muttered, "Okay, maybe I do feel bad about Melissa. It got way more intense than I figured. I'm giving you a heads up because I expect you're both going to be okay. That is, if you're smart enough to be practical. Are you the preacher's wife because you're crazy in love with him? Or because he pulled you out of a bad situation?"

She was going to answer, but he'd already turned away and was walking toward his rental car.

Watching Heston's car pull away, a dark mood descended on Loretta. She'd thought she was clear of the old life, that she'd emerged into a dazzling light, and that she deserved Evan's love, if not God's.

7

Ann Shackleton was sitting up in bed wearing a powder-blue cardigan over her hospital gown. The air conditioning had been cranked way up on this hot day, and the private room was downright chilly. Evan sat in the guest chair. He'd asked Luke to wait just outside in the hallway. Evan had bargained with the boy to come with him on the condition that they'd have some answer about Melissa by tomorrow. Evan knew that was a tall order. He'd asked Luke to stand outside until he could determine whether Ann was sufficiently aware of her surroundings and reasonably calm.

The old woman looked apple-cheeked and happy. She had oxygen tubes in her nostrils and was sipping juice from a straw.

"No one told me you are a faith healer!" she announced gleefully. "I'd have asked for the moon! Maybe you've come to give it to me now."

"Mrs. Shackleton, I'm so pleased you're feeling better but I'm not—"

"Oh, don't give me that. Last night I saw you plain as day, standing in that doorway. You were in your cassock, and you were wearing that purple stole. You were all dressed up to give me the last rites. But those angels wouldn't allow it."

She has me confused with the priest. She's remembering the night of her near-death experience.

"Angels?"

"Goodness, everyone was hovering around me in a panic. I didn't know what all the fuss was about. I was wide awake. But something was holding me down, this pressure on my chest. Well, I decide I'm just going to fly out of here. But then I'm on the ceiling, I'm looking down, and I hear them say I'm gone. They all leave! Except then the lady comes back in and grabs my teeth, takes off my rings. She had no business taking off my slippers!"

"You watched all this from above?"

"I was on the ceiling, bumping up against it. I wanted to fly out, but those angels wouldn't let me. They told me it wasn't my time, ordered me to go back. They asked nicely, of course. That's how I knew they were angels and not demons."

"What did they look like, those angels?"

"Oh, voices. Not faces. We're not supposed to see them, you know. I wanted a peek, but I didn't get it."

Evan was about to beckon Luke in when she said, "I'm so glad you'll be getting your medical degree. We both know you don't need it, but they're so picky here. They'll give you an office on this floor, then we'll get some things done. You can start by clearing up some things for me. And there are other folks here who need some looking after."

"Clearing up things?"

"If I'm not ready to go, I'll need to make a list. We don't have forever, do we? I plan to be ready next time. Maybe then they'll let me go."

She knows she's dying and seems not at all concerned.

Evan got up slowly, crossed to the door, and motioned for Luke to come in. The boy was wearing the obligatory mask and face shield, which Evan worried might make it even more difficult for his mother to recognize him. He announced in a gentle tone, "Ann, your son Luke has come to see you."

Luke was understandably uncomfortable, acting alternately jittery and listless. He'd seen enough of hospitals, he seemed to have a dread of invalids in general, and his fury with his mother were all mixed up with his denial that she was, in effect, already lost to him.

"Hello, Mother. I hope you're feeling okay," he said.

Ann didn't look at all surprised, continuing a conversation that must have been started years ago: "I've asked you three times to clean your room, young man, and you've stuck up your nose. It better be ship-shape by now, or you'll be sitting in it until it's done. And then there's the algebra. I know you haven't been doing it, so don't go fibbing to me."

"The algebra is too easy," Luke muttered. "No point."

She frowned. "Did you empty the trash like I asked?"

The boy replied, "There wasn't much in the bins. No point."

"That's no excuse. Your father likes a clean start." She appealed to Evan, "You see what I put up with? He's a sweet boy, but no sense of responsibility."

Evan gently reached over, took Luke's hand, and rested it on Ann's, which had a sensor clipped to the index finger. He placed his own hand on top and squeezed gently so that Luke's grasped hers.

Then, not wishing to offend either of them, his brief prayer was silent.

Right here and right now, the all-powerful presence of God is.

Evan asked Luke for his phone and took a photo of him standing at his mother's side.

8
_____

L uke didn't say anything until they were out of the building. "Did you take that selfie to show my dad?"

"No," Evan replied. "It's all yours. I took it so you'd have it to remember her — maybe not tomorrow — ten years from now?"

"I didn't say goodbye to her," Luke said.

Because of his diagnosis, Luke was not allowed to have a driver's license. This was a persistent sore point with him. Evan assured him, "I'll take you back here whenever you want."

Luke shook his head, "I don't think she has much longer."

"How do you know? Are you plugged into her the same way you are with Melissa?"

He shook his head again, this time more emphatically. "No, her soul is so afraid of demons, she won't let me in."

I don't know what to say to that. He's probably right.

As they reached Evan's car in the lot, Luke turned to plead with him. "Algebra is child's play. I could never make her understand."

Evan gripped Luke's shoulder firmly and said, "It really doesn't matter now. If she could understand what calculus is, I'm sure she'd be proud of you. I know I am."

As Luke went around to open the door on the passenger side, his face brightened, and he teased, "You know, people probably laugh when they see you coming in this thing."

"I hope so!" Evan shot back. "You just gave me an idea. Maybe all pastors should drive ice-cream trucks."

As Luke got in, he shook with a fit of giggles, "Okay, Preacher. I'll have a Dreamsicle."

EVAN DROPPED Luke at what they all persisted in calling "the Redwine house" and proceeded on to Route B toward Osceola, where he had an afternoon meeting scheduled with Chuck Holloman of Child and Family Services.

He was tooling along the interstate happily at top speed with the little Fiat's AC turned up full blast when the familiar voice came from the vacant back seat, "Miss me much?"

Evan shot a quick look back but didn't see Naomi. This time she was a disembodied voice.

"Why don't you come up here where I can see you? Or has time worn out your stunning good looks?"

"You're not permitted to lust after me now," she rebuked him. "You're a married man, a duly ordained minister, and a trusted pillar of the community."

"You forgot to mention 'faith healer.' How am I going to live that down?"

"My advice? Use it to your advantage. People will believe what they believe. You are as you do, and you're doing good."

"To what do I owe the pleasure?"

"I've told you to forget me, but you haven't."

Naomi's background was Jewish, and his was Baptist tending toward Unitarian or I-don't-knowist. He'd always thought they could make a go of it. He even enjoyed debating theology and science with her. Here was the dimension of intimate relationship he now missed with Loretta.

"How could I?" Evan asked her. "You're my conscience. Nobody has ever known me better, right down to my vices."

"Yes, I could write a book," she said. "But you'd be just one more evangelist with dirty hands, feet of clay, and a wayward pecker."

"Hey, I'm not evangelical! How can I tell other people what to do when I don't know myself?"

She insisted, "Your behavior is your testimony. Your walk is your talk. I'm sure you know that. You preach it."

"Wow," Evan said. "Since when did you become a Southern Baptist?"

"The rabbis call it practicing the cardinal virtues. Psychologists call it *moral persuasion*. Do as I do, whatever I may say. It's much more powerful than doling out righteous advice."

"Looks like I'm still Stuart Shackleton's puppet. How do I avoid walking into his next mess?"

She laughed. "Who said you're to avoid it? You're supposed to walk straight through it."

He was going to ask her what was coming next, but he knew she'd refuse to say. And she was gone as quickly as she'd come.

CHUCK HOLLOMAN WAS a dedicated state bureaucrat who liked his job, especially its generous benefits. He was a faithful Catholic, supporting a family of six with one on the way. He defined his duties as checking all the boxes on a myriad of official forms.

On a doctrinal basis, he opposed birth control, abortion, and the death penalty. Evan respected him for the consistency of those views. Holloman's job was to encourage and facilitate child adoptions. *Emancipation* was not a word he liked to hear.

His gray, all-weather, wash-and-wear suitcoat was hanging on the back of the door in his modest, one-room office. It was gray-painted cinderblock, but at least he'd graduated from a cubicle. He wore a freshly laundered, long-sleeve white shirt with a grease-stained rep tie at half-mast, collar unbuttoned. There being no AC in this state building, his office was hot and humid, even with its only window wide open.

Evan found him eating a peanut-butter-and-jelly sandwich from a paper bag, a can of vending-machine Diet Coke for his beverage. Holloman had recently been monitoring his body-mass index with the Fitbit his wife had given him for Christmas, and he now fretted that it showed him to be "moderately obese."

"Do you want me to come back, Chuck?" Evan asked. "You should take time to digest."

"Reverend — I have to get used to calling you that — if you don't mind, you can watch me gulp the rest down. These days, the hurrier I go, the behinder I get. Keep your mask on, if you don't mind."

"Melissa Benton?" Evan asked as he sat. He didn't mind keeping his mask on. It might encourage Chuck to do most of the talking.

"Yeah," the guy acknowledged, swallowing the last of his sandwich and chasing it with two swallows of soda, "I figured. Her epilepsy seems managcable with medication. Which she's taking — as near as we can tell. As for PTSD — well — we know she was raped at least once. That's when she was a massage therapist at Twin Dragons. She told her therapist it was consensual. She expected this gangster Churpov was going to make her a star. But it was slam-bam and she was out of his suite. Then after the kidnapping, when he had her on the boat, she says he didn't touch her. But the threat was there, had to be stressful. Understand, in my book, under eighteen and *consensual* are not in my dictionary. But from what I hear, the Feds let the guy go home. What they got in return, they don't tell grunts like me."

Chuck has heart. But I'd like the guy more if I thought he cared more about his wards than his paperwork.

Evan asked him, "How about we let her come home?"

"Where or what is home?"

"The new parsonage is a very old farmhouse — but spacious. Four bedrooms. My wife Loretta and I are guardians of her little boy Buzz, and we have custody of the boy's father Luke. You might say all we want to do is complete the family."

"Those two plan on getting married?"

"That's a reasonable guess. They want to be together, I'm sure of that. Both of them are already eighteen."

"Yeah, but Luke is on the spectrum, and she's still in treatment. Sounds like they both need to be heavily medicated just to be able to say hello to each other in the morning."

"Oh, they're more functional than that. Luke is maintaining quite well, the current drug cocktail is working, and he's taking advanced courses in science and math with a tutor."

"So does he have challenges socializing? Is that why he's not in school?"

"He's homeschooling because he's not enrolled, not because of the pandemic. The kid's a loner — what can I say? How about Melissa?"

"*Maintaining,* to use your word. Takes her meds. No episodes the last two months. They say she talks on the phone with this kid Luke nonstop."

"Hardly nonstop. After lights out, yes, every night. Content of those conversations not only confidential but unknown and top secret."

"So it'll be just one happy family? What does Stuart Shackleton have to say about all this?"

Evan pulled Shackleton's letter from his coat pocket. "I have his power of attorney for purposes of managing the healthcare of his wife, his son, and his grandson."

Holloman didn't bother to look at the document. His brow furrowed. "How come he needs you? Word is he's a free man these days, more's the pity."

"He hasn't been much of a husband or father — even before he was incarcerated. Now he's said he needs time to sort things out. But by the time he does, if those kids are no longer wards — they're of age, they'll be married, and he won't have anything to say about it. I'm guessing they'll see him Christmas and on their birthdays. Maybe."

"Is he paying you? You won't be getting rich on a pastor's salary, and they'll be a support burden for sure. Those kids won't be getting jobs anytime soon, I'd guess."

"We'll pray about it," Evan managed to say.

Might as well play the Reverend card. What's he going to say? Prayers don't work?

Holloman smiled and said, "Who am I to say prayers don't work?"

"What's the way forward? When can she come home?"

"She has an eval next Tuesday. I'll review the write-up and let you know. Could be soon after that."

"I'll be paying her a visit later today, if that's all right."

"Sure," Holloman said, grinning. "But you go casting out any demons, I got to write it up, okay?"

❦

EVAN WASN'T sure what to say to Melissa. On his drive to the Nurturing Nest Clinic in Sedalia, he rehearsed his speeches.

Your sister sends her love, urges you to call. Luke sends his love, but you know this already.

Luke wouldn't tell him what they say to each other on the phone, but he did admit to holding it up to Buzz on FaceTime calls so his mother could delight in the sight of his slobbering face. Buzzbomb, so named because he was a poop factory as an infant, seemed to know who she was, gurgled with delight at the sight of her face, and grabbed at her image on the screen.

Everybody wants you home, but this paperwork-obsessed social worker has to say yes first. He's a tough nut to crack, as the farmers say.

You'll have your own room. You'll have farm chores. Luke has his. There will always be enough to eat and a clean bed to sleep in.

You and Luke will be expected to go to Sunday-morning services. You can hold hands in public, but you can't kiss. You can hold Buzz, but if he starts screaming, you must both leave the sanctuary.

You can expect some people to say nasty things about you. Possessed of demons. Child of Satan. Whore. Try to forgive them. Pray about it. They just don't understand. Some of them never will.

In fact, in days gone by, they'd encircle you and stone you to death. But although they're doing that to this day in places like Iran, it's a rare event in this country — or, at least, it has been for about four hundred years (with a few exceptions for some honor killings in closed ethnic communities). But this could change. About some events on this Earth, I'm not an optimist anymore.

Evan had expected to say all this and more. But he found her incoherent, sobbing uncontrollably. Even though he followed their protocols faithfully, they almost didn't let him see her.

Until he played the Reverend card.

9

Loretta always said that her kid sister Melissa was the prettier one. And Loretta was gorgeous. When they were orphans at Sisters of Mercy, Loretta earned her diploma at Appleton City High while Melissa was placed in the work-study program that ended with her job in the spa at the resort. Loretta had survived on her wits. Melissa had only her beauty to sell.

The girl told Evan she never felt abused. He had trouble believing that. When she became pregnant while still working at the resort, she tried to kill herself. That got her remanded to the nuns, who promptly referred her to the adolescent treatment center of Myerson Clinic. The pregnancy proved to be a false positive, but then she got pregnant for real by her fellow sufferer Luke Shackleton. How that could happen with 24/7 monitoring and video surveillance Evan also found difficult to believe.

Unless someone let it happen.

Now here she was, sitting on the edge of her bed, heaving huge sobs.

Evan sat down, wanting to come close and give her a hug, but he had to keep his distance.

She looked up at him, her eyes swollen and red, her cheeks flushed and wet. "What do you want?" she asked.

"I promised Luke I'd bring you ice cream, and I've failed in my duty."

"He knows what kind I like, but I never told him."

"It wasn't because I don't know what kind. I'm thinking of buying an ice-cream truck. You could help me make the rounds."

She chuckled. "You know, Evan, we could put you in a clown suit. That would totally work."

He shrugged, "All we have to do is bust you out of here. But you've got to promise to lighten up. What's the matter?"

"That's the thing," she sniffed. "I don't know. It just came over me. Like some big gush."

Evan suggested, "Like you have all this hurt bottled up inside, and you finally popped your cork?"

She giggled. "Yeah, I guess it's like that."

"I call that progress," Evan said confidently. "Like when you have too many beers on an empty stomach and you just have to chuck it all up."

She looked at him, amazed. "And how would you know about that?"

He shrugged, "People tell me things."

MELISSA WAS CLEARLY in no mood for serious conversation. Evan's goal in visiting her was simply to see how she was getting along and for her to see that someone cared, to assure her that she'd be welcome when she came home. He didn't linger to speak to staff, and he had to trust that the psychologist's evaluation next week would find her stable and fit. He prayed she could dry her tears by then. He didn't have much experience managing depressive episodes, but he assumed, as he'd told her, that finally being able to regurgitate the emotional poisons she'd been forced to swallow was a step in the process of healing.

This Melissa, although not out of it because of drugs, was not the talkative teen he'd known. She was withdrawn, careful. Her strong personality had learned to protect its own space.

Now Evan was motoring north on the way to John Knox Village in Lee's Summit. On toward evening, he'd be rolling through the town of Peculiar.

It was an apt description of his mental state as well.

Why is there evil in the world? To make things interesting?

He could say, *to give humans a choice.* That seemed far too glib.

On Main Street in Peculiar was Evan's second-favorite diner, Merle's American Tavern — another local institution that had stayed open during the pandemic, perhaps because otherwise some of their regulars would be challenged making their own meals. He was looking forward to chicken-fried chicken, a ridiculous redundancy that somehow telegraphed the old-fashioned farm recipe of poultry parts dipped in milk, tossed in white flour, and fried up in a skillet filled with whatever mix of greases was handy, typically lard and Crisco. Then you take the residual grease, toss in more flour and milk as you stir over low heat, and soon you'd have a rich, thick gravy that would coat your insides as insulation from the frigid winter or hold wallpaper to a wall for a century.

Southern Missouri health food. How I miss it!

He pulled into Merle's fully intending to partake of the best of the worst, but he ended up with a bowl of freshly homemade chicken-rice soup and two slices of thick Texas toast slathered with garlic butter.

The coffee was too weak, and he was fresh out of packets of instant Folgers to add to it. Perhaps stressed by the sufferings he'd encountered on his visitations, his old habits were returning.

And why has Naomi come back? Is she trying to torment me? I don't believe in ghosts, granted that she's a manifestation of my own desires. But I thought I was happy with Loretta, who has given herself completely to a new life that can't be much fun for her. Here I am lusting after Naomi. Wayward pecker, indeed! Leave it to me to think only of myself and pick an unattainable goal.

Evan had parked the blue Easter Egg around the block from Merle's on a side street. It wasn't that he couldn't find a space in front, just that he didn't always want the distinctive automobile advertising his whereabouts. Sometimes a man of God needs to be alone with his thoughts.

Although the wise man knows he's never alone — but may doubt God cares.

As Evan drove down the empty street toward the connector to the interstate, up ahead he saw a black mass in the center of the road. From this distance, it looked like a pile of clothing, perhaps a rumpled overcoat. But as Evan drew closer, the form raised its head, and he realized it was a dog, a big one, most likely a black Lab. He stopped the car on the roadside short of the animal and got out. He worried it was wounded, perhaps having been struck by a passing car. As he approached the dog slowly, its gaze tracked him carefully and calmly. It didn't whimper, and it wasn't panting, as it might have done if it were in pain. Its paws were splayed in front, and its demeanor was like that of a cherished family dog sitting regally in front of a comforting fireplace. Only here it was boldly attempting to own a few square feet in the center of a roadway for two-ton metal beasts that could roll right over an animal and keep on going.

As Evan drew close, he held out his hand to the dog's muzzle. The dog sniffed and turned its head away. As Evan was bending down to its level, the dog got up slowly but then ran away at a sprint.

He noticed the dog was female, wearing a collar and tags that jingled with her trot. And she didn't appear to be hurt.

She was quickly around the corner and out of sight. Evan got back into his car and drove on.

Another omen? What the French call a bête noir, *a dreaded black beast that follows you around.*

Evan told himself he didn't believe in omens, but they were starting to pile up. First those slippers with the questioning monogram, and now this mysterious black dog. And Melissa hadn't been able to explain why she'd broken down at the sight of him. His new responsibilities for visitations, mostly involving sickness and death, could easily affect his mindset and his mood. Simplistic as it might sound, he resolved to keep looking on the brighter side.

Where I can if it's not irreverent, I'll make a joke of it. Bête noir? I'm going to call her 'Old Black Betty, the Most Peculiar Dog.' That should bring a smile if I see her again.

He was looking forward to seeing Arthur Redwine. The old coot had a wacky sense of humor and was just crazy enough to have some wisdom to impart.

~

EVAN RECALLED his visit to Angus Clapper here at the retirement village — on the day of the man's death. They'd had a spirited game of chess, during which the old lawyer had demonstrated not only sharpness but also deceptive cunning. And he'd been vigorous enough to ogle his nurse.

Hope springs eternal? Especially in horny old men.

Visitors' antivirus protocols had to be respected, of course. Seeing Redwine in the solarium seemed like an eerie replay of Evan's meeting with Clapper. As Clapper had been, this old man was in a wheelchair. Under his face mask, his nostrils were hooked up to an oxygen bottle affixed to the back of the chair. Sticking out from the mask, he still had his chin whiskers, which were becoming sparse, and his pate had only wisps. He'd once been proud of his full, white beard. His face looked sunken and sallow. Always a slender fellow, now he'd shed pounds he couldn't afford to lose.

But his mood was as sunny as the bright room. "Evan!" he grinned, crinkling his mask. "You've come to tell me the good news."

Evan pulled up a chair and asked as he sat, "Just what would you like to hear, Arthur?"

"Why, the gospel, of course. The wiping away of tears, the promise of salvation!"

In a low, soothing voice, Evan repeated the only prayer he used to comfort himself. "Right here and right now, the all-powerful presence of God is."

What else can I say that I truly believe?

Redwine nodded sagely, saying, "Whenever I hear you say it, it's always like the first time. Thank you."

"How are they treating you? Are you getting enough to eat?"

He frowned. "You could bring me a hunk of Emmenthaler next time. They won't let me have it."

Evan remembered dropping by the farmhouse when Redwine still lived there. Lunch was a pie-wedge slice of Swiss cheese and crusty wholegrain bread. And an apple from one of the old fellow's trees.

Evan eyed him, "Why would they fret about your cholesterol now? Your heart's been working for almost a century with no help from them."

Redwine whispered, "Constipation! They got charts on my bowel movements. Fluids in and out. This is what they learn in medical school? This is what I pay them for? You're right. How did I manage all these years without some college man keeping track of my shits and pisses?"

"They're supposed to make sure you eat and drink enough water. You didn't answer my question."

He huffed. "Oh, I do all right. Sick of red Jell-O with pineapple. Never get butter, just some yellow, waxy stuff. Same excuse as the cheese, I suppose." His grimace deepened, and he reached into the side pocket of the chair to produce an envelope, which he held out to Evan. "The car and the house are yours, whether you stay with the church or not. You've given me your thanks more times than I care to hear. But there is this one thing you must do for me."

Evan opened the envelope and read the formal document. It was an advance directive designating him as decider of critical-care questions should Redwine become incapacitated.

Redwine was quick to add, "I know it's a damn bother, but you see I don't have anybody else. And I know you'll do what's right."

"Arthur," Evan sighed, "I don't mind at all, but understand there's the law and there's accepted medical practice. But for much of it, there's no strict right or wrong. These are personal choices, whatever you want for yourself when you aren't able to say. And from what I see here, you haven't been specific. Don't make me guess. You might think I always know what's best, but I don't."

I know there are rules about these things, and I'm not sure what they are. Or how they might apply.

Redwine cackled. "If I can't feel the sun on my face, if I can't taste their crappy food — pull the plug! I'm chicken to die before I'm taken, but I want to be with Sedalia."

I always wondered whether the city was named for some woman. Could be the love of his life was named for the place. It is a lovely name, sounds like a state of grace. Sedate. Radiant.

Redwine's wife had been gone for almost fifty years now. He'd lived on their farm like a hermit since then. Just about the only visitors he received were fundraisers from the Daughters of Calvary, and word was he'd written them big checks.

I bet he planted that willow tree to weep for her.

"I understand you want to be with your wife," Evan said reluctantly. "You know I lost my Naomi. But I have Loretta now. Didn't you ever feel you wanted more than living with a memory?"

How can I promise he'll be with her? How can anyone promise anything about the afterlife — or whether there is such a thing at all?

Redwine shook his head. "There was never anyone else. You were brave, what you did. And you took in those kids. I admire you for that. And it's why I gave you what I did. To help."

"It's working out," Evan assured him. "And, yes, you've made it possible. And you hardly knew me."

"I knew you were a bright kid with a big heart. And I think you were the only real friend Bobby Taggart ever had. Such a shame. He went before his time, no good reason."

"And there's another thing," Redwine said. "My Model T."

Arthur's ancient Ford Model T Roadster was still in operating condition, parked on the side of the house. Even though Luke had no license, he kept pestering Evan about taking the thing out on the road. Evan couldn't allow that, but he did permit Luke and Walt to joyride around the property in it. A companion Model A Touring Car that Arthur had bought to take Sedalia into town on Saturday nights had not been driven since her death. It was still in the barn, propped up on blocks, and its sleek, black paint job by now had been overcome by a soft patina of rust.

"Your roadster is in fine shape," Evan said, "Although I believe the historic-vehicle plates need to be renewed. We don't ever take it out on the road."

"When I do pass…" the old man began.

"We could donate it to the historical society. Or to a vintage vehicles club."

"Let me ask, who fancies it most?"

Evan didn't hesitate to answer. "Luke gets his kicks driving it around the property. But he has this tutor, Walt Engstrom, about his age, who is fascinated by anything technical. First time he saw that car, he was telling me how Henry Ford ordered parts in wooden packing crates.

And specified the dimensions of those crates down to the fraction of an inch. Then when his workers unpacked those, the crates went right back on the assembly line and became the floorboards of the Model T." Evan teased, "There was a guy almost as tight with a buck as you. And of course I mean that as high praise."

Redwine's eyes misted over. "You got a kid there can do anything he sets his mind to. No doubt has a penchant for remembering names, dates, and events. Prominent forehead, I bet."

Evan remembered that Redwine, for whom phrenology was a lifelong hobby, had made the same pronouncement of him when he was ten years old. But then he'd said the same of Bob and any other young person he met.

"I believe you're right," Evan said. "Walt is curious about everything."

"Not many people know how many geniuses we've hatched from these parts," Redwine said. "My father Jake went on and on about Clarence Melton. His mind was spinning all the time, like this kid. They say he invented the superheterodyne radio. Built his own airplane with no plans. Figured out the pitch of the propeller from studying a spiral staircase. Worked in a little auto-repair shop in Rockville during the Great Depression. Moved to KC in thirty-one, joined up with Western Air Express, which became Transcontinental Western Airlines, which became TWA."

"I never heard that story," Evan remarked.

"Then there was Rufus Kamm. A chemist. Came up with the formula for RC Cola."

"I didn't know."

"All I'm saying is, when you find gold, you got to pick it up, polish it. Give the Model T to young Engstrom with my blessings. And don't wait until I die."

~

AFTER GETTING BACK into the Cinquecento and before leaving Knox, Evan searched Wikipedia on his phone to check out Redwine's stories about Melton and Kamm. As he might have guessed, Evan found that neither had the superstar reputation local lore had given them. Melton got no mention at all in the history of radio, and Kamm got some credit for reformulating the soda, but hardly for inventing it.

Maybe these guys made huge contributions after all. But just like local boys since, because of their humble backgrounds, they assumed they were second-rate, never got the credit they deserved. What will Engstrom do one day?

EVAN DECIDED to pass back through Peculiar on the way home. He'd cruise the Main Street area slowly, and perhaps he'd get a second look at Black Betty. He wanted to make sure she was okay.

But it was dusk and soon her dark surroundings would envelop her. If she were still on the streets, she'd disappear into the night.

Evan was about to get back on the interstate when a ping on his phone alerted him to an incoming text. The ID showed it was from Marcus Thurston.

PULL OVER AND CALL ME. NOW.

10

F rom his message, Thurston must have guessed Evan was on the road. The explicit instruction to pull over was puzzling though. Nevertheless, Evan found a parking space on Main Street in Peculiar and promptly phoned the Reverend.

"Evan, are you driving?" Marcus asked urgently.

"Yes, but I've stopped like you said. What's wrong?"

There was a long pause while Thurston thought about how to say what he had to say, which came out as a stammer, "Evan, there was… an accident. Loretta…"

An involuntary gasp, like a sock in the stomach, then, "How is she? Where is she?"

Thurston's message was disjointed. "She was in the Lincoln. By herself. On her way to the church, I believe. Vehicle registered to us, you see, why they called me. Broadsided by a semi."

Evan cried out, *"How* is she and *where* is she?"

"They're not saying much. She's in the ER at Oak Hill Memorial

Hospital. Chet's gone over there, and I was going to meet up with him. But where are you? How far out? Can you drive?"

"Of course I can drive," Evan insisted, although he knew he wasn't breathing normally. He was suddenly feeling dizzy and sick to his stomach.

"Where are you?"

"Main Street, Peculiar. Can you believe it?"

"Stay put. I'm coming to pick you up. There's a rainstorm headed this way, and I'd feel better if you weren't behind the wheel just now."

"Marcus, I'll manage. Just tell me where—"

"We'll all be fine, and we trust in God, but right now you're going to trust in me and my faithful Ford Focus. I'll be there as fast as I can."

As the call ended, Evan rolled down the window of the car to gulp fresh air. The dampness and the ozone smell of the approaching storm promised a heavy downpour.

And now curled up comfortably on the sidewalk right beside the car in the fading light was Black Betty.

"THAT DOG HAS TAGS." Evan declared as he climbed into the passenger seat of Marcus's well-traveled Focus. "Maybe there's a phone number I could call."

"Evan," the reverend said calmly, "if the dog has tags, it has an owner — or a guardian, if you will. And if it's hanging around here like you say, that person can't be far away. For sure, we're not taking any wet dog in my back seat. And especially not now. You want to occupy your overactive mind, give Merle's a call while we're on our way. I wouldn't be surprised if that dog is living on scraps from the place."

"Black Betty," Evan muttered as he cast a look back and Thurston's car pulled away.

"You got her name off the tags?"

"No," Evan sighed. "It was a poor joke."

On the way out of town, Evan called Merle's. According to the person who answered, the dog was familiar, but her owner unknown. Evan was going to ask them to check her tags, but the restaurant must have been busy because the background noise was chaotic, and they hung up before he could ask. He didn't bother to call back. The rain was coming down in a torrent now, and he figured Betty would know where to go to find shelter.

But in that moment of turbulent emotion, fretting about the dog was a welcome distraction. He needed to do *something*. He couldn't sit and wait.

Dr. Ravi Krishna could have played a charismatic doctor on TV. He was thirtysomething and trim, with a neat, close-cropped black beard that was as dark as his bushy monobrow and intense eyes. The guy was so cool and composed, with such an air of confidence, Evan wondered how he'd ended up here in farm country, from which brilliant boys and girls seem to flee at the earliest opportunity.

Dressed in scrubs and in full protective gear, the young doctor had emerged from the operating theater to address Evan. He lifted his face shield and introduced himself, explaining he preferred to be addressed as Dr. Ravi rather than by his surname. Thurston and Sheriff Otis were standing on either side of the preacher as if to catch him should he faint. To Ravi's questioning glance at the other two, Evan replied, "It's okay. They can hear whatever you have to tell me."

Ravi announced, "She sustained fractures to her clavicle and sternum."

Evan breathed a sigh of relief. "When can she come home?"

The doctor's face stiffened. He hadn't finished. "Actually, the injuries to her torso are not the primary concern. There was considerable head trauma, and as of now she's in a coma."

"This is…bad," Evan muttered, and the wind went out of him.

The sheriff laid a hand on Evan's shoulder and confided, "Evan, I wasn't at the scene, but I've gone over the accident report, and I inspected the vehicle. Like the man said, serious injury to the head. But for all we know, it's just a bad concussion, and she'll snap right out of it."

"That car has airbags all over!" Evan exclaimed, as if that fact made her injuries unbelievable.

The sheriff said, "Those work on first impact, then they're done. She swerved to avoid an oncoming truck, and it sideswiped her. I'm sure the bags deployed then. The car was thrown into the ditch, and it rolled over several times."

Ravi was uncomfortable again, correcting, "It's more than a concussion, I'm afraid. We did a CT scan, and she's sustained traumatic brain injury — hematoma and swelling. We installed a catheter to drain the bleeding, and we're treating the swelling with medication. We'll be doing more tests, but I have to say as of now she's on the low end of the Glasgow scale." He added, "That's a quantitative assessment of how deep the coma is, but it's not necessarily an accurate predictor of survival."

Evan gasped, *"Survival?"*

Ravi explained, "Coma is complex, difficult to assess, and nearly impossible to predict. But until we have more data for her, I can't even begin to advise you about her chances for recovery." The doctor extended his hand, and Evan hardly had the energy to grip it. "If there's any change, any change at all, we'll notify you right away."

"Can I see her?"

"She's being moved out of the OR now and into ICU. We're able to monitor her closely in there until she's stabilized. Give us some time to get her settled. You can look in on her briefly and at a distance. I'm afraid you won't be able to stay." He paused, regarding Evan more carefully. "You have to expect she'll be hospitalized for some days, very possibly longer. If she has responsibilities at home, make your arrangements."

As Ravi retreated, Thurston threw an arm around Evan. "You are not to worry, Evan. You can see she's in good hands. Clint's taken Coralie over to the house, and Leslie's there too. Loving Embrace will make sure you have round-the-clock coverage for the caregiving and house-work. For now, I think you'd better bunk with me. We'll pray about it."

Evan was tearing up and asked, "What are they telling Luke?"

Marcus replied, "They're saying Loretta has been hurt, and she'll be in treatment for a while. You can call him later, but for now, give yourself some time."

The preacher agreed, "He understands *in treatment,* all right. Almost everyone he loves is in some kind of care."

Evan turned to the sheriff, asking, "And what about the other driver?"

"Commercial truck driver. No injuries. High on khat."

"What's that?"

"An illegal drug those guys chew, especially when they have to drive long hours or all night. Keeps them up but also makes them daredev-ils. He was DUI and at fault. We'll get you lawyered up and you won't be worrying about the hospital bills."

WHEN EVAN WAS FINALLY ALLOWED to visit Loretta, she'd been moved out of the ICU and into a private room. He found her lying on her back, stretched out, with her arms folded across her chest, her hands slightly curled. It chilled him to think that's just how funeral directors pose corpses in their caskets for viewing. Her eyes were closed, the expression on her face blank, and she was intubated. He knew that meant she either couldn't breathe on her own or they'd done it in case her condition were to deteriorate. A catheter emerged from her bandaged head, and its clear plastic tube was filled with pink fluid. The tube reentered a place on her neck, also bandaged.

The room was dimly lit and deathly quiet except for the rhythmic *gasp-gasp* of the ventilator and the *blip-blip* of the heart monitor.

They'd given him latex gloves. He took her hand. It was limp, cool to his touch. He desperately hoped she'd squeeze back, but the delicate fingers stayed lax.

Her skin was ivory white and slightly pink where those endearing freckles crossed her nose. Her lips were pale, dry, and slack around the breathing tube, which was strapped to an elastic harness around her head. He resolved to tell the nursing staff to apply some moisturizer to her lips so they wouldn't become chapped.

Or perhaps they know to do that.

She had been on her way to deliver those sandwiches. Evan worried how terrorized and panicked she must have been as the accident was happening, but he was sure she wasn't suffering now. In this state, she must be far from worry, but also perhaps far from ever experiencing anything at all.

I wish I could be where she is, be with her and hold her.

The rain was coming down steadily now, creating long streaks on the outside window of the ward beyond the partition near the nursing station. Evan wanted to think the town was crying for their imperiled daughter. Or perhaps some of them thought the impudent sinner had gotten what she deserved.

A selfish thought struck him.

First Naomi and now Loretta? How much more can I take?

Then:

She's not gone! I won't let her go! Can I bargain with God? What do I have to offer that hasn't been already given or promised?

11

Thurston's bungalow, the former parsonage that he now rented, had just one bed. But he insisted Evan take it. The senior man stretched out on the couch. He was so tall that his calves stuck out over an armrest and his size-twelve feet dangled in the air. But he had a horsehair blanket and a stout pair of woolen socks.

It rained all night, and as dawn broke there was a perceptible chill in the room, not least because of his guest's mood. Now the dark clouds were retreating, and the sun was peeking through.

Evan hadn't slept at all. He'd counted every raindrop.

Marcus was up with the chickens, as was his habit. He had instant coffee made by the time the preacher decided it was no use pretending to sleep. He took care to make Evan's extra-strong, with a generous helping of sugar, which he never used himself.

"Did you manage to sleep at all?" the older man asked Evan. The young preacher was clad in a T-shirt and shorts. Thurston had lent him a terrycloth robe, which was so long on him it came down to his ankles and made him feel like a boy.

Evan smiled weakly. "My mother always said, if you can't sleep, at least close your eyes and rest. I couldn't even do that."

Thurston ventured to ask, "Shall we have a prayer?"

Evan sighed deeply. It was almost a sob. He replied, "Marcus, you know I have only the one prayer. And right now it seems if God was ever hanging out with us, he must be on vacation."

"You know that's not true. The power and the presence *is.*"

Evan smirked. "Grammatically speaking, the power and the presence *are.* But somehow it sounds wrong, so I never corrected you. Because the presence *is* the power. It's all one. Yeah, I get that. But right now I'll settle for an unhealthy dose of caffeine."

He took a mug from Thurston and drained half of it.

"We can go back today," Thurston assured him. "We'll go back as often as you want. And we'll keep asking questions. It's okay for us to pester them, you know."

Evan plunked himself down at the kitchen table and gulped more coffee. Then he announced, "I already called over there. All the nursing station could tell me was she's still unresponsive. That's not good, not good at all." Then he added as if it followed logically, "First thing, I want to check on that dog."

Thurston wondered whether his friend had become delirious, saying tenderly, "Evan, don't you think Loretta's care should be our first concern? And I'd say Luke needs you as well. Maybe not right away, but soon."

"When she wakes up, I'll be there. Luke is in his world. But for now, the dog is something I can do something about."

WAS it misguided to be fretting about a stray dog when his wife could be dying? Evan couldn't explain the pull the animal was exerting on him, but he felt he had to obey it.

Granted, Betty was apparently licensed, at least at one time, but what if her guardian has died? That could explain why she's on the street. There's so much death going around these days — like it's following me around. Maybe I should stay away from Ann? From Loretta? And what about Melissa? Redwine could already be doomed.

If the last of the dogs Bob called Brownie had been able to talk, we'd know a lot more about why he died.

In some states, Evan knew, the legal status of dogs was as livestock. In others, legal-aid organizations were circulating petitions to ensure them rights as conscious beings. In Missouri, which was a border state during the Civil War, much the same debate had once raged about slaves. And today many educated adults had no idea that Native Americans ever lived here. Or that they were forcibly driven off the land where their houses now sat.

Including the Emmett farm. Now Shackleton wants to use the land for a hotel. Or a luxury brothel. Or a war museum.

In all the years Evan had lived here, he'd never met the descendant of an indigenous tribe — at least no one who claimed the heritage.

Uh-oh. We're not supposed to say tribe. *Those are* ethnic societies. *But it might not matter what you call them if they're still here but are made invisible.*

To some, caring about the welfare of a dog might have seemed pointless, especially when Evan had serious responsibilities of his own.

If I go to Loretta's side, there's literally nothing to do. But how can I just keep going about church business, visiting the sick and the dying? Counseling the fearful and the suffering? Even if I can bear up in front of them, won't they see how frail and useless I am? I know it's not my own power I pretend to bring, but the messenger's hands are empty.

Thurston seemed to understand that having a focus and undertaking an assignment, however trivial but achievable, were vitally important to the young Reverend Wycliff just now. The older man shrugged as he sipped his own coffee. "I guess it won't take us long to run up there and look around," he agreed.

It was an easy task to find Black Betty. Now that the skies had cleared, she was lying in the same place in the middle of the side street behind Merle's. The street wasn't busy at all, but as Thurston pulled his Focus over to the curb, Evan could see an older-model F-150 slow down and cautiously drive around her as she stirred not at all. He concluded her presence here had become a fixture, and fortunately no one so far had run her over — accidentally or otherwise.

Evan and the old pastor got out and strolled over to the recumbent mutt. Betty raised her head slightly but seemed unconcerned. Evan crouched down, held out his hand for her to get his scent, then he cautiously massaged the top of her head and the crooks of her ears. She remained calm and didn't make a sound, neither a whimper of pain or complaint, nor a moan of pleasure.

Evan inspected her dog tags, of which there were two attached to her well-worn collar. One was a St. Clair County license with a registration number, the other bore the name "Murphy" and a local phone number.

Evan cast a look to Thurston, wondering, "Murphy?"

"Murphy Brown? Maybe this one is Murphy Black. Somebody's got a sense of humor."

Evan pulled his phone from his hip pocket and dialed the number. A robot answered stating it was no longer in service.

"That's not a good sign," Evan reported. "The owner has either expired or moved." Then he asked his phone to dial county animal control. He got someone on the line right away, but they balked at giving him any information unless he could identify himself by the owner name they had on file. But, as he often did, he played the Reverend card, stating that he feared a church member had fallen ill. The ploy worked (what

Evan called a *heuristic fiction,* a useful lie), and the clerk gave him a name and an address in Peculiar.

Dropping the sheriff's name and not having to lie probably would have worked just as well.

A late-model sedan swerved around them, going much too fast.

"We better get outta here before we're taken too soon!" Thurston exclaimed. He caught another questioning glance from Evan, then added, "Yeah, sure. We'll drive the dog to that address. But if I have to fumigate, I'm holding you responsible."

Not having a leash, Evan decided to carry the dog, which went along without any resistance. Then he said, "Let's stop in at Merle's first. Maybe they know this person. Wouldn't hurt to get some background before we go knocking on his door. Some of these friendly folk have shotguns, you know."

"That's right," Thurston chuckled as he started the car. "Always the crack investigator."

THIS TIME, Evan was able to ask the assistant manager at Merle's, who not only knew the dog well but also had an opinion of its owner.

"Granny Myra Longacre?" he smirked, adding, "the town wacko." And he gave a street address that coincided with the one animal control had on file.

The house on the outskirts of Peculiar was larger than a shack, but not much larger. The clapboard construction looked pre-Civil War. Chickens were running around the front yard, and a goat was tied up in back.

A sign in front of the house by the road read, "Dame Longacre, Psychic Readings."

Seeing the sign, Thurston turned to Evan with a raised eyebrow. "Are you sure you want to get into this? You're a sane man, but both you and I know you might be just a bit suggestible at this point."

"You don't have to come," Evan said as he got out then helped the dog from the car. "Don't worry. I just want to make sure she knows her dog shouldn't be living in the street."

Evan donned his mask. The front door was open, and there was no response to his knock. On a chintz-covered table in the middle of the modestly furnished room he saw a large magnifying glass, a deck of tarot cards, a small pile of blanched chicken bones, and a scarf of iridescent purple silk. The arrangement of these items was precise to the point of being geometric.

Portents from her last reading? Or carefully arranged props?

The room was also her sleeping quarters, outfitted with a narrow cot. An adjoining room scarcely larger than a closet was the kitchen. A gaunt old woman stepped out. With no mask, her sardonic smile bared tobacco-stained teeth with gaps. Her desiccated skin looked as fragile as crepe paper. When her thin lips parted in a weak smile, the pink of her gums was exposed where she had lost her front teeth. The condition of her mouth gave her a lisp, but she spoke hardly above a whisper. As if to reassure her new client, she moved with deliberate slowness. She kept smiling as she sat down, and the myriad wrinkle lines spread out from her sparkling eyes like stellar rays.

"Murphy has brought you to me," she said with obvious pleasure. "I'm Granny Myra Longacre."

Removing his own mask, Evan announced himself formally. "Reverend Evan Wycliff. The Reverend Marcus Thurston, my colleague, is waiting outside in his car." Evan risked adding sarcastically, "He may fear lower-level demons." This brought no visible reaction from the granny. The dog sat obediently by her as Evan took a place at the table. He asked, "Do you know she's living in the street?"

"Morphia is living," she stated. "She goes where she is called."

Morphia? You've got to be kidding.

Evan could feel his patience wearing thin. "Are you saying you sent her out to find me?"

She sat regally, saying, "You are here. That is the case."

'The world is whatever is the case.' Does she read Wittgenstein, or did she just pick it up from Deepak Chopra?

She asked calmly, "What is on your mind?"

He wondered whether she could stand some teasing. He had resolved to make more jokes, but what came out was almost mean. "Don't you know?"

She smiled. "I know you're not here to challenge me, although I'm not so sure about the fellow outside, from what you say. Yes, I know many things. But what is it you *think* has brought you to me?"

His upset overflowed as he blurted out, "My wife's in a coma."

She answered icily, "People assume I can see the future. But as you might, I see only possibilities and likelihoods. It's possible she will recover. It's likely you and everyone around her will do their best. Were you not in the trade, so to speak, I might take your money and assure you falsely that she will live. But you'd be wise to doubt I know more than you."

Evan shot back, "I didn't come to have my fortune told. I came because I found Murphy curled up in the middle of the street. She seems totally unaware of the passing cars, and I worry she's sick. And she could get run over."

Stroking the dog's head, she said, "I will make sure she has something to eat. And a restive nap. I appreciate your trouble, but I'm sure you have more urgent concerns."

"Besides feeling more helpless than ever, my responsibilities include a church of needy souls plus two mentally disturbed teenagers and a toddler, and I'm a pastor who on some days might not question God's existence but does wonder sincerely whether he's paying attention or has any interest or influence in this world."

"There's one other thing you haven't mentioned," she stated.

His jaw clenched. "I'm listening."

"There's a spirit following you around. You haven't let her go."

Now you're freaking me out.

Evan took a moment, then realized this woman was more than some carnival act. She'd seen into his soul, and there was no point hiding his secrets. "True enough. She was my fiancé. She died in an accident. In a war zone. She counsels me from time to time. I find her help valuable." Then he emphasized, "No one else knows this."

"You know you have all you need without her help," Granny said. "Without mine, for that matter."

Yes, that's the prayer, the one I preach. Why is everyone throwing it back at me?

He sighed deeply, "Then why do I feel so alone?"

She smiled, "Because you *are* alone on this plane of existence, my dear. We all are."

Is that supposed to be an answer? A comfort? All she's doing is infuriating me!

Expecting she might yet offer some hope, he asked, "Is that all you have to tell me?"

She gave him a studied look. "We will all be dead soon enough. Worry is a useless emotion."

He choked, "Soon?"

"In the scheme of things, we are a blink in the eye of those who watch over us."

We're done here. What she seems to know about Naomi must have been a lucky guess. How many of her clients are fretting over ex-lovers?

He was ready to get up, but he had to ask, "What about my passing? Will I go before my wife does?"

"As I've told you, it's not for any of us to know," she replied firmly. "Is there anything more you wish to ask me?"

As Evan was leaving, he shot back, "Okay, why do bad things happen to good people?"

She shrugged, "There is a crack in everything. That's how the light gets in."

The Gospel According to Leonard Cohen.

Evan was at the door when she said, "It's pay what you can. But then you've returned my dog, whose price is beyond measure. And wiser than myself."

He dug into his pants pocket and found a ten-dollar bill, which he tossed onto the table, saying, "That's a new one — paying for a witch's curse!"

Her face was expressionless as she quickly grabbed the bill.

He slammed the door on his way out.

As Evan got back into the car, Marcus asked him, "Well?"

Evan growled, "The dog's name isn't Murphy. It's Morphia. It cost me ten bucks to find out I'm not going to live forever. At least, not in this body. No predictions about Loretta."

Marcus warned his friend, "Your anger is finally boiling up. That's to be expected—"

Evan snapped, "Just drive, okay?"

12

They weren't yet out of Peculiar when Marcus suggested, "We should be heading back to the hospital."

"I've called them three times this morning," Evan muttered. "There's no news. They're advising me to talk to Ravi after his rounds."

"I'm sure he'll have more to say. You'll get more information at least. They must've done some more tests by now."

"I'll feel better when she wakes up. Or just flutters her eyelids or flinches from a pinprick. Until then, I'll have to focus on not losing my mind."

"We should pray about it."

"Marcus, I've already told you that's not working for me these days."

Thurston drew a breath, trying to summon patience, when he said, "I'll deliver the sermon on Sunday. You have enough on your mind."

Evan turned on him. "Is that the first step to relieving me? Are you all going to take my vocation away from me, too?"

Marcus pulled the car over to the side of the road. "You're in no shape to calm anyone's nerves this Sunday," he said, which was hardly an answer to Evan's question. Opening the car door, Marcus added, "Let's stretch our legs. I don't want to have an argument with you in a moving vehicle."

Their route in Peculiar had been circuitous, and as coincidence would have it, here they were on Highrise Trail, which bordered the lush lawn of a public park, along with a roadside marker that Evan had found amusing on his first trip through this town.

Historical Spotmarker

In 1861-1864

While bloody battles raged

throughout the southern states

nothing happened here.

On seeing the sign again, Evan shook his head. "It's not the least bit funny anymore. They must not have been paying attention. There can't be a town where nothing happens. Day after day, some people go to bed at night and don't wake up the next morning. And those might be the lucky ones. How many have family who fought and suffered and died in whichever war? And how many are like Ann, Loretta, Melissa, or Luke, suffering in silence?"

As they walked aimlessly on the dewy grass, Marcus began, "Evan, you have a lot on your shoulders just now—"

"Do you want me to resign? Is that it? Is it because we lost all those members? Has the board lost confidence in me?"

"I wasn't in there with you just now, but I can bet you got a strong dose of the superstition some of these farm folk believe, even if they won't admit it."

"What are you trying to say?"

"When the board voted to approve your ordination, some of them did it because they believed the rumors you're a faith healer. I should have corrected that impression, but I didn't."

"Oh, brother" was all Evan could say.

"It's not the best time to tell you, but now some of those same folks are saying this attack of Loretta's is a sign from God. A sign you're on the wrong road. Or being punished, even."

"You can't believe that."

"Of course I don't. But you need to take care of your own. Show you can hold onto your faith as you get through this. And you know I'll do everything I can to help you."

Evan stopped walking, bowed his head, and took a long moment. Then he asked quietly, "What if it is?"

"What if it is *what?*"

"A message."

Marcus answered carefully, "Evan, human beings are meaning-making machines. You're the one who keeps saying it, and you've preached on it. We can't help it. It's a survival instinct. We do it so we can adapt and use whatever we learn to go on. And as for me, I don't believe God punishes — at least, not in this life, and I expect not in the next. By our feelings of guilt, we punish ourselves, and in so doing we lose faith in our salvation. That's why we suffer, where we go wrong."

"Your reasoning is all very neat and tidy," Evan said. "But I can't help thinking there's a reason why all this is happening."

"Like I say, you can't help trying to make sense of it. It's to be expected, like these feelings of anger."

Evan admitted, "Granny called me on it." He paused before he delivered his blunt confession: "I've been cheating on my wife."

Marcus drew a breath, "Evan! You haven't!"

"Oh, not in any physical or sexual sense. But emotionally, I haven't let go of Naomi."

"You love Loretta. I know you do."

Evan was embarrassed to say, "Yes, yes. But I still talk to Naomi."

"Talk? Talk!" Evan had never shared anything about Naomi's visitations to him with Reverend Thurston.

Evan explained, "Luke says he hears voices and the doctors say he's afflicted. Me, I hear her *and* I see her. What does that make me?" Then he added, "You could be right. Even though it felt like you were pushing it on me, I thought I was led to this job. But maybe not. Maybe I am the wrong guy. And when Loretta recovers, maybe we should rethink things, make a fresh start somewhere. This could be a sign after all, but is so much suffering necessary? If you told me to go, I'd go without an argument, but it's not sounding like you want to get rid of me."

"Evan, believe me," Marcus pleaded, his eyes red and watering. "You're the best hope we have. You've opened hearts and changed minds. No way I want you to go. I'm just saying take some time for yourself and your new family. And I swear to you, maybe not now but someday, we'll find some meaning in all of this, no matter how painful it's been."

Marcus threw his arms around Evan, and they stood there in the middle of the park, swaying, both of them sobbing softly.

13

Luke and Melissa were closer back when they were confined separately and neither was permitted to have a phone. He would summon his superpowers by deliberately slacking off his meds. He'd then be able to reach out to her through etheric portals that were closed when he was in normal states of being. He would send his awareness on flights out-of-body to hover near her. He'd shoot laser beams of affection through wormholes in hyperspace — directly into her suffering heart. He'd listen to the slightest ripples on the ether to pick up the cries and whispers of her volatile moods.

And at those rare times she was experiencing an epileptic seizure, his mighty sage self would sit on her chest while holding her shoulders to the floor in a protective vice grip until her gyrations ceased.

The few times Luke had dared to share such an experience with one of his therapists, their reactions were always the same. "Understand," they'd say, "these episodes aren't real. You're hallucinating."

He understood hallucinations, and those were different. If he opened a door on a room full of writhing snakes, he knew they weren't actually there. He wasn't afraid of them. He was aware that his mind was playing tricks. He'd gotten used to those waking nightmares, including all manner of swarming insects, crawling worms, and snarling predators as well as disgusting carrion, fluids, and smells.

The voices did disturb him. But he refused to follow their directives, no matter how dire the threatened consequences.

He told himself the hallucinations were punishments. He wasn't sure for which sins, but he resolved those afflictions would have no effect on him. He'd eventually grown wise to them — perhaps because the drug cocktail they were giving him now worked better.

When he had been confined to the clinic, he had little motivation to be faithful about taking their medicine. They had ways of enforcing the regimen and controlling him, but he had his ways of deception. And being unpredictable was one of his most powerful weapons against their constraints.

But now that he was living with Evan and Loretta, he sincerely wanted to at least maintain. He followed orders. He took the handful of multi-colored pills regularly. He made his bed, showered, dressed in clean clothes, combed his hair, and reported to the family table for meals and assignment of household chores. He did his homeschooling assignments as well, although even when Walter tried to set challenges, the problems were boring.

But now came a double-dose of upsetting news. Both his mother and his stepmother were hovering at death's door. Visiting Ann, who'd been dead to him already, had been no more upsetting than seeing those snakes. And seemed no more real.

But Loretta was tugging at his heart. He'd only been in her care at the farmhouse for a few months, but her love already felt more genuine than all the years of careful attention his own mother had given him, in spite of her own frailties.

Despite having been warned the boy was sensitive, Coralie had gone so far as to use the word *coma* in her description to him of Loretta's condition.

Luke was no stranger to altered states. There was no question of his going to see Loretta bodily in the hospital. Whether or not he'd be allowed, visiting Ann in such a place had predictably given him the creeps, but he wondered whether any of the portals he'd used to join Melissa were open to where Loretta's spirit might now be.

Someone or some entity must have told Ann it wasn't her time to go. Perhaps he could do the same for Loretta.

LORETTA WAS STILL in the critical-care ward and under close observation. She didn't require a ventilator, but she was on oxygen. Dr. Ravi explained to Evan that they'd move her back into the ICU if there were any complications, including respiratory infection, which was a known risk. They weren't just worried about Covid. The mildest infection in her lungs could be life-threatening.

"She's breathing on her own," the doctor emphasized.

"That's good," Evan said, "isn't it?"

"Of course. We'll be looking for any movement, any responses to stimuli. Her eyes remain closed. When we lift the lids to take a look, the retinas are fixed and dilated, and there's no response to bright light. Eye movement is nil, not reactive. And I must tell you, even if she does open her eyes, it will be a positive sign, yes. But it does not necessarily mean she's yet awake or aware. Do you follow?"

Evan nodded meekly, asking, "Don't assume progress means success?"

"That's right. It's not only a matter of whether she will recover but by how much. Will she be awake and aware? Will she know who you are? Will she eventually be able to follow commands, even do tasks? These are all uncertainties, and progress is gradual. It will take time. From this type of injury, people don't snap out of comas, never mind what you see in the movies."

"No miracles then?"

Ravi allowed himself the hint of a smile. "Life itself is a miracle. We keep getting better at sustaining it, even prolonging it. But consciousness? We still have no clue how it arises, and we really don't know when it's gone…" Then he added, perhaps out of respect for the reverend, "…If it ever dies."

"So can I see her?"

"Yes, now that she's off the ventilator I would say come and stay as long as you like. Call her name, and especially any pet names. Talk to her. Read to her. Hold her hand. Stroke her arm. Play music she likes. Or, why not, music she hates. Why not? If she usually wakes to an alarm clock, bring it and set it for the same time she usually gets up. Bring her phone. Make it ring."

"Do you really think she can hear?"

"The technical answer is that a type of brain scan can show neurons firing in response to auditory stimuli, even in some patients with her condition. We have yet to do those tests on her. Short answer, we don't know for sure — in general or from one case to the next. But there is one more thing I'd try."

"Please."

"We want sensory triggers of all kinds. When you come, wear yesterday's clothes. And if you'll permit me to be so crude, don't shower. If she can hear you, I'd bet she can smell you."

Evan mused, "Ah, you don't know her. She's a neat freak."

Ravi replied, "Then let's make her sit up and scold you!"

NOW THAT EVAN was routinely visiting the sick and the dying, he should have known all the comforting words. He told Loretta he loved her, that she was needed and missed and adored, and that he was so sorry such an awful and unfair thing had happened to her, of all people, who had been making the mightiest effort to please not just him and their family but everyone in town.

It sounds like a bad greeting card.

He decided to tell her a story, not sure when he began how it would end or what healing value it might have for her.

"When I got the news, I was coming back from Knox, passing through Peculiar. Can you believe it? God's weird sense of humor. Anyhow, there was this dog. Big, black dog, and she was lying right in the middle of the road. I thought she might be injured, so I stopped to check on her. She seemed fine, maybe just old and lazy. When they told me here I couldn't see you right away, I don't know, I needed something to do, and I figured if I went home I might upset everybody. They tell me Coralie is cooking and calming nerves. I had Marcus drive me back up to Peculiar, and, sure enough, there was the old dog lying in the same place in the road. Unhurt. But she has tags and I tracked them down. Turns out she belongs to this old fortune-teller, Granny Longacre. So I go to see her because who can ignore the sign of a black dog in the middle of the road when you're not at all superstitious but you're worried every weird thing might be an omen?

"The dog's name on the tag is Murphy, but this granny is calling her Morphia. That's morphine — a drug to ease pain. I'm thinking maybe the dog is leading me to some relief from all that's happening to us."

It wasn't until Evan had gone this far in the story that he realized he couldn't tell Loretta that Granny had nothing to say about her recovery. This had to be a healing story, not some dire portent with no resolution, no hope.

He added, "She says you're going to snap out of this. And I even followed doctor's orders. I wore my old sweatshirt — you know the Jayhawk one I can't show anybody that's been on the floor of the closet for ages? He's saying you if you can hear me you can also smell me, so you can't pretend it's not me sitting here stinking up the place."

He resolved to spend the night at her side if they'd let him. By now his stomach was growling and he was thirsty. He wondered how long he could last on beef jerky and cheesy crackers from the vending machine.

I just know I can't leave her side now. I'll have to take it a day at a time.

As Evan was dozing off at Loretta's bedside, darkness had fallen. Dr. Ravi was about to climb into his rusted Volvo at the end of his shift when a shiny, silver Mercedes-AMG S65 sport sedan pulled up alongside him.

The driver's-side window rolled down in a whir, and the commanding voice came, "Doctor, permit me to buy an hour of your time." The resonant voice belonged to Stuart Shackleton, and he was not a man to be refused. "Please, get in," he said, sounding polite but firm.

The banker wore no mask, but the doctor had a pocketful of disposables, and before he would get in, he gestured for his host to comply. Ravi might have assumed they'd have a conversation right there in the privacy of the car, but no sooner had he gotten in than the luxury sedan began to move. Another commanding voice from the dashboard told him to buckle up, so he did.

"Where are you taking me?" Ravi asked nervously.

Instead of answering, the driver asked, "What's your favorite poison? Bombay Sapphire or Beefeater's?"

The doctor sniffed, "Are you assuming my drink is gin and tonic because I'm of Indian ancestry?"

"Okay, single malt," the man cracked. "You drive a hard bargain."

"I wasn't aware there was a bargain to be made. Again, where are you taking me and for what purpose?"

This time Shackleton explained, "I need to know about coma, its diagnosis and prognosis. Treatment durations and likely outcomes."

Ravi shook his head, "You understand, I cannot share any information about Mrs. Wycliff."

"We'll talk in the abstract then. The hypothetical. Think of me as your nonspecialist associate. I'm an intern and you're briefing me on what to expect when presented with such a case."

"What is your interest? And why should I do this?"

"My interest is that I have a stake in the welfare of certain individuals, including the patient's extended family. And I must make a calculated determination of the extent to which I am willing to support them financially." Then he added, lightly but meaningfully, "As for why you might want to help me, I believe you still have a sizable student loan balance."

Unnerved, Ravi admitted, "That I do. How is this relevant?"

Shackleton said simply, "A protracted coma treatment will be expensive, even with the best insurance — which Reverend Wycliff doesn't have. And accident coverage will have limits. An interested party might be motivated to make sure your bill gets paid."

At the bar of the Flaming Lantern Restaurant in Butler, no doubt in reaction to the stresses of his workday and his nervousness about this interrogation, Dr. Ravi did indeed knock back several single-malt Macallan whiskies, neat. Shackleton matched him shot for shot with what looked like vodka, but unbeknownst to his guest, he'd tipped the bartender to keep refilling his glass with plain water. He fully intended to drink this callow youth under the table while loosening his tongue.

And after he got started, Ravi's responses to hypotheticals sounded a lot like his actual assessment of Loretta's condition. It didn't take long for the banker to learn what he wanted to know. There were possibilities and likelihoods that Ravi hadn't shared with Evan because the doctor refused to speculate: Coma, unless artificially induced as a treatment, usually didn't last longer than four weeks. If it did, it may be long-term. During that time, risk of life-threatening cardiovascular or respiratory complications was high. Statistically, twenty-percent of patients with low initial Glasgow scores survived. Of those, about ten percent would achieve an outcome above the level of severe disability. All but five percent of patients who showed no response in retina or eye movements within six hours of admission would die.

The doctor qualified his answers. "Understand, there is considerable variability. Circumstances differ widely, and the technology is improving all the time. It's possible today to keep the body viable long after there is little or no hope of the brain's regaining consciousness. We do this with transplant donors, for example. But I've read in the literature that seventy percent of coma-patient deaths in hospital are because their families decide it's more merciful to take them off life support."

Shackleton asked, "Could you be more precise about what's involved in pulling the plug?"

"We're talking about patients who can't express their wishes at the time. The question is both legal and moral. In Missouri, I can take a patient off the ventilator if there is either an advance directive or the family requests it. However, for a patient who is breathing on their own, no matter what the family wants, I can't remove a feeding tube unless the patient has authorized it in an advance directive."

Shackleton lowered his voice to ask, "And the decision to pull the plug, how often do you think the motivations are financial? Limit the expenses of prolonging life, perhaps uselessly?"

Dr. Ravi bowed his head, perhaps reflecting on the seriousness of the question or simply dizzy because he'd had too much Scotch. Then he said, "Those who want it done on religious grounds seem to feel it's wrong for anyone except God — including the patient — to decide to end life. Insurance companies, of course, must follow the law but obviously want to mitigate exposure. It's no coincidence that the healthcare industry is pushing advance directives. From the standpoint of caregivers like myself, it's more a matter of wanting clear instructions — not only reducing our risk of getting sued but also simply being able to sleep at night."

"I'll drive you home," Shackleton offered. "Will building security be alerted if they see your car has been in the lot until morning?"

Ravi was amused. "Will they think it's unusual if a critical-care doctor is working a double shift?"

Shackleton drove the inebriated doctor to his modest apartment building in Butler. There was no conversation because Ravi had dozed off. After getting nudged awake at their destination, he asked his host groggily, "What about my loan?"

Shackleton didn't hesitate to answer. "Doctor, I haven't made any requests of you, and I'd expect your recommendations to always be in the best interests of your patients, with due consideration for the welfare of their families."

"What's that supposed to mean?"

"It means," the banker said, "always remember that I'm prepared to help you do the right and lawful thing."

14

Luke feared the worst because Evan hadn't come home since the accident. The consequences for the young man might be to send him back to the mental health clinic or make him live with his father. Much as he was beginning to think of himself as an adult, he appreciated that being in the care of Evan and Loretta was somehow keeping him from these nasty alternatives, possibly affording him the best life he could have. Even though Luke was wildly worshipful of Melissa, he'd come to adore Loretta. Not only because of the sisterly resemblance but also because, even though Loretta was only two years older, it had always fallen to her to be the responsible one. Luke felt safe with her. He took his meds faithfully to please her. She'd left a void, and he worried that in time her absence could become unbearable.

It was the second night after her accident, and Luke had been told Evan was camping out at the hospital. Coralie had been helping here, and Luke liked her well enough, but that guy Clint always dropped her off and picked her up when she stayed at the house, and Luke had mixed feelings about him. Clint was still working as a caretaker in the adolescent wing at Myerson, and there had been times when he'd had to enforce Luke's timeouts. Some healthy suspicion lingered.

Luke couldn't sleep, and he was lying awake on his back in his bed, staring up at the ceiling. His mind was clear, and he wasn't tripping. Those times when he wanted to be close to Melissa, he would close his eyes, focusing inward on his breathing while ignoring sounds, the room temperature, breezes, and the occasional twinge or itch. Locked in the universe of his head, he'd will himself upward. He'd be hovering above his bed, then above the house, then above the rolling farmland. Following heart-tugs, he'd fly to wherever his bride-to-be was.

This worked, Luke assumed, because Melissa's body and soul were fused together in the same place. He knew that Loretta's comatose body was in the hospital. But where was her soul? It might not be there. It might not be anywhere that Luke could find. It might not even be a physical place. More like a state of being. This was all new territory, and he'd have to learn how to find his way around in it.

In his mind's eye, he pictured Loretta's face and the warmth of her smile. He recalled the reassurance of her touch on his arm or his shoulder or his cheek, casual brushes that didn't seem so significant at the time, but in retrospect charged with spiritual electricity. Comforting. Thrilling. Angelic.

Somehow he knew she was still alive. If she was still bound to this Earth, he thought he could find her. Venturing out into the cosmos might be a bigger journey than he could yet undertake.

He didn't have to look out of the window to know the Moon was full tonight. Its beneficent glow flooded the grassy landscape. As if searching for a distant radio signal, he tried to tune to Loretta's emotional channel. Melissa communicated that way. Her sister must as well.

Longing came through as a signal like a continuous, sustained moaning. Loretta had gone off somewhere and couldn't find the way back to her suffering body.

Luke willed himself to be in that somewhere.

He found her sitting by the edge of a babbling brook. He knew it wasn't water. It was an image. But its rippling effect on his feelings was the same. She wasn't in a panic, but her mood was sad. He hovered over her, tried to speak, but no words came. He wasn't surprised. When he'd encountered people in dreams, he couldn't speak to them either. She didn't even act as though she knew he was there.

He could pick up on her thoughts though. She wanted Evan by her side more than anything, but she knew he shouldn't join her. He'd told her a story about a black dog named Morphia, and now its etheric self was sitting at her side watching the imaginary clear water flow over the rocks.

Luke sensed that Morphia could comfort her but not transport her. The kind dog was a familiar spirit, a messenger, and a helpmeet.

Luke was frustrated because he couldn't find a way to make his presence known. He was comforted that he'd found Loretta existing in a kind of spiritual waiting room.

He'd learned there was hope. Now he'd have to find his way home.

And if he found his way, would he be able to guide her back the next time?

Stuart Shackleton had requested a meeting with the hospital administrator. Although the medical status of patients was strictly confidential, apparently discussing financial matters was a gray area open to discussion with interested parties.

Shackleton announced, "I'm considering setting up a trust fund for one of your patients, Loretta Wycliff."

"I've reviewed the case file," Clyde Barstow acknowledged. He was a slightly built, balding, middle-aged man in an unremarkable suit. Another weary bureaucrat for whom precision in accounting was akin to righteousness. "High likelihood of long-term treatment, and, assuming survival and discharge, assisted living indefinitely. You're extended family, I understand?"

"As you may know, I've designated her and her husband, Reverend Wycliff, as my son Luke's guardians. My boy's been diagnosed with schizophrenia, and my wife Ann is in assisted living at Myerson with late-stage dementia. My personal circumstances have been uncertain, at best, and I'm deeply indebted to the Wycliffs for their help and support. In return, I am still a man of means, and at the very least I can help pay the bills."

"I'll tell you that the church carries medical insurance for their employees, but of course those benefits have limits. I believe there is an accident claim, but I haven't been informed of its status. I expect the church would be the guarantor, but as you can imagine, a rural congregation will not have unlimited resources."

The banker closed his eyes while he took a deep breath as if to say he already understood as much. Then he offered, "I'm prepared to guarantee the expenses of her care. Inpatient, of course, as well as going forward. And, if I might, perhaps a stipend for Dr. Ravi as a research grant?"

Barstow grinned, "Most generous. I'll have those papers drawn up." Then he added, "From time to time we have openings on our board…"

"I'd be honored," Shackleton assured him, "should I plan to stay in the area."

EVAN HAD BEEN LIVING at Loretta's side in the hospital despite repeated urgings of staff to go home and get some rest and wholesome food. They'd only allowed him to stay after he'd agreed to submit to a Covid test. Thankfully, he was negative. The hospital had specific visiting hours, but in this pathetic case no one had the heart to enforce the rules — as long as the patient was out of the ICU and still breathing on her own.

In coma cases, visitors might understandably hope they'd be at the bedside to witness a spontaneous recovery. The patient would open her eyes and spring back to life. But as Dr. Ravi had advised Evan, coma patients typically didn't regain consciousness all of a sudden. It was usually a groggy wakeup, as if from some brutal bender, followed by a protracted period of therapy, cognitive exercises, and slow, stepwise progress.

Follow my finger. Does this pinprick feel dull or sharp? Are you feeling hot or cold? What day of the week is it? What's your birthday? Who is president of the United States? (This last question was becoming more controversial than it used to be, especially in this part of the country.)

Emotionally, Evan felt as though he was willing Loretta to hang onto life. He feared that if he left her side she'd expire. But by the end of the third day, he was beginning to think this would be a long pull. And unless he were willing to give up his other responsibilities, he'd better attend to those as well.

He drove up to his house at midday. Coralie had already left for her morning shift at the C'mon. He found Leslie in the kitchen with Buzz perched in his highchair as she was trying to get him to accept a gloppy spoonful of cooked cereal.

"So how is the missus, Pastor?" Leslie grinned. "We all just know she's gonna be right as rain."

What's so right about rain? No use asking her. She's trying to be sweet. No telling how much Coralie, who hears everything, has shared with her.

"We appreciate so much what you're doing, Leslie," Evan said as he made his way to the coffee pot. "Did you spend the night?"

"That I did," she said proudly. "No trouble. No trouble at all."

"Don't you have to be in school today?"

She wrinkled her nose. "I'm done with that. Beauty school starts next month." She was quick to add, "You probably won't be needing me at all by then."

She'd stopped waving the spoon in front of the toddler's face to have the conversation, and now Buzz was protesting by literally buzzing.

He'd learned to make the sound with his wet lips, and he was spewing spittle, milk, and chunks of oatmeal. Evan knew the child wasn't fussing. He was just being Buzz.

Leslie obliged Buzz with another spoonful, which he snapped up and swallowed, issuing a belch as a thank-you. She asked Evan, "Do you want me to fix you some lunch, or maybe you just want to settle yourself down for a nap? You look all tuckered, if you don't mind my sayin'."

"I do think I'll lie down for a while," Evan told her. "But where is Luke? I should check in with him first."

If Luke were another boy, I'd worry he'd be hitting on her. But I can't imagine it, and I'm not going to add that concern to my list of terrors.

She sighed. "Where would he be? In his room with his eyes glued to that laptop. Hey, don't go getting him those VR goggles he wants. If you think he's in his own world now, he won't have any friends except some avatar in another time zone."

Evan had to ask, "How is he with you? Do you think girls like him? I mean, of course he's stuck on Melissa, but assuming he can take those goggles off, he has to learn how to live in the real world."

A bigger sigh came from her this time, one of exasperation. "Oh, Luke is cute and all. People will always say he's weird, even when he's minding his meds and all mellowed out. Now, Walter, that boy's got the beginnings of a build on him, and he could be ripped if he wanted. I've told him he needs some more meat on those wings. He's like Luke with his know-it-all attitude, but if he wants any dates he's going to have to learn to shut up and listen when a girl tries to tell him what's what."

Evan wasn't sure whether to share this, but he said, "You know, Walt's probably going to end up with a Ph.D. If you hook up with him, what will you two have to talk about?"

Hardly offended, she shook with a fit of giggles, "Pastor, I don't have to tell you that lovebirds don't spend all their time billing and cooing. I mean, Loretta only made it through high school, but you two seem to get on just fine."

Evan smiled, "That we do." As he stirred his coffee, he realized he hadn't thought much since the wedding about how different his background was from his wife's. Naomi had been more or less an intellectual equal, and often their conversations were more like spirited debates. But he met Loretta at the heart level, and that bond was just as strong. He didn't think she worried that her education was inadequate. She was sharp and she was quick. No, it was the transition in social roles that must challenge her. He worried she was much too serious about acting the part of conscientious church lady.

I must remember to tell her that when she wakes up.

LUKE WAS INDEED HUNCHED over his desk and staring at his laptop, but Evan could tell it wasn't a video game on the screen. The boy was scrolling through pages of dense text, some with diagrams and charts.

He'd heard Evan come in but didn't look up. Still focused on the screen he asked, "Where is she on the Glasgow scale?"

Does everybody but me know about this score? Is it a topic of everyday conversation like batting averages and RBIs?

Evan rested his hand on Luke's shoulder. "Somewhere between three and four. I hope you haven't been spending all your time researching this."

The boy grumbled, "Don't worry. I can stop whenever I want."

This is his idea of a joke. Like I'm accusing him of being addicted. As if anyone could stop him when his curious mind is plagued with a question.

"There's a very bright guy on her case," Evan assured him. "Dr. Ravi Krishna."

Still without looking up, Luke muttered, "Krishna means *black* in Sanskrit, you know."

There's that sense of humor nagging at me, taunting me. Am I supposed to be amused — or warned?

But to Luke, all he said was, "No, I didn't know. But it's also the name of a Hindu god, so maybe we have that going for us." Giving the boy's shoulder a reassuring pat, he turned and said as he left the room, "I'm going to try and get some sleep. You should try."

15

———

Perhaps Stuart Shackleton's most satisfying achievement after his acquittal was the return of his cherished boat, the yacht *Namouna*. As far as he knew, it was still the largest private motor yacht on Truman Lake. After the showdown with Dmitri Churpov, who had commandeered it during his attempted kidnapping of Melissa Benton, the Feds had impounded it as evidence. If Evan's brilliant deception of Churpov hadn't worked, there almost certainly would have been a shoot-out between the mobster's bodyguards and the SWAT team, and the *Namouna* would today be a pile of bullet-shredded rubble at the bottom of the lake. After the Feds were done with it, Shackleton had intended to pledge it toward his bail, but even his high-powered legal team could not convince the judge that he wasn't a flight risk. The boat had stayed in dry-dock until today when it slid down the boat launch at Osceola marina and the banker's rehired captain fired up its twin diesels.

At the time of the showdown, Shackleton had actually been prepared to sacrifice his boat to get back at Churpov. He hadn't known about Evan's scheme to rescue the girl, and, sure that the mobster had betrayed him many times over, he was prepared that morning to take the guy out with his own deer rifle from the distant vantage point of a rented houseboat. He'd worried about the girl's safety, but he'd lusted after revenge more.

The miracle that Evan worked that day not only saved Melissa and caused Churpov's capture, but it also prevented Shackleton from actually committing murder. If it were true that he really didn't assassinate Father Coyle, he was only guilty of evil intent. And even though he'd coveted Bob Taggart's farmland, he'd played no active part in the man's suicide. Wanting these three people dead had not made it so.

Soon after the launch, the captain steered the boat into its slip, where Shackleton and his attorney Bert Harrison boarded. The ship's stores had already been richly stocked per the owner's instructions, and as the *Namouna* headed out, Shackleton and Harrison made themselves comfortable lounging on the fantail as they sipped tall vodka tonics served by a cook-steward, the only other crewman onboard.

With the boat out on the water and underway for mid-channel, the captain at the helm, and the steward belowdecks, the two men could have a private conversation.

"Well, Stu, are you rested?" Harrison asked. "Up to your old schemes?"

The banker chuckled. "What would you know about any of those, Bert? You've kept your hands clean, as far as I know. As for me, I'm fit as can be, fighting weight. All I could do in prison was eat, sleep, and work on the weight pile. They stuff you full of the starches, lots of beans and rice for our brown brothers, but I managed to stay trim." Then he asked, "How about you? You ready for another fight?"

"You mean the Emmett farm? That's still hung up in probate. Discovery's done. That one's a waiting game. You'll need me for a hearing or two, but it really depends on how difficult Edith Taggart is going to be about pressing her claims to her husband's estate."

"Edie *Clark,*" he corrected. "She's already dropped the guy's name. No, I'm talking about something else. Much bigger — potentially much, much bigger."

"Bigger than your development deals? You were smart to sell off your shares in the casino, but I figured you were far from done with the resort business in this neck of the woods."

Harrison's middle-aged demeanor was even more conservative than Shackleton's. The man could tolerate his client not only because of sizable fees but also because the lawyer never asked questions to which he didn't require answers.

"We're going after Green Monster Global Logistics," Shackleton told him.

Harrison looked appalled. "With my little firm? What the hell for? I haven't seen the numbers, but aren't they the largest cargo operation in the world? Greek ownership backed by Russian hoods and German banks. Pockets so deep they can't find the bottom. And when I say an *army* of lawyers, I mean a goddamn army. Including goons, I'd guess. Can you share the facts of the case?"

"A semi hauling a container right here on Highway P sideswiped a resident's SUV in a rainstorm. The car swerved into the ditch, flipped over a few times, and the driver's in Oak Hill Hospital in a coma. Brain injuries, early tests not good, prognosis bleak. No passengers in her car. The truck driver is unhurt, but he was loony on some Ethiopian weed — khat. The truckers chew it like tobacco to keep awake. They can also lose their inhibitions, take risks."

The lawyer observed, "Sounds like a pretty straightforward insurance case. A few million, and for sure it'll take a while if they don't settle."

"The operator is Green Monster. The victim is the pretty new wife of the town's young Baptist minister."

"Okay, like I say, the two carriers will duke it out on liability — property and medical, along with pain and suffering. Then the family could pile it on in a separate civil suit. This kind of thing happens every day, unfortunately. But, hell, it's routine. Far from a scheme. Personal injury isn't our thing at the firm."

"I'm not necessarily talking about a lawsuit. The potential is for an international news scandal. A huge globalist corporation. Green Monster has been buying up other operators left and right. Their diversification plan includes leveraging the brand into waste management — and pushing their way onto the fashionable side of the international environmental movement. Meanwhile they go shopping for politicians in every country they care about, typically lefties. They're also going to go big in robotic trucks, and to get that done they'll be fighting the unions day and night. But from what my sources tell me, abuse of this khat drug is a common thing. It's been scandal fodder in Africa for years, but the story never broke here. We've got the corruption story that the big operators could be looking the other way on drug abuse. Then we've got this huge sympathy factor — tragically injured gorgeous victim, righteous family. It's a big story — a story with *heat.*"

"But isn't this up to the preacher and the family? How do you plan to benefit?" The lawyer frowned, then advised, "Heat? I hope you're not thinking of threatening the company with some kind of smear campaign. Or a stockholders' revolt? Okay, you could help the family bring a lawsuit, but that's small money for a guy in your league. It could drag on for years. As for bad publicity, threatening a civil case might not be extortion, but if they do pay to make the bad man go away, you won't be able to prevent the story from leaking. Like they say, if you let the cat out of the bag, you can't get it back in."

"I've already offered to underwrite the victim's medical expenses. The preacher will owe me. Suing Green Monster would be a sideshow."

Harrison shook his head. "What do you want from him? I know you've thought this through. You always do."

"We use the publicity to make that preacher a star. Once he's the new Oral Roberts, the accident will just be backstory."

"Don't tell me you've found religion. Again, what's in it for you?"

Shackleton grinned. "What all could you do with a multinational, tax-free organization?"

Harrison chuckled admiringly, "I'd suppose just about everything you could do with casinos — without the rackets, I hope. Understand — accounting isn't my field, and we'd keep it that way." He thought a moment. "What about the woman? If she recovers soon and it's not particularly debilitating, the sympathy factor with the public won't be so great."

Shackleton smirked. "I've dug into her case, and I'm betting she won't do well. Not well at all. But I'm not betting on her dying anytime soon. As a matter of fact, she could grow old in that bed."

16

A restorative sleep was just what Evan needed. Despite his emotional upheaval, he was so exhausted he slept through until mid-morning and woke up refreshed. He was aware his dreams had been vivid and active, but seconds after waking he couldn't recall the slightest detail.

Probably just as well.

Before he was even dressed or had his coffee, he was calling the hospital. By now he knew all the names on all the shifts at the nursing station.

No change, favorable or otherwise. Loretta was being nourished through a feeding tube inserted in her nose, threaded past her throat to deposit a high-carb slurry directly into her esophagus. The nurse explained this way the diet could be richer than providing it through the IV. The patient urinated through a catheter into a bedside bag, and the output volume was measured and noted. The feeding was low-residue, so she simply wore a diaper that was changed as necessary. They massaged and sponge-washed her arms and legs once a day, and they turned her body on a regular schedule to prevent bedsores and promote circulation.

"She's doing just fine," they had told him. That was the bottom-line statement, although relative to what was the question.

Evan appreciated that professional training for nurses had to include counseling and supporting the family, and he wondered in the case of comatose patients which was more difficult.

He well knew that his wife's simply maintaining was an achievement, although he couldn't manage to draw encouragement from the fact.

Leslie had been up for hours, had fed Buzz, and now she was in the parlor trying to amuse him with his toys as he romped in his playpen. Her patience and her good humor seemed unlimited.

Luke was in his room with the door closed, which signaled to stay away, something Evan had learned to respect and not worry too much about as long as the boy at least emerged for meals.

Evan helped himself to a bowl of cornflakes and was surprised to find fresh bananas on the sideboard. The shopper from Loving Embrace was being attentive. He'd think to ask who it was.

He phoned Marcus to give him an update, only able to offer the same mundane details the nursing staff had shared with him. The old pastor said he had business matters to discuss with Evan — hardly urgent, but important — so they agreed to meet for lunch at the C'mon.

Evan fully intended to check in on Ann Shackleton again soon, but maybe not today. Visiting Redwine would have to remain on his list, but the fellow's immediate plight didn't seem as dire. No doubt there were others Evan would need to see, and he guessed those responsibilities might be among the business matters Reverend Thurston wanted to discuss.

Not sure I could deal with any funerals — or even a wedding.

It occurred to Evan that just now he needed to have a heart-to-heart with a friend. Naomi's appearances were not predictable. She couldn't be summoned, and he was too dependent on her still. Cora was a friend and an ally, but she was also a gossip. Bob Taggart would have been the listener he craved. He was too bewildered to have burning questions. He just wanted to start sharing without censoring himself. He might even indulge himself in a cry.

If he were counseling someone in the congregation, he'd advise them to pray. He told himself he'd do that, just not now.

There's too much static on the line!

He decided he knew just the person. And it had been too long since he'd paid her a visit.

HE FOUND the Reverend Mother Bernadette working in the rose garden at Sisters of Mercy, just as he had first met Father Coyle busy in the same place at the same task.

He'd always seen her in full-dress habit, and her informal appearance was startling. She was wearing denim overalls, a baggy T-shirt, and a cloth skullcap to cover her thinning hair. Her rimless glasses were the only remnant of her familiar austere look.

She wore canvas gardening gloves that were too big for her hands. Evan guessed they must have been Coyle's. She stopped working with her shears when she saw Evan approach.

The nun looked up at him and smiled serenely, saying "My dear friend, take off that mask. Feel the sweet breeze! How is it you trouble to see me at a time when your cross has become so heavy? I am so sorry."

She's heard the rumors.

"So you know," he said. "Thank you. I can't presume to unburden myself, but some intuition told me if I sat down with you, I could take a breath."

She gestured toward a wooden bench on the edge of the bricked walkway, and they sat.

"Do take a deep breath," she advised. "Our roses are in full bloom. The Lincolns are almost as big as pie plates."

"This is where I first met Father Coyle," Evan told her as he surveyed the lush foliage and delighted in the floral scent as he took that deep breath. "You've done a wonderful job with what he left you."

She admitted, "I wish I could say the same of the abbey. He had a head for the accounts, and besides administering the charities, he supervised our operations and expenses. Seriously, I don't know how much longer we'll be able to keep this facility. And if we lose it, I have no idea how we will continue to provide services." She shook her head in apology. "But that's not why you came to see me."

"I didn't have a reason. I should be praying about what's happened, asking for mercy and healing and patience, but it seems I've run out of words. If it's my cross, I don't know how to bear it or what to do with it. For my wife, it's unfair beyond belief, and my only consolation is I must believe she can't feel grief where she is just now." Then he added, "Besides, the only prayer that works for me is to affirm that with God's grace I already have whatever I'm asking for — even if I can't see it just yet. But you know as I do there are times when that's not much of an answer."

She smiled. "I do. Yes, I do."

Evan expected her to say more, but she didn't right away. That made him ask, "If you were facing this challenge, what would you do?"

She thought a moment, then said, "Exactly what you're doing. We'd be sitting here, having this conversation. What would *you* be telling *me?*"

Her clever reversal stunned him. He choked back a sob before the answer flowed out, "I'd tell you, as much as you might think this is about you, it isn't. Yes, you're suffering through it, but the fate is Loretta's. Has she decided to be where she is now? Is she having a debate with God about what's next? We talk about God's will, but humans have to make choices. And souls must reflect on those consequences."

Bernadette seemed amused. "That sounds like pretty good advice, Preacher."

"It's easier to say when it's not me," Evan admitted. "But it seems cold."

"No," she insisted. "Not at all. If she makes her transition, now will be her time, and you must come to accept it. If she returns to us, that will be a compact she's made with God, and she will know better than you what her mission will be going forward."

"Wow," Evan said. "You're a hot knife through butter."

"It's much easier for me to see," she assured him.

"Thank you," he said. "I don't know what that changes, if anything. But I expect I *will* know."

"Yes, you will. I am sure," she said.

"The roses are amazing," he said finally.

"They remind me of our little lives," she said. "So beautiful, so fleeting, so precious. Such an awesome testimony to the grandeur and the complexity of the universe. And yet, not despite their inevitable decay but because of it, come the new season, they are reborn. And if these are not tended here — they will arise somewhere, for as long as anyone will be here to appreciate them."

Evan decided to ask, "How about you? I know there are money problems, but you seem fit."

She looked at her muddy black shoes for a long time. Then she asked meekly, "Reverend, will you hear my confession?"

She's not joking!

The Reverend Mother led Evan in silence up to her modest office on the second floor of the abbey, closed the door, and locked it from the inside. He sat opposite her at her desk, where he'd confronted her the day the sheriff's team was downstairs investigating the untimely demise of the priest.

Evan was uneasy as he said, "You know I'm not reluctant at all to hear this as a friend and colleague, but according to your own doctrine I could hardly offer absolution or penance. Certainly, whatever you tell me will be in confidence—"

"No," she said. "Don't promise that. I trust you to decide what you must do."

"What *I* must do? Now you really have me worried."

She held up a cautioning hand. Then she fetched a small key from her pencil holder, reached down, and unlocked the file drawer of her desk.

And from the drawer, she produced a two-foot-long metal cylinder. She placed it decisively on the desktop and then looked up. Evan saw her eyes were filling with tears.

"You know what this means" was all she said.

It's the cattle prod! The murder weapon.

"Yes," Evan said cautiously, "I know what it is, and I believe I know how it was used. You told me this would be a confession, so I must tell you that you really shouldn't say anything more."

"Oh, but I must," she sniffed. "Understand, I didn't kill him."

"That's a relief, but I don't understand. All the more reason you could have handed this over to the authorities sooner."

"I followed Mr. Shackleton's case closely. If the charges hadn't been dropped and it had gone to trial, I tell myself eventually I would have claimed to have found this on the property. And I firmly believe I would have summoned the courage to testify to my role in the matter."

"Which was…?"

"I knew that Father received placement fees from the resort for sending our girls into the work-study program, but I wasn't aware of the abuses. I also knew he worked with Social Services on the adoptions, both of our girls and their infants. I was aware that Stuart Shackleton handled the placement fees, and I did know he'd brokered the adoption of Melissa Benton. But my only contact with the adoptive father was through his representative, a Mr. Olachek."

"Are you saying you thought Coyle's actions were legitimate? Appropriate?"

"I did think that. Or, in retrospect, for a long time I allowed myself to assume Father Coyle was acting righteously. After all, those fees were keeping our doors open, and we were one of the few organizations in this area serving the underserved."

"You *were?* Past tense?"

Are they closing this place down? She hasn't said. Maybe she doesn't want to tell me. Or perhaps she won't know until the higher-ups tell her she has to retire.

"I've been in charge since Michael's passing, and I ended the internship program right away. And the casino has new owners. We do no business with them."

She's saying they've run out of money. I'm not going to press it.

Evan had to ask, "So who killed Father Coyle? You must know."

"First I must tell you what happened the morning he died. He called me into his office, and he warned me that a courier would be coming to pick up Melissa's adoption papers and also to give us a check. A very sizable check. We were desperate for the funds, and I expected he'd be overjoyed to tell me. But he was anxious and overwrought. He made the mistake of confessing to me and asking my advice. He told me he was aware of the abuse, had been for quite a while, perhaps even from the beginnings of the program. And he was sure this adoptive father was not only a rich hoodlum but also one who ran the operation that took advantage of our girls. To say he was having second thoughts is an understatement. He had the nerve to ask me what he should do."

"I'm sure you were shocked. What could you possibly say?"

"I told him to refuse the check and shred the adoption papers, which he said he would do. As for his own guilt in the matter, I told him if he didn't make a confession to the Bishop and show me some proof he'd done that, I'd have to turn him in, possibly to the sheriff."

"You must know Shackleton was the courier. According to his story, Coyle did refuse the check and sent him away without the papers."

"I was here in the office when I heard the motorcycle arrive as well as when it left minutes later. Naturally, I wanted to know what had transpired. I went downstairs to Michael's office, and I found him on the floor, curled up, no breath, no pulse. Yes, I could have called the paramedics, but I didn't. I'm not proud of my actions. Sister Margaret was napping at the reception desk. She hadn't seen me go in, and she was still asleep after I'd come back down from my office with this device. I administered the wound on his forehead postmortem, and, yes, I added the irony of the symbol with a smudge from Michael's ashtray."

"Why?"

"I felt Michael had been stricken and taken as he deserved to be. He'd had heart trouble, and no doubt he was overcome by the stress of the confrontation. But since that morning, I had begun to realize that Stuart Shackleton was somehow to blame for much that had happened."

"You know he's a Mason. Explains the wound in Coyle's third eye and that cross on top of it. You did it to frame the guy for murder."

"I did it hoping to implicate him. And I did it to shame Michael. I did it because I didn't have the courage to do anything else, and yet I was furious! And, as I say, if Stuart Shackleton had gone to trial, I tell myself now I wouldn't have let him be convicted." She added quickly, "But I'm not the least bit sorry for his suffering, if indeed a man with no conscience can suffer at all."

Evan eyed the device. "The sheriff and I wondered whether one of those would have enough juice to kill a person. As I understand it, probably not. But then it might have been enough to push a cardiac patient over the edge."

"This one was my brother's. He has a ranch up in Chillicothe. And it has a painful sting, but only enough to startle a cow."

Evan was almost afraid to ask, "Do you want me to take custody of it?"

She replied simply, "Please."

"I'm not sure what I should do with it. Or your story."

She assured him, "Pray on it, and you will. And I'll accept your decision."

"You say it was your brother's. How did you come to have it?"

She stood, came around the desk, and raised the cuff of her jeans, revealing multiple burn marks on her leg.

"Penance," she said flatly.

17

Evan put the cattle prod in the trunk of his Fiat. He'd told Bernadette the truth that he didn't know what to do with it. From a legal standpoint, at a minimum, he was sure the Reverend Mother had withheld evidence from a criminal investigation. Failing to call for an ambulance upon finding the corpse was surely a serious mistake, if not a crime. But she'd had every reason to believe Michael Coyle was already dead. Although an autopsy was done, the examiner had not been able to determine whether the wound on the priest's forehead had been delivered before or after he died.

And now that the murder charge against Shackleton had been dismissed, what was the status of the case? Like it or not, Evan was involved in it again.

What am I obliged to do? What do I feel I ought to do?

If he shared Bernadette's story, would it close or reopen the investigation? Forensic testing of the device would no doubt show that the shock it delivers was not sufficient to kill a person — a healthy person, that is.

Evan did indeed want to pray about it, but he also wanted to think through all the earthly complications his decision might cause.

As he drove from Sisters of Mercy into Appleton City to meet up with Thurston, he reflected on these things. In the past, this would have been one of the times Naomi would pop into the passenger seat and tell him in coldly logical terms what precisely he was doing wrong. But not today.

It occurred to him his own sense of guilt about hanging onto her spirit was keeping her away. He even had the chilling thought that Loretta was being taken from him because he didn't appreciate her enough.

Okay, I've learned my lesson. Don't tell me it's too late.

Cora's morning shift at the C'mon Inn didn't end until after the lunch crowd had thinned out. Social distancing was still required, except the restaurant was permitting friends and family to sit together. Marcus had arrived first and found a booth. As Evan entered, those two were conferring heatedly. And at that moment, the buzz of conversation in the place hushed abruptly, and all eyes were on him. Cora straightened up and put on a big smile as she saw him. She'd already made sure there was a pair of mugs on the table, so she promptly poured Evan's coffee from her permanently attached Pyrex carafe.

She hurried off, telling him, "Lots to say but it'll keep till the end of my shift. I'll be back to get your order in two shakes."

Evan greeted Thurston, sat down, and promptly focused on doctoring his coffee. He didn't look up as he muttered, "When I took the job, I hoped I'd become more popular in town. But not this way."

Thurston's only reaction to the comment was a fatherly smile. He reached across the table and laid a hand on Evan's forearm to calm his nervous stirring. "Whatever did you do to Stuart Shackleton?"

Evan finally looked up. "Last time I saw him was that day in court. I told you and Chet what he said. I mostly listened."

"He paid me a visit at the parsonage this morning. Unannounced. He was his jovial self — a face I'd not seen before. If it was any other man, I'd say he suddenly got religion. But you and I know better."

"What did he want?"

"At first, he didn't want anything. He informed me he's set up a trust fund for Loretta's care. 'For however long it takes,' his words. This from a guy you put behind bars with an accusation some folks might have thought was wild speculation. And maybe it was. We both know he's not guiltless in lots of ways, but apparently not about that. Granted you've taken in Luke and Buzz, and you're ministering to Ann, but until now I'd guess revenge would be his usual response to anyone he thought had wronged him."

Blinding light on the road to Damascus? What would make a man like him do a one-eighty on the road to Hell?

Evan mused, "I've never asked him for any kind of help. And, yes, this is a huge burden lifted. I hadn't even begun to think through all the paperwork, much less what we'd end up owing. But this? I'm prepared to believe in miracles, even though I can't bring them, but you're right. This strikes hollow. Gives me the creeps, frankly."

"He did make a request. He said it's not an obligation."

"Uh-oh. Here it comes."

"As far as I can see, it's not dishonorable. Nothing to compromise your integrity — or your honesty."

"Okay, spit it out!"

"Not right away, nothing urgent. But no matter how it goes—"

"How *what* goes?"

"Loretta's... recovery..."

"This is really making me uncomfortable, but go ahead."

"No matter how it goes, he'd like you to agree to tell your story on TV."

Evan's face grew red. "That snake! And say *what*, exactly? What a great and good and generous man he is?"

They'd been keeping their voices down, but some heads turned.

Thurston insisted, "Not at all. Yes, you'd think he has an agenda. We must assume he does. But he made it clear he would never tell you what to say."

I'm sure he has trouble keeping his agreements even when they're in writing.

Evan choked back his rage. "Right this minute, I don't know how to take this or what to do. Maybe one day I'll wake up and it'll dawn on me how he plans to exploit our grief, but this is like the money for the house multiplied a thousand times over. I took that gift, and you told me how to think about it, why I could accept it with a clear conscience. This time, I don't care whether I'm selling my soul. Loretta's going to get whatever she needs, and this might be the only way." Evan added, "When we do find out how he expects to be paid back, I'll have to be ready."

"I wasn't going to try to talk you out of it," Marcus said. "Unbelievable as it might sound, it's not impossible that God could be working through Stuart Shackleton. Consider that the man has a lot to regret, much to confess, and just maybe he wants to put things right."

Evan squinted and looked Marcus in the eye. "Tell me you really believe that."

"What I believe doesn't matter. Maybe not even what you believe. What I do know is, if some divine plan gives you an opportunity like this, it's your duty to take it. I admit, down the road, Stuart may try to control you. But not many preachers get a worldwide platform handed to them. Your testimony could do a lot more than save Loretta. You want my advice, you best step up."

Evan took a deep breath, sipped his coffee a couple of times, then said, "I can't say anything because I need to speak to Chet about it first, but this morning I was given a piece of evidence that proves Shackleton is telling the truth about Coyle. He might have provoked the guy, but now I'm sure he didn't kill him."

18

After lunch, Evan had intended to head over to the sheriff's office and unburden himself to Chet Otis. He wasn't yet sure what he would say, only that he'd ease his way onto the subject and decide how far to go depending on the sheriff's reaction. With the case now cold, if not closed, he didn't see the urgency. And if they'd want to interrogate Bernadette, he didn't think she'd be going anywhere.

I can imagine how angry she must have become when she finally realized Coyle had made a deal with those criminals. She'd been in denial about her own suspicions, and she may have assumed he was looking the other way as well. Only to find out he must have known he was selling the prettiest girls in his flock into slavery.

Evan was about to get into his car when Cora caught up with him at the curb. "Could I get a lift?" she asked sweetly. "Goin' to your place, of course."

Evan looked puzzled. "You just came off your shift. I'm betting you haven't had lunch yourself."

"Oh, taken care of. I grab a smoothie now and then."

Is she fibbing? She's looking downright skinny. If this drags on, I can't be taking advantage of her kindness forever.

He knew that, for a hash-slinger who ladled red-eye gravy, she was something of a health nut. He also knew she and Loretta had conferred on the benefits of vegan diets, although neither had turned enforcer.

She was about to let herself into the passenger side when he raised a hand. "Actually, I wasn't planning to go right home…"

She shot him a look. "Yes you *are*. You're gonna have a man-to-man with Luke."

"Is he okay? Is he cooperating, taking his meds?"

She didn't answer right away but held her stern look. No way she was going to be dissuaded. He got in, so did she, and they drove off.

"Oh," she cooed sarcastically as they settled in, "he's sweet as pie — when I see him. That's usually just long enough to grab a glass of milk and a baloney sandwich that he makes himself with white bread and ketchup. Then he dives right back into his room and closes the door."

"I thought we had a rule he's not to eat in his room. He's supposed to take all his meals at the table. We say grace. Discipline, you know. Set mealtimes, clean up, wash your hands. His doctors say he needs the routine. And he's to take walks in the afternoons. Fresh air."

"I'm pretty sure he's not sulking or cramming for some test. Damned if I know what occupies him. He's not about to stroll around outside, neither." Then she insisted, "You'll speak with him."

"Sure," Evan said. "It's a lot of stress on all of us, but in his condition there's no telling how he'll cope."

Cora hesitated, then asked, "What have you told Melissa?"

She might not like this, but we've stayed awake nights trying to decide what's best.

Evan was sad to say, "We haven't told her anything at all. When I visited her right before the accident, she was having bouts of emotion but maybe not so different from a troubled teenager with a bad case of the blues. She's been showing improvement. No more night terrors and most important no seizures. It seemed like there would be a real possibility of her coming home soon. I met with her social worker, and he let me think it would happen if he could get the necessary approvals. But now? If we wait to tell her until after she comes home, she could have a breakdown that we can't manage, and the episode could get her thrown right back in. But if I tell her now, even if it's only to say her sister's been laid up, how can I explain she shouldn't go see her in the hospital? Covid regulations? No matter what we do, who knows how she'll react? And if Melissa gets worse, they'll sin on the side of caution and maybe keep her in the clinic a good, long time. I don't know what to do."

"And Luke's counting the days until she's with him, you know."

"Oh, yes. And he doesn't handle disappointment well. Frustration can send him into a rage. That's the main reason he never wanted to visit his mother. He'd become furious when she couldn't recognize him. Maybe he even thought she'd withdrawn her love because of something he'd done."

"He's remarkable, that kid," Cora said. "Considering all he's had to overcome."

"Yes, he has special gifts," Evan said somberly. The unspoken hurt he shared with Cora was Loretta's condition and care. A solemn moment passed. "You know we could lose her. She's been under for a week now, and from what the doctor tells me, if we don't see some positive signs soon, her chances aren't good."

She stiffened and snapped, "Preacher, you're not to talk that way! You say, 'Cancel! Cancel!'"

They rode in silence the rest of the way.

"WHEN IS MELISSA COMING HOME?" Luke's fretful question echoed in Evan's ears like the wail of an emergency siren. The boy had no patience with hello despite the fact that he hadn't seen his presumptive stepfather in four days.

Cora was busy with Leslie and Buzz in the kitchen. Evan lowered his voice. "Why don't we take a walk?"

Luke shook his head emphatically. "We'll go in my room and close the door. That's where I feel safe."

So they did.

If I'm going to follow through with the duties of this ministry, I'll be sitting on the edges of their beds with clients as a matter of routine for the rest of my life.

Evan began cautiously, "You know I visited her last week, and I told you she's making progress."

Luke smirked. He always claimed to know more about Melissa's emotional states than anyone, and Evan wasn't about to contradict him.

Evan continued, "I also met with her social worker Chuck Holloman to get the approvals started for her release from the clinic. And then I'll be filing an application for guardianship, just as I had to do for you to live with us."

Luke was frowning now and kicking his legs nervously, which caused his whole body to shake. An angry pressure was building, and an outburst was inevitable unless Evan said just the right words to satisfy him.

Evan rested a hand on the boy's shoulder because what he had to say next was more likely to trigger the explosion than prevent it. "It will all work out someday, and I hope soon, but Loretta's accident has made things even more difficult than they were before. Mainly because I haven't yet told Melissa anything about it. While she's in care and doing better, we can't do anything to upset her. And we can't invite her to move in with us until we can give her the care and attention she needs. The plan was for both you and Loretta to support her, especially as she becomes a mother to Buzz again."

Through this speech, Luke had stopped shaking, but now he clenched his teeth as he stared at Evan defiantly.

Evan went on, "You already know all this, I believe. But what you might not yet understand is that, whenever Loretta does come home from the hospital, she is likely to need a lot of care herself. She might even be in bed for a long time. It's that kind of… illness."

Luke informed Evan plainly, as a lecturer would, "I've been studying the literature on coma. I have a suggestion, but you still haven't answered my question."

A suggestion? Is this going to be medicinal or supernatural?

Evan summoned his courage to say, "We are going to have to wait to see how Loretta's recovery progresses, then find out what she will need here at home, then we'll know how to make a welcoming place for Melissa. It's not just about housework or childcare. But if — and I have a hard time picturing this or even saying it — if Loretta will be bedridden, when Melissa sees her sister in that state every day, it might be more than she can bear. I mean, we will all of us be challenged, but I think you'd agree Melissa will be more fragile than the rest of us even as she continues to grow stronger."

Luke had expected a simpler and more definitive explanation. "But how long?"

There were times when Evan hadn't known whether to approach his quirky ward as a teenager with an ominous disability or as an adult who by now probably understood more quantum physics than he did. Luke was not only bonded with Melissa as her lover, but he'd also grown close to Loretta as his stepmother.

Can I speak to Luke objectively about the facts and consequences of Loretta's condition? Or might talking about it crush Luke as much as it would doubtlessly hurt Melissa?

Evan decided to risk addressing the senior scientist in the room, "Since you've been reading the research, why don't you tell me?"

Luke had his answer ready. "The clinical assessment would be, if she improves at all, showing some functions above brain stem, she could be out of it, lying flat on her back, for months or even years…" When the boy hesitated, Evan sensed he wanted to say more.

What can't he say? Otherwise, there's no hope?

"What else, Luke? I know this is incredibly hard to talk about. I believe I do understand the possibilities. I can't say I'm prepared for them, but her doctor has given me the facts."

"You're going to think I'm crazy," the boy stated by way of introduction.

Evan actually chuckled. "Yes, of course, some people hear about your diagnosis and maybe that's what they think, but it didn't take me long after I met you to realize you're a seer. I'm not sure that any of those words describe you correctly. Maybe more like a shaman? I imagine having those visions and insights would be difficult for anyone to deal with."

"You know I visit Melissa. I send my spirit to be with her."

"Yes, you've told me. I have no reason to doubt."

"What I haven't told you, I tried to find Loretta. She's sitting on the edge of a river. She wants you there, but she knows you mustn't join her. She doesn't know why she's there, and she doesn't know what to do. She's not unhappy. She's like us. She's waiting,"

A river?

Noting Evan's astonishment, Luke continued, "Understand, it's not a physical place. Another dimension? I don't know how to describe it to you."

She's stuck on the bank of the River Styx, waiting for Charon the boatman to ferry her across to the afterlife!

Evan shuddered with a chill. He wished he'd never read Dante.

How ridiculous to think any of the poet's metaphorical hallucinations could be real!

Even now, he had no reason to doubt Luke's experiences. The boy's insights about Melissa had always proved true, as the incident when she faked demonic possession to freak out her Russian kidnapper had demonstrated.

Evan chose to focus instead on the here-and-now when he asked, "You said you have a suggestion. Can you go back and plead with Loretta to come home?"

Luke answered, "It may not be her decision to make. I know it's not mine. No, my suggestion is about an experimental medical procedure. There has been some success stimulating the thalamus with ultrasound to rouse the patient from a minimally conscious state."

19

_____

"Insurance won't cover it," Dr. Ravi said tersely.

No sooner had Evan stepped out of Luke's room than he'd called the doctor. He was surprised to get him on the phone. He described briefly what Luke had told him about the experimental treatment.

Evan insisted eagerly, "But there's the trust fund. Cost shouldn't be a question."

The doctor seemed reluctant to say anything more. He finally explained, "I've read about it, yes. I have no experience with it."

"Then call in whoever does!"

A reluctant pause followed. "I wouldn't recommend any extraordinary intervention until there are some signs of responsiveness — some indication of activity at a higher level than the brain stem. As of now, she's breathing on her own. That's something. Hopefully, healing is taking place. We must allow it to continue."

"For how much longer?"

"All I can say is it's day to day and week to week. Let me put it this way. If it were possible to shock her awake now, the lights would be on, but there might be no one home."

The words were brutal, but coming from this sensitive fellow they were simply a statement of fact. Evan's excitement evaporated, and he added weakly, "There must be something…"

"Are you talking to her?"

"Yes," Evan said. "I'm going back there this evening. Same old sweatshirt."

Some warmth returned to Ravi's voice when he suggested, "Tell her a story, one with a happy ending."

Evan's next call was to Chet Otis. He might as well stop in to see the sheriff on his way to the hospital.

Get it over with?

WHEN EVAN HINTED that their meeting would involve the Coyle case, Otis suggested they meet in the pastor's private office at the church with the excuse, "The walls have ears at the station."

Evan told the sheriff almost verbatim everything Bernadette had shared with him. He laid the electroshock device on his desk, and he was ready to turn it over. Although he hadn't taken the precaution of handling it with gloves, he had wrapped it in a clean plastic bag.

"Fingerprints won't mean a thing, of course," Otis told him as he reached for it reluctantly. He turned it over repeatedly in his hands as if its heft might be a clue. "But could be some blood is here on the end of it, so I'll send it to the lab. If there's a match with what they have on file for the priest, I suppose it gives some credence to her story — although it won't tell us one way or t'other as to whether she actually offed the guy with it."

"If you find blood, it won't be his," Evan said.

"Why not?"

"Because the thing has been used a lot since then."

"On cattle, you mean?"

"Nope. You've heard how some priests use scourges to punish themselves?"

"No! The nun?"

Evan nodded. "Frankly, Chet, I worried about whether to tell you any of this. I mean, really, what more is there to find out? Unless someone comes forward who saw someone else go into Coyle's office — or who confesses they did it themselves."

Otis mused, "Technically and legally you really had no choice. But I'll say to you and no one else, I'd just as soon you hadn't. Not sure I know the difference between a case that's closed and one that's downright pointless. If the guy had lived, he'd be facing trafficking and child endangerment, for starters. Then there's fraud. And that's as much as we know about until the Feds get done sweating those Russians." Then he muttered, "Hell, if I'd known what he did to those kids, I might have shot him and planted the gun myself!" And added, "Those cops on TV do it."

"Do you feel you have to depose the Reverend Mother now? From what she told me, I'd expect her to cooperate."

"Serious threat of too much information. I mean, what you've given me is hearsay, but you've got this dingus to show me you're not just making shit up. Yeah, I guess I got to record an interview with her, then try to convince the DA it's not worth chasin' his own tail." Then he had to ask, "Do you believe her? I don't have any trouble trusting that a saintly nun didn't intend to murder a priest, but what she's telling you she did is almost harder to accept. She finds him dead and has to desecrate the body? And she didn't just whack at him. She puts that burn between his eyes and then smudges him like it's Ash Wednesday. Sounds like cult nonsense. Rage, certainly. You say you know her some. What made her do it?"

"Like you say," Evan replied. "Rage? Righteous anger? She'd been in denial the whole time the girls were being exploited. When she found out, I'm guessing she was not only furious with Coyle but also wracked with guilt herself."

Otis was clearly skeptical. "Is that how she expressed it to you?"

Evan told him, "Think about it. She carried suspicions about him for months, maybe years — maintaining that serene demeanor of hers. She had it all pent up inside. Then she finds out he's not only skimming placement fees but some of her cherished students are literally getting raped."

"Still," the sheriff insisted. "Speculative."

"No," Evan pronounced at last. "You didn't see those self-inflicted burn marks on her leg."

The sheriff got up slowly, tucked the bag under his arm, and grinned broadly. "Thanks for nothin', Preacher. Don't sweat this. I haven't said it, but you got enough on your plate."

Moments after the sheriff had closed the office door behind him, the gentlest knock came back. At first, Evan thought it might be Chet wanting to apologize for his sarcasm or for not asking after Loretta.

But the door opened slowly, and there stood the church's aged sexton, who went by the name of Birch and was so grizzled, gaunt, and frail he looked like an old-timey slave who was near starvation.

Although the man's janitorial duties involved all manner of messy chores, Evan had never seen the fellow in anything but a suit, always the same one, its fabric worn and shiny in places.

Maybe I can get the Loving Embrace ladies to love him with some new duds.

His voice was low and gentle. "Pastor, I hear about your missus. Such a shame. I been prayin' night and day."

"Thank you, Birch. I'm headed over there to see her now, and the doc told me to tell her a story. He said a story with a happy ending. Any suggestions?"

Birch smiled meekly. "There is that story about the man goes into the underworld to pull his girlfriend outta there. Seems like that's a miracle you could do."

Evan was perplexed. "That's not a Bible story."

"Nossir. Nossir, it isn't. It's in one of your books there." And he pointed to the library shelves on the wall beside Evan's desk. The preacher had brought his college textbooks to add to the religious-studies collection Thurston had left him.

Evan teased, "Birch, don't tell me you've been sneaking off with my books!"

The sexton smiled. "That I have. There's times I'm done with my chores I'm just hanging out here. Yeah, I lock up and go home eventually, but all I got is my cat, and my being here is better than leaving the place empty, don't you reckon?"

Evan smiled back. "You're a watchman. I know that about you. You care about us, and you watch over us. That's a more important part of your mission than sweeping up."

"I do my best," Birch agreed.

"Please. Show me the book."

"It's a poem," Birch said, taking a leather-covered edition from the shelf. "Perhaps you know it? Orpheus goes down there to rescue his girlfriend."

"Orpheus and Eurydice. It's a Greek myth. A few thousand years old."

"Well," Birch said, turning the pages. "I don't think this poem is that old, but I liked it."

He handed the open book to Evan, who got up from his chair to take it, saying, "From what I remember of the myth, it didn't have a happy ending. Orpheus found her, and he was leading her out of there, but he made the mistake of looking back, and he lost her forever."

He saw it was a retelling of the story by Edward Burrough Brownlow. Evan found the chorus and read aloud:

> Thus Orpheus stood; but now no longer mute,
> For to the rich-wrought tremblings of his lute
> He raised his rare-heard voice and stilled the word
> On Pluto's lips, and then all Hades heard:
> Persephone! Persephone!
> Give back my soul's delight to me!
> Eurydice! Eurydice!

Evan said, "He's appealing to the goddess, asking her to reflect on how much she adores her own lover — Pluto, the ruler of Hades." Then he muttered, "My soul's delight? Oh, yes, yes," and the overdue tears started.

Birch stepped closer, embraced his pastor, and whispered, "I guess you got yourself your next sermon."

"How's that?" Evan asked, sniffling and wiping his eyes with the back of his hand.

"If you look back, you're doubting you already got what you need to get it done. You're always tellin' us, whenever you pray, you already got what you need. What the poem's saying, you lose faith and you're lost!"

20

Thrown alongside the hateful cattle prod in the trunk of Evan's Easter-egg vehicle was the embarrassingly stinky sweatshirt that Dr. Ravi had advised might rouse the olfactory centers and memory of Loretta's sleeping brain.

Before entering the hospital, Evan popped the trunk and exchanged the time-honored sport coat he usually wore with the grubby over-garment.

I smell like the locker room in high school.

He found Loretta as he'd feared she still was — stretched out in bed, lying on her back, hands curled at her chest.

I've prayed a thousand times just to see her blink. Why not yet?

He flashed on unbidden images of medieval knights recumbent on the tops of their tombs laid beneath the stones of Westminster Abbey. Their brass effigies lay for centuries posed just as she was now, but dressed in chain mail and clutching their swords like righteous crosses over their chests.

They died for Jesus, the churchmen said. The hilt of the sword was the cross they bore.

Evan had never been to London. But another of his great-grandmother's prize possessions was a "tomb rubbing." It had been a hobby of Victorian ladies to capture portraits of those knights by rubbing gold-colored crayons on black paper laid over the deathly images engraved on the brass lids of their caskets.

For reasons Evan never understood or bothered to research, elegant women of the time seemed to be fascinated with death and dying. Some even took small doses of arsenic to make their white faces even whiter. The sickly look was fashionable, the suffering attitude thought to be virtuous.

And Loretta's face was pale. Gone was the blush he'd seen before. Her lips were almost colorless.

Is this progress? Does her doctor just want to 'let go and let God?' That's supposed to be my thing, but I can't do nothing! Has Ravi given up hope and not been able to tell me?

For the storytelling Ravi had prescribed, Evan had intended to tell Loretta about Orpheus and his devotion to his beloved Eurydice.

You'd think a Baptist minister could summon a Bible story instead of some Greek fantasy, but I can't think of one.

Not for this reason, Evan decided in the moment that his story needed to have the required happy ending. Innocent fib though it might seem in the Orpheus story, Evan didn't want to change the ending. Perhaps Loretta knew the story — maybe she'd studied it in high-school English class — and she'd be dismayed he wasn't being straight with her.

You'd think she wouldn't know she's in danger. But Luke says she's worried.

Evan had been thinking about the poem on the way over to the hospital. It was a nineteenth-century romance on the story, the kind of syrupy stuff Victorian ladies lapped up like treacle. Besides those tomb rubbings, he remembered a vintage poster that used to hang in his great-grandmother's parlor.

And that was the story he decided to tell his sleeping lover.

"Know that poster we have in the parlor? The one in the circular copper frame? I never told you why it's special to me. There's a lady in a full-flowing dress strolling barefoot along the seashore. She's wistful, looking down, hoping to find something — she isn't sure what. She bends gracefully to pick up a tiny thing that's caught her eye. She cradles it in her upturned palm, gazing at it, studying it for a sign, a message.

"Now, the words printed on the picture's frame read, 'The Sea Hath Its Pearls.'

"That picture belonged to my great-grandmother. I remember seeing it in the parlor of her house when I was about five. I thought it was pretty, but I never knew the story behind it. And then when I was older, after I'd gone to school and come back, I thought the picture and the rest of my family's old things had been lost or given away. You see, I had to sell the farmhouse after Mother's death to pay for Dad's medical bills, and I didn't pay much attention to what happened to their keepsakes. I didn't put much store by objects. Then about a year ago, just as we were making our new home and scrounging for furnishings, I found that picture in a resale shop. It was only then I got curious about what the caption on the frame meant. I don't know why I didn't think to tell you at the time.

"It's the title of a German poem by Heinrich Heine, and it became hugely popular back in the day when it was translated by Henry Wadsworth Longfellow. This poster and its poem must have been like a hit love song."

And he recited it from memory:

> The sea hath its pearls,
> The heaven hath its stars;
> But my heart, my heart,

My heart hath its love.
Great are the sea, and the heaven;
Yet greater is my heart,
And fairer than pearls or stars
Flashes and beams my love.
Thou little, youthful maiden,
Come unto my great heart;
My heart, and the sea and the heaven
Are melting away with love!

"And there's more to the story. Among my great-grandmother's prized possessions was a small, glass-covered coffee table. It's lost now. Beneath the glass, resting on a bed of fluffy cotton, were seashells — of clams and mussels and little conchs and starfish. And I remembered that my mother told me her parents had honeymooned in Cuba — on the beach!

"And then I knew my mother was a love-child, and that's why her middle name was Pearl! Magdalena Pearl Zorn Wycliff."

Evan took Loretta's limp hand, the one that wasn't attached to an IV line, gave it a loving squeeze, then cradled it gently in both of his hands, hoping his warmth could flow into her body. He leaned forward, close to her ear, and told her, "Loretta, you're my pearl! My soul's delight! Let's have a love child! Please — *please,* don't go!"

21

Evan left the hospital around midnight. Her eyes hadn't opened, not even for a blink. He didn't want to sleep in that chair again, and holding onto that ripening sweatshirt was downright depressing.

He'd cried when he'd pleaded with her. Now the well was dry. He'd managed to sleep last night, but the exhaustion was wearing him down emotionally, then physically.

He had to force his eyes open as he drove home, and he knew he was in danger of blacking out. The night was moonless, and the highway home was pitch black.

The Dark Night of the Soul. What more can I do? How many times do I have to ask? I keep telling my little flock they already have the answer before they ask. But if I truly believed, I wouldn't need to ask. Please! Please! Show me the way out of here!

Revival preachers liked to admonish worshippers that dark days are times of testing. Then they'd trot out the Book of Job.

Testing — for what? I don't believe in a vengeful God. Never have.

Evan remembered the afternoon he'd picked up the hitchhiking Leon Weiss on this same road. It was during a drenching rain when Evan's only intention was to fetch a miserable homeless man from the cold mire of the ditch. He came to believe Leon was an angel, but a human one, sent by Naomi to watch over him. People like Birch — the quiet ones who sit in the pews in the back, who do the menial jobs, who live to serve — they are angels too.

Oh, for a world full of people like Birch!

Birch had nailed it: Don't look back.

But looking behind or ahead, all Evan could see was a dark road. The lit striped centerline was his only guidance, the limit of his foresight. Fellow travelers had come and gone. Dear ones had been here and passed on. Some were waiting to be born, if only Loretta could manage to live. On the roadside, no angels were standing by, even though he vowed he wouldn't hesitate to accept their help, however discouraging or unlikely their outward appearance.

22

Evan didn't drive home. He headed north on the interstate toward Peculiar, the little community of self-proclaimed misfits, and from there to the Ak-Sar-Ben Motor Lodge, which had once been his refuge from the world and from nefarious people who might be stalking him.

No one ever said why it's Nebraska *spelled backward. 'Peculiar' seems to be the explanation for everything that goes on in these parts.*

This time he lacked the anonymous rental car, but after he checked in with the night manager, he made sure to park the Easter Egg around the back of his cabin.

He dove into bed with his clothes on and, like his dear wife, slept the sleep of the near-dead.

❧

In the morning, he awoke at seven and promptly sent separate texts to Leslie and Marcus. He hoped both would assume he'd spent the night at Loretta's bedside. He added that he'd gone away on an urgent matter and might not be back for several days. In the note to

Thurston, he asked the pastor to cover for him on Sunday, two days from now.

An urgent matter? That's no lie. But it's more likely I'm running away from it than heading toward a solution. Why am I here? Aren't I failing everybody?

Then he placed his regular early-morning call to the nursing station. He'd come to know the staff by their first names, and their friendly voices never hinted annoyance that he kept asking the same question that made them give him the same answer.

What if she doesn't wake up?

The thought kept playing in his head like a mantra. He wanted to replace it with some positive affirmation, but he was discovering that fear was a stronger motivator than hope. As Thurston had reminded him, humans are wired to respect fear. It's a survival mechanism.

Faith is a vision you summon in the moments when you are most afraid. Why else would you cling desperately to the illogical, to the fanciful, to useful fictions? How can you deny the evidence of your senses, the consistent results of repeated experiments, the inevitable conclusions of careful and rigorous logic?

Loretta was hesitating at death's door, but her body was functioning automatically, just as it had since she'd taken her first breath. The urgent question was whether her brain was now already dead. And whether her consciousness had gone somewhere else — or simply winked out.

At times when he sat beside her, he'd actually been preparing for his Sunday sermon. He'd been reading books by astrophysicists on the notion of a "godless universe." The theoreticians were claiming that the dual processes of entropy and evolution could account for everything that is — without the need for a creator or divine engineering.

Oh, and by the way, there's no such thing as eternity. Entropy will win, and the stars will wink out. Or the universe will collapse back in on itself. Granted, the fourteen-billion-year-old universe is still young, and it should take that much time and more before it expires. But what human living today has any reason to care?

No one has been able to answer the question of how it all started — of who or what decreed, 'Let there be math!' Other than pure faith in ancient stories about creation, there is no rational explanation whatever for 'Why is there something rather than nothing?'

He'd wanted to tell his Sunday-morning worshippers that common sense might work in the grocery store or deciding what and when to plant or how to fix leaky plumbing. But when the doctors say you're terminal or when you're contemplating the prospect of your own death, you won't be able to think or explain your way out of fear. Fear and faith defy all explanations, all reason.

You can't have faith you will survive if you jump off a building.

Faith won't take you one inch farther when your car runs out of gas.

But for anyone who has ever grasped even a hint of faith, life without it is a horror.

Evan made do with the modest, single-serving coffee setup the motel management had provided in the room. Besides the coffeemaker, there was a microwave and a mini-fridge. Evan's plan for the next few days, such as it was, would have been to scrounge frozen prepared meals at the supermarket.

An obvious question is how many to buy.

He had a vague notion that a spiritual retreat — if he wasn't simply running away — called for a program of fasting. But although he'd reluctantly gone without meals from time to time, he'd never engaged in a deliberate fast. Besides not knowing what to expect, he didn't know how to undertake it safely. He was still a man with responsibilities, after all. He wasn't profoundly depressed to the point of inaction. He wasn't suicidal. Not yet, anyway.

I just want some clarity. A way forward.

Then he had the guilty thought that he'd think better on a hearty breakfast.

Here's the Evan I recognize!

He was thinking oatmeal was healthier but pancakes would better satisfy his cravings, when there came the sound of tires on gravel, the slamming of a car door, and an insistent knock at his door.

Having slept in his clothes, Evan was already suitably dressed, if unkempt. He wasn't afraid of who might be out there. He couldn't remember whether he'd ever told anyone about this place, but the most likely visitor would be Marcus Thurston, who would be urging him politely to get his head screwed on straight and come home.

But standing there boldly on the stoop was Reverend Mother Bernadette, although she was no more recognizable than the last time when he caught her working in the garden. She wore a lumberjack's plaid shirt over a pair of well-worn jeans. Her hair was tucked up almost entirely under a Royals baseball cap.

Dark glasses made her look both inscrutable and mysterious.

Absent was her serene smile and calm demeanor. She seemed more annoyed than angry. Removing the glasses, she snapped at him, "You know, if you want to hide from the world, you could drive a different car."

She's been following me? For how long?

He couldn't summon anything to say, so he gestured for her to come in. He beckoned her to sit in the only chair, the one that fit under the desk, and he sat on the edge of the bed across from her.

Again, the edge of the bed. Why is she here?

Evan guessed the answer to the question must surely be that she was worried about whether or how much he'd shared with the sheriff about her confession. "I've told Otis pretty much everything, and I gave him the cattle prod."

"That's not why I came to see you," she said.

Evan was perplexed. He didn't know her all that well, but he'd come to regard her as a kindred soul. "Is there something you need from me?"

"I'll begin with an apology…"

"Whatever for?"

"When we spoke, I was concerned about myself. I needed to tell you my story, and I don't regret that I did. As I said at the time, the sheriff will do what he must. I'm prepared to accept the consequences."

"This might be the end of it. If you came to tell me you've changed your mind, it's too late. I have nothing more to tell him. He didn't say whether he'd want to question you, but if it's any comfort, I don't think he's eager to reopen the case."

"I know you must be beside yourself with worry about Loretta, and I failed to offer you my support. She's been in my prayers. And you. And yours."

"Thank you," he said. "I assumed you knew, but I understand you've had your own challenges."

"Indeed." She nodded but didn't elaborate. "I don't know whether you're aware, but Loretta was the brightest student it was ever my privilege to serve." Then she added, "Also the sweetest, the most sincere."

"I knew she did well in high school."

"We don't often place our wards in the public schools. We have our own curriculum, combining religious education with the state requirements. But in her case, we quickly saw that our course offerings were no match for her talents — or her curiosity."

"She never talked about academics. She told me she was on the cheerleading squad."

"She was. But she excelled in science and math."

"Wow," Evan said. "She never mentioned it."

"Those were your own interests, I believe."

"Yes," he said. "After I completed my divinity studies, I took some graduate courses in astrophysics. I thought I'd head into research, then my mother died, and I moved back here to care for my father. By that time I'd lost my enthusiasm for both the ministry and science."

She smiled. "No answers anywhere?"

He nodded. "I don't understand why Loretta never shared those interests with me. Or why she didn't go on to college if she was doing so well."

"She dropped out of school because she decided it was more important to find a way to support her sister. She didn't think Melissa was doing well under our care. And it didn't help that some of our sisters thought Melissa's epilepsy was evidence she was possessed by demons. As for why Loretta never talked more about her interests with you, I expect she worried she wasn't on your level."

Evan had always known that Loretta's emotional sensitivity and insights were more than a match for his. And her cleverness and resourcefulness never failed to surprise him. But he hadn't suspected that at one time she'd excelled at academics.

"I have a lot to learn," Evan muttered.

"You've run away," the nun stated.

He sighed. "I need a breather. Reverend Thurston has stepped in for me at church, and it's more than I should expect. We have volunteer caregivers at the house, but that can't go on forever. As for me, I sit at her bedside, and I tell her stories, and I even wear a nasty old sweatshirt that makes me smell like a fieldhand. The doctor says she might recognize my body odor. I've prayed every way I know how — I even tried bargaining — and there hasn't been the slightest sign. And all the doctor can say is hurry up and wait."

Bernadette stiffened, gazing at him intently. "Here's what I came to say. And it may be no help, no help at all. Loretta may be beyond help. It's not for any of us to decide where she should be or how she should serve. You've obviously come here to have a think." She paused as if it was difficult to say. "You must tell her, if it's her time, you will let her go."

Evan could feel the blood rising into his face as he growled, "That's impossible! How could it be her time? Excuse me, but that's a ridiculous thing to say."

She was undeterred, saying calmly, "Evan, consider what your life was like before you met her. Also consider everything that's happened since. You've been drawn into the ministry. You now have family responsibilities. When you returned to your roots here in farm country, you lived like a vagrant. Your personal habits were perhaps not healthy. You had no focus, no mission. Then you were drawn to help people who had no other helpers. And you met her."

"Okay, maybe it's all because of her. But how is that enough for her? For us? Why must this be the end?"

"It's not for us to know. But one answer might be that she's needed somewhere else."

AFTER THE REVEREND Mother left him, Evan was quiet for an hour — quiet, except being wracked with sobs was anything but peaceful.

He was reaching to turn off his phone when a call broke his solitude. It was his attorney, Jeremy Bailey. "Evan! For once I have good news!" he announced without waiting for a greeting. "You'll be pleased to hear—"

"Jeremy—" Evan tried to stop his friend, but the enthusiasm gushing through the phone was unstoppable.

"Edie Taggart is out of the picture," Bailey announced. "She's withdrawn her protest of Bob's will. He'd given her their residence, of course, and it was going to be all about her claim to the Emmett farm. But she's walking away from it. What's more, she put her house up for sale yesterday, and it sold today. And you'll never guess who bought it."

"Stuart Shackleton," Evan muttered.

"How did you know?"

"Scientific wild-assed guess," the preacher said. "And it suits his personality. Revenge, control — take your pick." He sighed and added, "I shouldn't go disparaging him. Since he was acquitted, he's acting like a new man. He set up that fund, and I don't want to think about how we'd manage without it. I just worry it comes at a price — which he hasn't named yet."

"I'm sorry," Bailey said, shifting his tone to concern. "You sound upset. Was there something you needed to ask me?"

"Yes, but thank you for the news. And for all your effort on our behalf. One big burden lifted. Anything more?"

"Actually, yes. There won't be any legal objections now to the Emmett's taking title to the farm. But Shackleton has already made them an offer — considerably above market. In fact, *way* above market. I'd be very surprised if Josh and Linda don't decide to take it."

"It's theirs to do with," Evan said.

"I know you have a lot on your shoulders," Bailey said. "Is there anything I can do?"

"I wasn't quite ready to call you about it, but I'll need to engage you on another matter."

"Anything," Bailey said.

"The doctor won't come right out and say it, but I have to consider that Loretta won't make it. She might not want to stay with us, assuming she has a choice."

"Evan, Evan" was all the lawyer could say.

"I need you to tell me what's involved. Legally."

"Does she have an advance directive?"

"No, neither of us do. We'd intended—"

"Is she on a respirator?"

"No. She can breathe, and they give her oxygen."

"I don't know how you'd know she doesn't want to live, but you must understand there's nothing you can do one way or the other."

"Isn't removing life support an act of compassion? Of mercy?"

"Not in this state. Missouri has no 'right to die.' If she didn't do a written directive when she was capable, you're allowed to take her off a respirator, but they can't stop feeding her body."

"So what happens?"

"She lingers. Indefinitely. Until God decides to take her — or, that's what the people who wrote the law seem to believe. I take it you don't."

Evan took a deep breath and blew out his discouragement and frustration. "I think God gives us choices. Deciding whether to believe might be the most important, but choosing when to go would be a big one."

PART II

Six months later…

23

The pandemic was waning, if not entirely gone. It was November, a thick blanket of snow covered the farmland, and the ponds on Evan's property had frozen thickly enough to skate on, although no one had.

"Five minutes," came a voice from behind Evan. He was propped up in an uncomfortable chair in front of a blindingly lit mirror in the green room of a TV station in Springfield. The makeup-and-hair technician was putting a last-minute trim on his bushy eyebrows, which he had to admit made him look at best like an intelligent Neanderthal. A protective paper collar was tucked into the neckband of his white shirt, and his new suit was hung on a rack behind him. He hadn't yet worn it to be seen, but he'd liked how it looked on him when he'd tried it on for the tailor's second fitting. The fellow had needlessly pointed out Evan's paunch and advised that the suit-coat button would be located a bit lower than the younger men were wearing it. Evan had agreed that, paunch or not, he didn't favor the look of a button well above his navel. In his opinion, the suits for men these days were designed to look a size too small, perhaps to make fortysomething men like himself look twentysomething, as if they were fast outgrowing their britches. But he and the tailor agreed that an ordained minister shouldn't look like a kid.

Shackleton had paid for the suit, of course. He obviously intended to be the newsmaker, although no one would be mentioning his name. Given the banker's conservative tastes, Evan feared he looked like a banker himself in the gray pinstripe they'd selected for him. They'd thought about a country-and-western look, a tan coat with those piped pockets, along with a string tie instead of a Windsor in silk. But the judgment was he didn't have the folksy accent, nor the winning smile, to fit the stereotype.

They meaning Shackleton and his publicist-assistant, a post-grad named Emilie Shinn who wore an equally conservative suit and informed everyone they had better trust her wired and unerring instincts about social media.

Emilie was sitting beside Evan, no doubt to breathe courage and wisdom into him before he was to step in front of the cameras. Her expression was both concerned and fretful. She was restraining herself from coaching the makeup person.

"You understand," she told Evan in a low voice, although the tech could hear, "this isn't a Christian station or network. It won't be all softballs. You may get challenged, and in that case you simply smile and, if necessary, say something off-topic. They don't care what you say, really. Just how you look, how you're coming across. You're a new face. A friendly face. Someone people will want to trust. That's the message — *your* message."

"Challenging questions?" Evan asked. "What about?"

"They want to know you're for real. That you're not selling something."

Evan chuckled. "Hey, I'm supposed to be an evangelist. I'm selling salvation, aren't I?"

"Not to this audience," she said sternly. "You don't have an agenda. You're answering questions. Questions about who you are and your values."

Evan looked over at Emilie, which caused the tech to smirk because he was in mid-snip. Evan asked her, "Isn't there something Stu wants me to say? This was his idea, and I still don't know what he's trying to achieve."

She answered calmly, "You will become an influencer. That's what this is about. As to the message, it's none other than your own. Above all, be honest. Don't try to guess what others might want you to say. That's what they'll like about you."

How can she be so sure? That's not how it works when I'm behind the pulpit.

THE SHOW HOST was not much older than Emilie. Her name was Nora Gibbons. The name didn't betray her ethnicity, which might be any of several fashionable nonwhite mixtures, a diverse blend for broad audience appeal. Her practiced stage voice had a region-less, plain-sounding, news-anchor accent. She came off as articulate and charming, and she was no weekend substitute. This was her show, and, if you included the streaming services, it would be on an international feed.

The show, "Religion Matters," aired on Sunday afternoons. Some might regard it as filler for a slow news day. But in the age of post-truth digital media, there was no such thing. If there was no news, it would have to be invented — or at least a new spin would have to be applied to yesterday's stories.

Nora led off with, "Joining us today is Reverend Evan Wycliff, pastor of Evangel Baptist Church in Appleton City, Missouri. Tell us why 'Religion Matters,' Reverend."

"Thank you for having me, Nora," Evan had been coached to say. "Religion matters because it's the fabric that binds society. As a community, we agree to be governed by a system of laws. However, the legal system tells us how to behave but doesn't call us to anything higher, doesn't nurture our best aspirations. The laws demand our respect but don't encourage our love of one another. A community

needs a system of *beliefs* to sustain us through life's challenges and diffi-
culties, to give us goals along with the hope our efforts can make a
difference."

"No separation between laws and beliefs? Between church and state?"

No softball here!

"Separation, yes. That's the wisdom of our democracy in this country.
We can live with one another, love one another, and yet we don't all
have to share the same beliefs."

"Is that the ideal? Constitutional democracy?"

"That's what works, yes."

"But as a new Baptist minister, don't you expect to be active
politically?"

"You know, Nora, I can't speak for Baptists generally, but I do regret
the involvement of the church in politics of any persuasion. My fore-
bears, who settled their farms here a hundred and fifty years ago,
didn't call themselves Baptists. They were Freethinkers. They were
fleeing the tyranny of Otto von Bismarck because they were afraid
he'd draft them into the Prussian army to fight his imperial wars
against people who weren't their enemies. Nowadays, we don't have a
draft, but we're sending our young people off to fight foreign wars —
why? Because they need the practice? Because we need to show people
who *might* be our enemies someday that we have the right stuff to
resist them? Or just to provoke another war because it's good for
business?"

Evan thought she was stepping over the line when she asked him,
"Does religion have any place in politics? It seems you evangelicals are
playing a big role these days. You take influential positions on
everything."

"Let's go back to the Freethinkers. They called themselves *separatists,*
like some of the Amish are today. They claim God's kingdom is not of
this world. Their treasure is in heaven. This place, this Earth, is a
stopover for them. It matters what we do here, but in our daily lives,

we must walk apart. Our testimony is that we're not like everyone else. Our mission is not to preach but to walk, to walk the more difficult path. Our lives are humble examples. We don't have to advertise."

"I have to admit," Nora said, "that's refreshing. And hardly evangelical. Is this what you believe? Are you a separatist?"

"You know, I doubt there are many people in our audience who are old enough to remember a time when Baptists were not caught up in politics. I remember my father telling me about the election of 1960. No one in their church would dare mention politics back then. As I say, the affairs of the world were not the concern. But then in that year, his Sunday-school teacher warned them that, if this John Fitzgerald Kennedy were to become president — this man, a Catholic — would make sure that the Pope would rule America."

"Didn't work out that way, did it?"

"Not only did JFK get elected, but, as my father told it, our pastor informed the Sunday-school teacher he was never to mention such vicious gossip ever again."

"Where are you on vaccinations, wearing masks, abortion, the death penalty…?"

Evan shook his head. "Respectfully, those are secular issues, Nora. When you attend our church, no one should ask you your views on any of those questions. What we want to know is — not because we require it but because we care about you and your soul — are you struggling with your faith? How can we help you face the trials and tribulations of this life on Earth? How can we offer hope?"

"That's refreshing, Reverend. A real breath of fresh air. Particularly when we've all been through so much."

"As you say, 'Religion Matters.' It shouldn't be a burden or an obligation. Our beliefs — and our faithful walk — should be a source of hope and joy."

Nora shifted in her chair as if preparing for a frontal attack. Then she shot him a frank look and asked, "Reverend, I have to ask you —

because so many of our viewers have posted the question on our site
— do you consider yourself a faith healer?"

Here it is. The curveball!

Evan smiled. "I have faith. And faith can heal. If healing takes place,
it's none of my doing."

"You've had results though…," she began suggestively.

Evan shrugged.

"For example," she went on, "everyone in Appleton City assumed your
close friend Bob Taggart had taken his own life. You refused to believe
it, and you conducted your own investigation."

"Ah, but I found that he *had* chosen to end his life. I did find evidence
that others pushed him to do it though. And they had their own
reasons for coveting his earthly possessions. Suffice it to say, those
people have not prospered."

"And you tracked down an afflicted teenage girl. You cast the demons
out of her and won her release from kidnappers."

"Before I was pastor, I had some on-the-job experience as an investigator. And, yes, I did track her down. She suffered from epilepsy, and her
captors were superstitious enough to think Satan had got hold of her.
In fact, I encouraged her to fake a seizure, they drew their own horrific
conclusions, and then they released her."

The host paused for dramatic effect, then asked, "And what about
your wife? She's been hospitalized, in a coma since an automobile accident — in a persistent vegetative state. Why can't you do anything for
her?"

Oh, for an answer to this one!

Evan answered soberly, "Yes, she's been that way for some time. I like
to think she's having conversations with God, perhaps getting instructions she can share when she's back with us. But it's a profound
mystery. I want to believe there's a reason. But if she doesn't stay with
us, whether it's God's decision to take her or she decides it's her time to

go, all I can do is pray and wait." Then he added but hardly meant it, "Thanks for your concern."

He thought he was off the hook and it was the end of the segment, but then she asked, "And what about the Shining Waters Temple?"

Evan had no brief. He smiled and said simply, "Early days, Nora. Not much more than a hope and a vision."

Evan wondered, *The Shining Waters Temple? Whose idea was that?*

He could guess. It sounded like the catchy name of a new casino.

"You did great out there," Emilie assured him as he smeared cold cream over his face to remove the stage makeup.

He asked her, "Shackleton wants to build a megachurch? Is that what this is all about? You might have bothered to tell me."

"He doesn't want to commit to it just yet," she said dismissively. "And the less you know, the less you'll be able to promise. We don't want to make you a liar."

"I'm relieved," Evan said. "Might it be built on the farmland where the Emmett place now sits? Shackleton probably won't say anything until he's sure the bulldozers can go back in there."

"May I call you Evan? Relax. You're a media personality now. You have a new platform, and it's the whole world."

"Are you sure there's no agenda? Or are you just afraid of what I might say about it?"

Despite what they've told me, I'd think Shackleton would have coached me by now. It's worrisome — not because I don't want to carry his messages but because I don't know where he stands.

"Mr. Shackleton is a visionary developer. He always has all kinds of plans. Not all of them can go forward. Like I said, he only wants you to be honest. It's your sincerity that works, not so much what you say."

"That's kind of ridiculous," Evan said.

"I guess you never read Marshall McLuhan," she muttered.

24

Recently Evan had worked a miracle he was justly proud of. He'd found a way to convince Luke to spend time with his mother. The solution was a matter of simple math.

Having recovered from her heart attack, Ann had been moved back into the assisted-living wing of Myerson that served patients with dementia. On his visits to her, Evan had found her mood consistently cheery. She had a wardrobe of three brightly colored sweatsuits, which made it easier for the caregivers to dress her, and the patient delighted in mix-and-match. No one had ever explained to him why people in her condition are prone to shucking off their clothes at odd times. The benefits of easy dressing could work the other way. On one occasion the patient had asked him with a giggle to help her take her top off, a suggestion he simply ignored, and the next moment she'd forgotten she'd asked.

The magic lay in a deck of playing cards. And the math problem was whether the face value of the card he drew was greater or less than hers. Ann called the game *Canasta,* but she couldn't remember the rules. Evan might have learned them at one time (his mother had loved to play cards with him), but the simpler game he actually played with Ann was called *War*. From a shuffled deck placed face-down on the table, she'd draw a card, then he would draw one. She often had trouble deciding whether her card outranked his. So it fell to Evan to declare, "You won!" or "I won!" depending on which of their cards was higher. Beset with giggles again, she'd snatch the two cards covetously if she won. She'd frown and give him the raspberries each time she lost, knocking the offending pair of cards onto the floor.

And whether she won or lost, she'd giggle as they drew again. The game seemed to make her enormously happy.

When Evan set out from the house for his next visit with her, he asked Luke, "You're good at games, right?"

Luke shrugged and said, "Sure."

It was one of those rare times when Luke seemed to have nothing to do. Melissa was out with Leslie running pre-Christmas errands, and they'd taken the toddler. Other times, Luke might have been home alone with Buzz and still trying to find ways to amuse him when he fussed. Playing with toy trucks on the carpet usually held his attention, but Luke would become bored or impatient after a few minutes. He couldn't understand why glowing screens seemed to hold no fascination for a son of his.

Since she'd come home, Evan had observed Melissa's withdrawn personality much as he'd seen it when he'd visited her in the clinic. She wasn't depressed. She wasn't timid. She was someone who had found herself — especially in devoted motherhood — and didn't feel obliged to provide explanations.

Besides caring for her baby, her life's mission included protecting Luke from anyone who made the mistake of underestimating his sanity and his talents.

If Luke's frustration drove him to anger, which was possible even when he was faithful about taking his meds, he'd been told to simply take a walk outside to cool off. But if they were alone in the house, he wasn't to leave Buzz by himself. At those times, he'd have to step quickly into his bedroom and scream into a pillow or put a paper sack over his mouth to calm his hyperventilation.

Evan saw his opportunity, asking, "I have a math question."

"Shoot."

"Do you know the card game War?"

"Sure, it's dumb."

"What are the odds of winning on each draw?"

"Fifty-fifty. Always fifty-fifty. That's why it's lame."

"But what if I win three draws in a row? What are the odds of my winning on the fourth draw?"

Luke smirked. "Like I said. Fifty-fifty."

"Really? Are you sure?"

"Yes, I'm sure. Why do you need to know?"

"But what are the odds of winning four times in a row?"

The young man brightened and shot back, "One in sixteen."

Evan asked him, "Then, having won three, why isn't the probability one in sixteen that I'll win again on the fourth draw?"

Luke replied slowly as if explaining to a child. "It's the difference between likelihood and possibility. Winning four in a row is unlikely. But winning or losing on the next draw are always equally possible — no matter how many times you've already drawn."

Evan asked cautiously, "Did you know your mother loves to play cards?"

"Yeah," Luke said, and his voice dropped. "She was crazy about Canasta. Not exactly her thing now, I'd guess."

"Right. We play War, but she calls it Canasta," Evan said. "Funny thing is, she wins on every draw!"

"That's impossible!" Luke said immediately and made a face. But then he looked startled, got serious, and added, "No, it's actually not impossible. But it's colossally unlikely."

"So you went with me to see her today, the odds are you'd win as many times as she does?"

Here's hoping the ego he has invested in the math problem will overcome his fear of seeing her.

Luke now suspected Evan was working a con, but he remained intrigued. "If we played one game, the likelihood is I would win approximately half the draws. Fifty-two cards in a deck, twenty-six draws, about thirteen wins either way. Either she's cheating or you're telling her she wins when she doesn't."

Evan shook his head. "I'm stumped. Why don't you come along, and no doubt you can tell me what's going on."

Luke must have decided to humor Evan and replied, "No doubt," as he grabbed his coat.

EVAN INTRODUCED Luke as "Here's Mr. Canasta, the guy who can't lose!"

Ann sniffed, "We'll just see about that."

She didn't let on whether she recognized him as her son. He was Mr. Canasta, after all, and her mind was locked on the challenge, as was his. If the meeting upset him, he didn't show it. Perhaps he found it easy to hide behind his new personality, the card wiz, an illustrious stranger.

The game between them went predictably, adhering unerringly to the math, and by Evan's scorekeeping, Luke won twelve of the draws, and Ann won fourteen. As before, whether she'd won or lost on the previous draw, she giggled each time she grabbed a new card.

Luke turned to challenge Evan. "You see, I've won pretty much half the time. I don't know what you're talking about."

Evan smiled. "It's true. You don't know what I'm talking about."

"I don't understand."

No need to be discreet in front of her. Bless her, she won't be shaken out of her good mood.

Evan explained, "She's delighted every time she takes a new card."

"Yeah, so?"

"I submit to you, her attention span is so short, she doesn't know whether she won the last draw. She refuses to think she could ever lose."

Luke thought a moment, then said, "It's not about the math, is it?"

Evan smiled and said, "It's not at all about the math. It's about faith."

25

———

L ife in the Wycliff household had become remarkably uneventful, even though two of the residents had serious chronic conditions that required regimens of potent drugs. Melissa had moved in a month ago, and that transition was not as difficult as Evan feared. Chuck Holloman wanted the girl off his caseload for his own reasons, and her attending physician at the clinic supported the move, assuming she could be carefully prepared in advance for a soft landing.

A week before they broke the news of her sister's condition to her, they put Melissa on a daily regimen of diazepam, and she got a mild sedative each night to make sure she was well-rested. The dosages would be tapered gradually after she got home. Talk therapy accompanied this program, eventually getting around to informing her about Loretta's accident and hospitalization.

Melissa finally got the news with Evan attending the session. Had she not been so heavily medicated, she probably would have demanded to see Loretta, and she could have become understandably enraged when told it wasn't a good idea just now. All of the professionals agreed that seeing Loretta in a persistent vegetative state could be devastating for

Melissa. Keep it as a promise for the future, "after your sister is better," they advised.

Once home, Melissa's thrill at being reunited with Luke and Buzz seemed to absorb all her attention. Her counseling sessions focused on the responsibilities of motherhood, and she seemed to be taking those seriously, even with enthusiasm. Working diligently at her chores helped her maintain, just as Luke's studious curiosities sustained him.

Evan saw no sin in allowing her and Luke to live as an unmarried couple. The greater risk, in his view, would have been to try to convince the congregation and the community to condone the match. Of course, he could have held a private ceremony in their home, but surrounding events were moving too fast. Certainly, Stuart Shackleton's views mattered, but both of the young people were now over eighteen. However, legally they were both still Evan's wards until the state welfare system ruled they were competent and stable. Evan preferred for them both to be fully empowered as adults before he'd gladly officiate at their wedding.

A comfortable life for them would have been impossible were it not for the trust fund Stuart Shackleton had set up for Loretta's care. Her absence as housekeeper and caregiver justified a much-needed, full-time salary for Leslie, who eagerly gave up her trade-school enrollment to take the job. And Coralie had kept her place in the daily schedule, being paid as part-time cook.

Perhaps most amazing of all, Shackleton had stopped by a few times. Evan doubted the man would balk at seeing his son and grandson in Melissa's tender loving care. But the first meeting was awkward. He'd brought those toy trucks as gifts for Buzz, who was now a chunky toddler. Luke spoke not a word to his father but grabbed the toys and stared at them intently, rubbing his fingers along their contours to make sure there were no dangerous sharp edges.

But Shackleton didn't seem unnerved by it all. Evan appreciated how much of an effort it must have taken for this notoriously hard-hearted fellow just to walk in the door.

Then there was the question of what leverage Shackleton hoped to gain from insisting Evan do those TV appearances.

And the show host's mention of plans for the Shining Waters Temple had come out of the blue.

Evan visited Loretta daily. Now that he'd resumed most of his ministerial responsibilities, he didn't have the time or the energy for round-the-clock vigils. Instead, he stopped in at the hospital at precisely 7 p.m. every evening. He reasoned that, if she did sense his presence, showing up faithfully might rouse some anticipation in her.

Although Loretta's condition didn't change from day to day, Dr. Ravi advised keeping her in a private room at the hospital, within steps of the ICU where she could be treated if a serious complication should occur. Since Ravi couldn't offer any further advice on how to help, Evan found it comforting to have a reason for everything he did.

His mainstay was telling her stories. Yes, he would sometimes read to her from the Bible, but only red-lettered passages that he judged conveyed hope and inspiration. He remembered she used to rebuke him when he sounded too preachy, even from the pulpit. He wasn't about to test her patience.

I know better than to assume her silence means approval.

He had two favorite stories, which he often repeated, embellishing them more each time. The simplest was "Spunky," about a beloved family dog who went missing one day. Somehow the little dog had clambered into the back of a moving van unnoticed and been carted off out of the neighborhood. The family tried everything to find him. They looked and looked all over town. The children told all their friends, they put up signs, and, yes, they prayed fervently. But nothing seemed to work. Weeks passed, and eventually the parents became so concerned about how sad their children were that they said they'd better pick out another dog to adopt. But the children wouldn't have it. They had faith Spunky would return. And, miraculously, one bright morning he showed up on their doorstep. Spunky had found his way home on his own, and he wanted no other home than this one with the children who loved him so.

Evan had heard the story many times from his grandmother. The tale was beautiful in its simplicity, and it always struck him that there was no cautionary lesson to be learned. The children didn't promise they'd do their homework or finish their chores or not fuss at bath time. No, they just held firm in their belief that Spunky would come home unharmed because they knew he loved them as much as they loved him.

It was in his retellings that Evan eventually appreciated his grandmother's fondness and insistence on telling the story of Spunky. She had taught Sunday school for young children, and it was the only story in her repertoire because it was a modern parable of salvation.

It's about the power of faith.

The other story Evan liked to tell Loretta was "The Velveteen Rabbit." It's about a child's favorite plush toy that, after serving years of loving companionship to a boy, gets discarded on a rubbish heap. But before the toy can be consumed by flames, a fairy appears and, because the toy had been so faithful to the boy who loved him, she turns him into a real rabbit, and he joins the other living rabbits in the forest, able to use his hind legs and hop joyfully for the very first time.

A story of resurrection.

At times, Evan had to admit to himself that these stories were hopelessly cute, downright syrupy. He imagined that, if he were sitting across from Loretta as they relaxed at home, she'd tease him for thinking these messages were so profound. She'd no doubt find his earnest delivery particularly amusing.

But the sight of Loretta giggling, just as Ann always did when she'd grab her winning cards, was just the result Evan yearned to achieve.

26

"Why does Stuart Shackleton want to meet with me?" Thurston demanded. It was late on a chilly Saturday, and Evan had stopped by the parsonage on his way to the hospital.

"No idea," Evan shrugged. "But you can bet it's transactional. I never had a meeting with him when he didn't make a request."

The old pastor smiled. "Evan, haven't you learned by now that all human relations are transactional?"

"What about unconditional love? Doesn't it go just one way?"

Thurston chuckled. "Not at all. If I love you unconditionally, I'm giving myself a huge gift. I won't lose sleep worrying about whether you're going to do something stupid."

Evan's voice softened when he said, "Marcus, you've worried about all of us for a living, and now that you've retired, you haven't managed to stop. Please don't."

Thurston laid a hand on the younger man's back as he beckoned him to sit in an easy chair that had a blanket thrown over the place in the cushion where a spring protruded. Thurston reclined on the couch with his hands folded behind his head and his legs thrown over the armrest as he'd done when Evan was his houseguest. It was a thoughtful pose, as if Thurston was prepared to listen to a long story.

"I don't mean to be disrespectful, Evan. I was about to take a nap, but I'll try to stay awake through your account of whatever stupid thing you've done."

On previous occasions, the two of them had already cried and prayed, agonizing over Loretta's illness, and this sarcasm was Thurston's way of lightening the mood.

Evan asked cautiously, "You act as if it won't be news. Is there something I've done that's got your scruffy tail in a twist?"

"This faith healer rumor is a worry. You might have known they'd go there. On that show, you didn't brag about it, but you also didn't deny it."

"I tried to answer honestly. That's been the agreement from the beginning. Shackleton says he doesn't have an agenda. Of course, he does. But they're not giving me talking points. They're not making me carry water for some politician or cause. And I tried to make it clear that, unlike some of our religious leaders, I won't get pulled into those debates."

"Yes, the separatist doctrine," Thurston mused. "That's really old-school, you know. Folks don't think that way these days. Oh, Arthur Redwine, maybe. But that's his personality. He delights in being a stubborn old cuss. But look around you. I'm sure you've noticed all the Christmas lights around town. The house next door, they're living on food stamps, but they've got a four-foot-high lit Santa from the bargain store out front. If we were genuine separatists, we'd refuse to participate in the commercial holiday. With all this gift-giving, it's a month-long shopping spree, and God is our Santa in the sky. Pray hard enough and you'll get that car you want. Maybe you're not old enough to remember, but I recall a time when we preached that coveting earthly possessions was a sin. Now, to hear these evangelists, if you're not rich, you must not be righteous! Gone are the days when poverty was a virtue and rich people had trouble getting into the kingdom."

"Would those preachers say, 'Pray hard enough, and your wife will walk again?'"

"Come on, Evan. In our prayers, we're not asking for a miracle. We're asking for God's plan to be revealed and for us to accept it, learn from it. As humans who miss Loretta and crave her love, we selfishly want to keep her with us, and that is our fervent hope."

Evan knew this was the honest truth. He wouldn't pretend otherwise, even though in his boyish dreams all he wanted for Christmas was just such a miracle. He admitted, "I thought that Nora Gibbons was going to try to lead me there. She stopped short, this time."

"Aren't you afraid that might be Shackleton's angle? If Loretta recovers, he'll make it a payday for both of you. I don't see how it works the other way."

"You mean, if she doesn't make it?"

Thurston was quick to say, "Evan, I'm not thinking that's a possibility. There's still hope. We must hold the thought, all of us. We can't judge what the lesson is when we're in the midst of the trial."

"Shackleton has set up the trust fund to give her the very best chances of surviving. But it could also keep her body alive long after her mind is gone. None of us know when the spirit leaves. Sitting beside her, as still as she is, I feel her soul is in there. But Jeremy Bailey is telling me the law says they have to keep her on life support until her body gives up on its own."

"Many folks believe God chooses when you're to be taken."

"And are those the same ones who are praying for a new car? Reverend Mother Bernadette tells me Loretta's soul will choose to go when her work is done."

Thurston said, "I'm sorry. I wasn't going to get into this. I express my concerns because I doubt Shackleton, for all his generosity, is a new man. I'm worried about how he might be planning to use you. And what's the Shining Waters Temple?"

"The first time I heard of it was when Gibbons asked me about it. Shackleton has this publicist. I asked her and got a non-answer. I searched online, and I can't find anything. I thought maybe you knew. That's what I came to talk about, and I have to say I'm worried too. You've answered before I've asked. Then again, without his help, I don't know what we'd do. We'd be a charity case. You'd be back in the pulpit and shopping for a young pastor."

Thurston wondered, "But he's asked to meet with *me* — not *us* — so I'm thinking his request this time will be to me. And I'm at a loss to figure out what I have to give him that you can't. It sounds like he intends to build you a new church!"

"Have I made a deal with the devil?"

"Let's say, you've made a deal with a human being who, at the very least, still has allies on the other side."

27

"I thought there'd be more people," Nora Gibbons complained stiffly. "Emilie made this sound like a cocktail party." She was seated across from Shackleton and his assistant on the fantail of the *Namouna*. It was a balmy, breezy day out on the lake, and the banker was drinking gin and tonic, which the steward had learned to mix with more Boodles than soda. The ladies were cautiously sipping mimosas.

"What do you mean?" Shackleton asked as if he didn't know. "You got your cocktail. Didn't you bring your party mood?"

"We were docked, and I assumed more people would be coming, but before I knew it, you'd put out to sea!"

Shackleton chuckled. "It's more like a big pond, Nora. And shore is just minutes away if you get uncomfortable."

"What's this about?" the news anchor asked impatiently.

Emilie had the brief, and she thought this was supposed to be her meeting. "Stuart was very pleased with the interview, and we wanted to cover talking points for the next one."

Nora fumed, "You're coaching me? You've got your nerve! This isn't how it works."

Stuart kept his tone cordial. "As Emilie said, we couldn't have hoped for better. You must know we're grooming him, and frankly we want your star to rise as well."

"What does the preacher think about all this? He's full of opinions, but at times he looked like he'd rather be somewhere else. And what stake do you have in his future?"

Shackleton leaned forward to make his point. "Evan Wycliff is a rarity among the clergy. He doesn't sell Jesus. People can sense he's like them — that he has his doubts. And yet, he's exceptionally well informed. On science, he's got the depth of Neil deGrasse Tyson. But he speaks to the religious audience of the Schullers and the Grahams. He's honest to a fault, which is why we've promised him we have no agenda, no talking points *for him*. Don't you see? He's credible across the board. If your politics are blue, he talks science. If you're red, he's a man of God, even if, like so many these days, he's struggling to hold to his faith."

Nora looked skeptical. "So, are you going to run him for office?"

"No," Shackleton was quick to say. "We're going to build a brand around him. We don't want to tell him what to say. He'll back off."

"And the brand is…?"

"Whatever we say it is," the banker replied. "For whoever has a message. And is ready to pay."

Nora rolled her eyes. "This is crass, to say the least. But I won't say it'll be ineffective."

Shackleton nodded his approval. "Emilie here has the social media expertise to spin anything any way we want. In the kids' language, this guy is eyeballs and clicks. He never has to say anything we tell him to say. That's the beauty of the strategy."

Nora protested, "Sooner or later, and maybe even now, he's going to wake up to how he's being exploited."

"His wife is in a coma. I've set up a trust fund for her care and for the support of her family. Without my money, they'd be living in a car. As long as we don't ask Evan to deliver our messages, he won't mind stepping into the spotlight. I need to get his church leaders to go along, but I think they'll be just as pragmatic. These Protestants are warring factions, as they've always been, and Evan's supporters won't mind having an edge. Again, that's as long as they think they're deciding how they stand on the issues."

"But what about the wife?" Nora asked. "If she recovers, I can see how you could spin it so it's an answer to his prayers. But what if she doesn't?"

Emilie spoke up, "It's a sympathy angle. Hearts will bleed for him. And she's gorgeous. Hollywood couldn't manage better casting."

"Wow" was all Nora could say.

Shackleton elaborated with his no-nonsense banker's tone. "If she shows no signs of recovery, Missouri law says her doctors still have to try to keep her alive — her body, if not her mind. Indefinitely. It's like some long-running cable series. Any sign, any symptom, any reversal — it'll be news." He took a big gulp of his drink. "And if she expires, that's also big news. He's the miracle worker who could work miracles on anyone but his own precious love! Isn't that tragic? You'll ask for his reaction on camera. You guys will know how to milk that."

"Wow," Nora said again. "You're like a pack of wolves with advanced degrees. I'm getting chills. Let me ask again, what do you hope to achieve?"

"For starters," Shackleton said, "we'll build the Shining Waters Temple. I'd thought I'd build a military museum as a tourist attraction around that spot, but this plan is so much better. Casinos have a pull, but this is a magnet the politicos won't touch — and tax-free. Let the Branson boys go after the gambling and the music. They won't have anything to top this."

"You're building a platform, I get that," Nora nodded. "But where do we go from here?"

"Okay," Shackleton said. "Now you're getting to the heart of the meeting today. The truck driver who forced Loretta Wycliff off the road was employed by Green Monster Global Logistics. He was driving under the influence of the drug khat, which is a national scandal ready to break. Lots of long-haul truckers are staying awake with it. My lawyers say suing Green Monster would be tricky, but you can gut them quicker with a media campaign."

"And why would we want to do that?"

Shackleton chuckled, "Why, to show anyone we *can*. And I'll short-sell their stock."

He shot Emilie a look, which was her cue to speak up. "You know, I'm going to change clothes and stretch out on the sun deck. If you don't mind."

Nora guessed it was a ploy and said, "Emilie, I think I'll join you."

But Shackleton said, "Nora, let's have some time to ourselves."

Nora hesitated. Emilie went off to change, and then Shackleton said, "I'm not putting the moves on you. But you must know you're an attractive woman. Do I have political aspirations? Who knows? Do you? I think we'd make a helluva team."

28

Events moved rapidly after Evan's television appearance, which was now racking up megaclicks on the streaming services. Phone calls offering both sympathy and donations poured in to the church office. Mrs. Olinger became so flustered Evan had to tell her it was okay not to answer and to increase the storage allowance on voicemail. She was to add a recorded greeting directing callers to a new website, developed with funding from Shackleton and directed by Ms. Shinn and her team of website developers.

The decision for a website came after Thurston called Evan to tell him why Shackleton had wanted to meet. The old pastor's husky voice came through Evan's phone. "Can you believe it? He actually told me not to turn down donations. I told him that's up to you, but he insisted he needs to make sure the deacons and the board will back you up."

Evan replied, "Are you comfortable with it? I have to hold my breath when I'm taking his money for our expenses, but accepting funds from the public means the church must be accountable, and we're still not sure what his motivations are."

Thurston didn't seem concerned. "The way he's got it set up, any donations specifically for Loretta's care go into the trust fund you're already using. Everything else goes into a Shining Waters Temple building fund. The donation buttons on the website will go there. His name won't appear on the accounts, and he'll have no signature authority. Checks and transfers will require two signers — one me, the other you. The accounts aren't even at his bank."

"So have you bought the story he's a new man?"

Thurston chuckled. "No, I'd be amazed just to hear he's gone back to attending services in his parish. But I'd pity the priest who has to keep mum after hearing his confessions."

"Nora Gibbons' producer called to book me on some more interviews. The original deal was I only had to do the one. But now his publicist Emilie Shinn is my new best friend."

"Is anyone telling you what to say?"

"No. No agenda. Difficult as that is to believe."

"How about this? Go along until they start telling you what to say. You'll be getting your message out, and I trust whatever you say will be what people need to hear. The minute you feel compromised, cut the cord. He could find a way to pull back his money, but we never had it to begin with."

"Remember, I'm living on that trust fund."

"Evan, we both know, whatever the technicalities, he could pull the plug at any time, no matter what you say or do. Okay, we're helping him clean up his act. Maybe he's planning to run for office. If so, the platform and the issues and the policies will be his. If he's smart — and we can assume he's even sharper than we think — he won't ask you to be his mouthpiece. But you can expect there will be a day when he wants a photo op with you standing beside him."

"That could be awkward, depending on what he's pushing at the time."

"Your stand has been, you're honest. You've already declared you want to separate church and state. You're not in the political game and not willing to join in, even to comment. I admire that about you, and I think it's high time as a ministry we stopped peddling these divisive side issues and started reminding people what's truly important about behaving as a loving community."

"Careful, Marcus. You're sounding like a reformer, maybe even a revolutionary. What could be more controversial these days than refusing to take a position on current events? This may come as news to you, but that's a stand as political as any other."

Thurston assured him, "I'm retired. You're the messenger."

THE NEXT EVENTFUL call was from Josh Emmett, who took a roundabout way of thanking Evan for everything he'd done for their family, keeping them in their home, and barring bankers, wolves, and government operatives from their door. But then he admitted sheepishly that, after discussing it and praying about it, he and Linda were accepting Shackleton's over-market offer on the land and buildings of the farm that had been the center of contention for so long.

Evan assured Josh they must be making the right decision and closed by hoping he'd see them in church, where he knew they'd been absent. Josh repeated his concern for Loretta.

Then Evan called Shackleton. He was surprised and a bit irked that the banker had gone to Thurston first with his plans, but he was learning to be pragmatic, as long as he could maintain his honesty.

His first question was, "So, will the Emmett farmhouse get bulldozed after all?"

"Yes," Shackleton replied, "but it won't be the Corps of Engineers going in there. They've already decided to go the long way around, and the hazmat work on the adjoining government site is already underway. No, Evan, the Emmett land will be the site of your new sanctuary. I've got a guy in Springfield who walks the paperwork through. The Shining Waters Temple!"

"Sounds ambitious. Won't it take time to design and build something so grand?"

"Oh, it'll be a showcase someday. But we'll do a temporary meeting hall first. Lay down a slab, and then do a tilt-up."

"What's a tilt-up?"

"It's how they build big warehouses quickly. Pour a slab, no basement. The crew lays out framing and rebar for a long wall flat on the ground, pour concrete into it, and when it hardens, they tilt it up. Steel roofing, all prefab. We'll have the structure done in a couple of months and the interior outfitted a month after that. Count on preaching to thousands in that place this spring. Meanwhile, we'll be designing the permanent edifice, which, I assure you, will one day be a world destination."

"Do I get to ask why you're doing all this?"

The banker's explanation was straightforward. "You're a force to be reckoned with, Evan. And I want you at my side when life in this country gets a whole lot more interesting." And he ended the call.

Shackleton made it sound as though he feared the Apocalypse. But the preacher shrugged it off as a figure of speech. Evan judged his nemesis as a man who would be more likely to cause a cataclysm than to suffer through it.

29

"She blinked," Dr. Ravi announced. Evan would have expected more excitement from the voice on the phone, but the young doctor was simply stating a clinical fact. The guy was deliberately underplaying the news.

By Evan's reckoning, Loretta had been on retreat from the land of the living for six months, one week, three days, and six hours.

"So she's awake!" Evan was suddenly hyper-alert.

"No," came the sober answer. "We can't say that. There are some other encouraging signs, however. When the nurse saw her lids react, she followed a series of tests. Oculovestibular testing is very simple, harmless. We use an eyedropper to put some warm water in one ear. We lift the eyelids, and if the eyeballs move to the opposite side, that's the normal response. We repeat the procedure in the other ear. Then we use cold water in each ear, and the eyes should move *toward* the stimulus rather than away. It's a good test of brain-stem function. Loretta's eyes reacted normally, and the size of her pupils responds to our bright exam light."

"This has to be encouraging," Evan insisted.

"Yes," Ravi said. "That's how I would describe it. Encouraging. Hopeful. Now we watch for signs of further improvement. Pinpricks. Washcloths. Hold her hand, gentle squeeze."

"But doesn't this mean she's trying to wake up?"

"Not necessarily," the doctor replied dryly. "It means there is renewed activity in the primitive, involuntary regions of her brain, most probably because the swelling has subsided. But it doesn't mean she's having thoughts. Or capable of having them."

"Should I go see her?"

"It's not urgent. But of course. Whenever you can. Nothing's changed in that respect."

"Is there anything more you can do — to help her along?"

Ravi's tone warmed slightly when he answered, "You do the praying and the visits. We'll continue to provide the medication."

Before Evan could thank the doctor, he'd ended the call. Evan had wanted to ask about whether now might be the time to try the innovative procedure Luke had mentioned. But he judged Ravi didn't need or want to be reminded.

EVAN DECIDED NOT to share the news with Luke and Melissa right away. He was acutely aware that Ravi was being cautious about igniting new hope. If and when Loretta progressed from a vegetative to a minimally conscious state, he'd take both of them to see her. At that point, she might be dimly aware of their presence. But for now, from what Evan understood of the prognosis, even expecting that she could hear his stories might be wishful thinking. He wanted to believe he was doing everything he could, and whenever he sat with her, he kept telling himself that her soul was hovering near him and paying close attention.

Hadn't Ann Shackleton's spirit come unfettered from her body for a time? They were sure she was further gone than Loretta is now.

Medical science could explain with some precision the mapping of brain functions to its structures and regions. But so far, no theorist had a provable explanation of how or where consciousness arises. Evan's religious doctrine held that the soul occupies a body for a time, then departs. Many if not most medical practitioners theorized that soul is nothing more than the biological processes of personality and psychology, having no existence apart from or outside of the mortal brain.

Evan wondered whether Luke had made any more attempts to communicate with Loretta. The boy hadn't said anything more about it, and now having Melissa around all the time, Evan didn't think he dared speak as freely with him. Since she'd come to live with them, Evan had to figure that anything he confided in Luke would reach her ears. She seemed stable now, but Evan feared her emotions could spin out of control in a heartbeat — no, in the wink of an eye.

What about the dog in Luke's vision? Why didn't I think to ask why Murphy's spirit is there?

Luke's vision of Loretta sitting by the river could have been a product of his imagination — forming mental images of situations that weren't real. Or perhaps they did occur in some realm beyond our physical senses. A black dog is a common enough symbol, understandable in Luke's revelation as death patiently waiting at Loretta's side.

Why hadn't I made the connection?

Evan had no idea what more the dog's presence could mean, but somehow having received a glimmer of hope — literally a twinkle in his lover's eye — he suddenly had a strong urge to seek out Murphy.

He'd visit Loretta tonight, but first he must make the trip to Peculiar.

30

For Evan, driving to Peculiar had become a shift of mindset, a suspension of the rules. He could go off his diet at Merle's, and he could reflect on everything that "didn't happen here" during the Civil War. And if he didn't mind indulging superstition, he could stop in at Granny Longacre's.

I don't dare ask her about Loretta, do I?

Except Granny's house was boarded up. And there was no for-sale sign with information so he could investigate.

He drove to Merle's, the only place where he'd met anyone who knew the old lady. Ned, the assistant manager he'd spoken with before, was at the register.

"Reverend, I got some news," the fellow said quietly.

"Granny moved out?"

"You must've seen the place all shut up. Not sure how close you were, but she's moved on, as in passed away."

Was my urge to see the dog a last message from her? I thought I couldn't buy what she was selling, but I can't deny the effect she's had on me.

Evan asked, "Had she been ill?"

"Nope. They say she probably went in her sleep. Some folks know it's their time. She's got a daughter in Topeka, but the gal ain't showed up yet. You can figure she'll have that shack torn down before she sells the lot. Clean start for somebody who wants to build in town."

"Do you know if there are arrangements? Will there be a service?"

Should I volunteer to officiate? Being seen as the friend of a fortune-teller would only stoke the rumors I'm trying to work magic.

"Mortician told me he's to ship her ashes to the daughter. I'm going to guess she'll do everything by remote control. They got no folks here."

"What about the dog?"

Ned made an extra effort to smile wide. "Now that's the glad part. She's all yours! We got her tied up around back."

"It's cold out there!" Evan scolded him.

The guy shrugged. "We kept her fed. It's only been a coupla days. I was going to call the church and track you down, but then here you are!"

"How do you figure Murphy is mine? Maybe I can't manage to keep her."

The man reached under the counter, pulled out a small envelope, and handed it to Evan. "They say Granny spelled it out. The daughter gets the house and the furniture. You get the dog and this note. The funeral director give it to me. You'll notice it ain't been opened."

Evan hurried to get Murphy and put her in his car. He noticed her eyes were watering, perhaps from the cold air, but she seemed otherwise fit. He started the engine, flipped on the heater, and let it warm up before he took off his gloves to open the note, which was written in a careful, old-fashioned cursive hand:

My wise and wonderful friend,

Morphia must be with you now. Please see that what life she has left on this Earth is comfortable. I know she will have a loving home. She is already devoted to you, as she has been to me. Please remember that she doesn't run off. She explores!

I will be watching, and I will glory in what I see unfold.

Yours in Christ,

E. Longacre

Evan turned the paper over hoping there would be a contact number for the daughter written on the back, but it was blank. And Ned had no information about her.

Murphy sat at attention on her hind legs in the passenger seat with her front paws braced and her head up so she could see the road ahead as if she were set to be the navigator. Evan glanced over at her, and she returned the look.

Those are tears.

31

"What in blazes makes you think it's a jolly old time for us to be adopting some fleabag mutt?" Cora complained. She was at the sink chopping vegetables for stew, and her fury wielding the knife emphasized her aggravation.

"Murphy won't be a bother," Evan assured her as he took off his coat and draped it over a kitchen chair. "A meal and a blanket to curl up on at night are all she needs. During the day, she'll have the run of the property. She's very independent, you'll see."

Cora turned back to get another look at Murphy and pronounced, "She's old. I hope you didn't have to pay for her."

"Old and wise," Evan said. "And no, she's a gift from a dear friend who couldn't be with her anymore."

"Couldn't manage the vet bills, you mean," Cora sniffed as she resumed her chopping.

Luke and Melissa had been huddled in their room and came into the kitchen with Baby Buzz clomping along. He was walking now, if unsteadily, and he held tightly to Melissa's hand. His eyes grew big when he saw the dog.

"Ahhhhhhh!" he yelled as he let go of his mother, charged at Murphy, and fell onto the dog's neck, clasping and hugging her with his outstretched arms to break his fall.

Cora gasped, sure this wild beast would snarl, counterattack, maybe even bite.

But Murphy sat regally, solid and unmovable as the statue of a saint.

"Hey!" Melissa exclaimed, "He must be good with kids. Is he ours?"

Evan explained, "This is Murphy, and she's a *she*. Whether she's ours or we're hers, we'll find out. But, yes, she'll be living with us."

"I think she's kind of old," Luke muttered.

"Didn't you say you had a dream about a black dog?" Evan asked cautiously.

Luke glanced at Evan, fully alert. They were tuned-in to a private telepathic channel now. The boy answered, "Yeah, now that you mention it. The dog in my dream looked a lot like her, sat still and straight like her."

Evan's next hopeful question was, "Just the one time? Or have you had that dream again?"

Luke didn't want to answer. "Nothing's changed. People in my dreams don't talk."

After a hearty dinner of Cora's stew with fresh-baked cornbread, Evan was putting on his coat to head back out when Luke came up to him. "There's something I've got to show you," the boy said.

Melissa and Cora were sitting by the fire in the parlor as Buzz played at stacking building blocks on the floor. Cora would be leaving soon with Evan, who would be dropping her off in town.

Evan followed Luke into his bedroom, which at one time had been old Redwine's preferred sitting room. Luke crouched down to lift a loose floorboard beside the bed. He dug down, lifted out a stack of old magazines, and handed them to Evan.

It was all vintage pornographic material from the 1950s, dating well before the Hefner era when men's magazines began to contain presumably tasteful pictures of scantily clad women. Here were black-and-white photos of naked people in poses the worldly-wise Evan had never seen — along with scenes involving sadomasochistic costuming and devices of torture.

"And some folks call me a sicko," Luke muttered. "They have no idea. I guess the old guy was no saint."

Arthur Redwine. Feet of clay.

Evan gave the stuff back to Luke with the advice, "After everyone's in bed, toss them in the fireplace. And you know it should never be mentioned. I doubt anyone besides Arthur knows about these. I'll be going to see him tomorrow. They're telling me he's in hospice." He added, "Thanks for showing me. You did the right thing."

"Do you think it's a sin to have these?"

Evan was more concerned about Luke's reaction to them, asking, "Does seeing these upset you? I know they make me uncomfortable."

"No, I just don't understand why people would act that way."

"For sure, it's a sin to do things to people they don't want done to them. As for what adults agree to do with each other or what goes on in someone's imagination, I have no advice to give. You might have no control over your impulses — you know that, I'm sure, from when you didn't get the right meds — but when you decide to act on those thoughts, that's where you can go wrong."

THAT NIGHT AT THE HOSPITAL, Evan told Loretta that Luke had seen her sitting on the bank of a river with this miraculous dog Morphia at her side. This beloved animal must be a healer, he told her, maybe an angel. They'd share her presence and their affection for her, along with the comfort they would so desperately need as a family.

Evan yearned to be rewarded with a blink, but his wife's face might as well have been made of wax. He wouldn't be discouraged, so after he kissed her lightly on the forehead (which he'd been told not to do), he gently lifted an eyelid and was heartened to see the iris contract. His tears welled up. Here was a gift, slight and subtle, but he would hold to it as a promise.

32

The next morning Evan woke around five. The others were still asleep. Peering out the window of his bedroom, the full moon made the night's fresh snowfall glisten. He went to the kitchen and was brewing a pot of coffee when he felt Murphy's nose nudge the back of his leg. He turned to ruffle the fur on the top of her head and stroke her muzzle. She licked his hand and nudged back. He resolved to buy some dog biscuits, but not having anything like that, he went to the fridge and fetched some cheese. As he cut a small piece for her, he flashed on the first time Arthur Redwine had served him lunch in this house — and then the old man's pleading for the contraband of his favorite Emmenthaler. Evan would buy some of that, too, just for Arthur.

So many expectations, responsibilities. There was a time not so long ago when no one needed me. How could I believe I was happier then?

Evan poured the coffee into a thermos, dressed, bundled up in his winter wear, and grabbed a thick blanket. Moving quietly, he went outside with Murphy at his side. He led her down to the pond and spread the blanket double-thick on the soft snow on the bank under the sorrowful and meditative weeping willow tree.

With his back against the tree and Murphy curled up and warm in his lap, he sipped his coffee and watched the ridge of the horizon in the east begin to glow, then the sunrise over the wispy gray silhouettes of the endless tree-line.

The pond was still frozen over, with patches of snow on the ice. The light of the two bright celestial bodies played on the glistening surface. Evan felt a stiff, bracing breeze.

He wondered at the choice of *Shining Waters Temple* as the new home Shackleton wanted to build for the Evangel Baptist congregation. Never mind whether the flock was sheepish enough to be led there.

Before Granny Longacre's death, when Evan had gone to find Murphy, he hoped his urge to see the dog again was a helpful portent. Then after he'd adopted the animal, he sensed Granny's spirit had pulled him to Peculiar. Since Luke had seen Murphy by Loretta's side, Evan hoped — as he'd shared with his sleeping wife — that the dog would bring not only comfort but insight.

Morphia, can you convince her to come back?

The dog had no telepathic messages to give Evan, but her warmth was much more comforting than any blanket.

33

Evan had officiated at four funerals so far in December. The interval between Thanksgiving and Christmas seemed to be a time when old souls chose to depart. It was almost as if they didn't want to be a bother to their families during the holidays. Or perhaps they had no families — or none who were close or welcoming — and the prospect of feeling isolated during the festive time was just too grim to bear.

Apparently, Granny Longacre had been cremated, and Evan wondered whether the choice was hers or her daughter's. In his experience, it seemed the young folks thought returning quickly to ashes to be the greener way, requiring less or perhaps no real estate for a plot, and it was certainly less expensive. But traditional Baptist doctrine teaches resurrection of the body. In days gone by, some people thought wanting to be cremated suggested a lack of faith. When Evan reflected on these things — as he tried not to do, especially now — his scientific mind knew that the smallest scrap of intact DNA should be sufficient for the Creator to reconstitute a human form. That assumes God must operate within the universal physical laws decreed just before the Big Bang.

As well, you must somehow believe a happy afterlife for eternity requires a physical body.

Funerals were challenging for Evan — but not because death was hovering at his family's door. In his official role, he couldn't find much to say with sincerity. All of the people who had passed this month had been old and had succumbed to natural causes. (The teenage auto accidents and drug overdoses, which were more prevalent during the spring and summer, were torturous events for everyone involved.) In the case of an older congregant, if they'd ever attended the church at all, it probably was before Evan had become pastor. Thurston might have been acquainted with the person. Evan might know some members of the family. But when it came to composing a eulogy, Evan had to fall back on formula. He'd have to interview family members and make careful notes about the deceased's admirable and beloved character traits, along with a few lighter anecdotes about their fads and foibles. Evan always dreaded having to start with, "I wasn't fortunate enough to know Mary, but…"

Then at the gravesite, he would read directly from the published liturgy, and rather than injecting emotion, he'd try, as the prescribed words were meant to do, to convey a calm confidence that this person was now at rest and in a better place.

He doubted his congregants knew — if they gave it any thought at all — what the time-honored pronouncement, "Rest in Peace," was meant to convey. It wasn't intended to describe an eternity of doing nothing. Rather, it was a wish that the soul wouldn't be troubled — as in, haunt anyone — while it waited, perhaps eons — to be resurrected. After which the Christian program is mostly unpublished.

Unless you believe Dante actually got a tour.

To say that the deceased is with God, of course, could be a polite fib. No earthly being could know the fate of a soul — no matter how outwardly righteous they'd been in life. And of all the ministries he was called upon to perform, funerals tended to bring on Evan's more agnostic moods.

The brutal thought he avoided these days was whether there would be anything left of Loretta after her brain was cold. And then there was the awful fear she was dead already in a brainless warm body.

He could have asked Thurston to do the funerals, but he had too much respect for his mentor's retirement to ask for help. Evan suspected that Marcus judged presiding at ceremonies to be work, as he did.

But Evan had learned that visiting the sick could be as uplifting for him as it was for the patient.

EVAN INDEED FOUND Arthur Redwine in the hospice wing of the retirement complex. The old man was bedridden, stretched out on his back much as Loretta was, except there were no life-sustaining or even monitoring devices attached to him.

Evan had brought the promised cheese, but this man wouldn't be able to eat it. He was breathing on his own, with an audible, wheezy rattle with each gasp of air.

They must think he's present enough to tell them not to bother with life support. If he was out of it, they'd have asked me as his executor, and they haven't.

Evan sat, leaned in close, and took the man's hand in both of his. "You're hanging in there, Arthur. Are they making you comfortable? Anything you need? All you have to do is ask."

Redwine smiled weakly, turning his head toward his pastor. "No need to pack my bags, son. I'll be going over soon."

"Shall we pray?"

"You can say your words. I'm fresh out." No sooner had he closed his eyes as if to rest than they popped open again and he said, "There is something."

"Anything, Arthur."

"My room, under the floor. Dirty pictures. Get rid of them. My fault, I forgot to clear them out."

"It's already done. Don't worry."

"You saw them?"

"Yes."

He became alarmed. "Children see them?"

"No," Evan said. "Of course not. Ashes in the fireplace."

Not a fib. Luke's hardly a child anymore. If he ever was.

"Good man. Thank you."

Evan assured his friend, "I know it must have been hard on you, all those years with Sedalia gone."

He actually chuckled. "Oh, she was there. Couldn't get rid of her if I'd wanted to, and of course I wanted her by me. I had no desire to remarry, and she never scolded me for looking at them pictures."

His Naomi. Of course.

"I won't either, Arthur. I can only imagine how lonely you were."

Arthur seemed to want to lift his head but couldn't. He looked up at Evan and his eyes were wet. "I worry, my boy, you'll be like me. Your missus is in a bad way, they say."

"No, she's going to make it. I'm sure."

The old man chuckled again, saying, "She's such a pretty thing. If I was a hundred years younger, I'd be fighting you for her." He grew serious again when he added, "Evan, if she goes over before you do, I'm gonna look after her real good until you show up." His swelling emotion brought on a coughing fit. Evan put a hand on his chest, and Redwine calmed down so he could catch his breath. Then he continued with a wicked grin, "A man's got to have a reason to get up in the morning. You know as well as me, since the dawn of time, three things get us goin'— *What's there to eat? Who or what wants to kill me? And who can I fuck?"*

Evan could have amended that with something like "What does God want me to do today?" but all he said was "I can't disagree."

"Now you get out of here," Redwine ordered. "We come in alone, we go out alone."

"You'll be seeing Sedalia," Evan said.

I know that's what he wants to hear.

Redwine whispered, "God grant. God grant."

If I have to wait until I'm on the other side to see Loretta again, yes, I hope I have a body!

EVAN HAD a difficult time leading the Christmas Eve service. Arthur's passing was still on his mind. He owed it to the man to arrange a fitting memorial, but he wondered who would bother to pay respects to an old recluse nobody in the present generation had ever met. Tonight, many of them must have been either celebrating elsewhere or shut-in, because attendance was sparse. While the choir was singing, Evan counted twenty-four heads, most of them gray or white.

He'd found no inspiration for a sermon. Instead, he simply read the Nativity story from the book of Matthew and hoped against his own doubt he sounded sincere.

Evan's mood was glum, his outlook grim. Yes, he'd received that blink, the gift he'd prayed for, but he felt like a kid who'd asked for a bicycle and been given socks.

PART III

Four months later…

34

Loretta sat stiffly in her wheelchair on the stage-left side of the platform. The choir, which now numbered thirty voices, was arrayed behind her in their new electric-blue robes with gilt stoles. Evan stood at the pulpit on the opposite side. His sharp new suit was jet black, and his silk tie was a blood-red burgundy. She was wearing makeup for the first time since before the accident, and she worried it looked overdone. Emilie Shinn had encouraged her to glam up, including getting her hair done in town, and they'd bought her a white-satin dress with a gold scoop collar and sash for the occasion.

This would be her first public appearance, and the occasion was to announce her recovery to the congregation and the TV cameras that were now permanent fixtures in the sanctuary. The platform was flooded with too-bright stage lighting that could cycle through all the colors of the spectrum, adjusted and switched to fit the order of service. She'd been coached that squinting might be seen as frowning and was told to put on a pleasant face and smile as much as she could manage.

In the hospital, once she'd shown responsive signs, her recovery from coma had been much more rapid than Dr. Ravi expected. Four months after she blinked, here she was, ready for the spotlight.

The moment was approaching. She'd rehearsed it several times at home with only the watchful Leslie standing by. She was pretty sure Evan didn't know what was coming. Today was the first service in the new sanctuary of the warehouse-style temporary church, and Emilie had assured her that the surprise would not only make him overjoyed but would also be an inspiration for the worshippers, a highlight of the momentous day.

Evan was saying to the congregation, "And many of you know this lovely lady sitting by me is my dear wife Loretta. She's made a brave and remarkable recovery from a long illness, and she wants to share her own words of thanks to you for your faith, your fervent prayers, and your donations."

He turned and started to cross the chancel toward her because the plan was for him to wheel her over to a microphone that was suspended above the altar.

She'd been careful to set the brakes so the wheels were locked. Gripping tightly to the chair arms, she raised her body a few inches, pitched her weight forward, planted her satin shoes firmly on the floor, and slowly stood up!

The congregation had grown quiet for Evan's announcement, but the sudden silence was unbelievable for a crowd of more than two thousand. Then came gasps, followed by shouts, "Praise God!" "Hallelujah!" and "Amen!"

Evan was so startled his movement toward his wife was frozen by the shock.

She managed a nervous smile, and gazing at him in adoration, she stepped haltingly forward.

He held out his arms, beckoning her to a joyous embrace.

One step, then another, but no sooner had she lifted her chin and straightened up than her body began to sag.

He rushed to her and caught her in his arms before she was on her knees.

Tears were streaming down his face as he hugged her tightly and lifted her back up on her feet.

As fortune would have it — or as a stage manager might have directed it — they were standing at the altar directly beneath the suspended microphone.

The congregants applauded and cheered amid more enthusiastic shouts of praise.

Breathlessly, Loretta raised her head toward the microphone and said, "God bless you all! I'm so grateful to be back!"

And she kissed her husband.

EVAN MUST HAVE BEEN THRILLED at the sight, but now he was furious. After the service, he'd wheeled her into his private office and closed the door. They'd come from standing out in front of the building, where, with her in her chair beside him, Evan had stood greeting worshippers as they slowly made their way out of the sanctuary. He hadn't seemed upset then, but she knew his smile was pasted-on. After all, neither of them knew most of these people. The membership of Evangel Baptist numbered less than a hundred, and the size of the congregation there on Sundays was typically less than half that. The opening of the Shining Waters Temple, although this interim facility was no grander than a decorated warehouse, had attracted people from all over the tri-county area, perhaps some even driving down from KC or St. Louis, even planning to stay the night, as if the new edifice and its preacher were a tourist attraction.

"Why didn't you tell me what you were planning to do?" Evan demanded. "You might have been hurt! That's worry enough, but don't you realize how this looks? Do you have any idea what we'll have to deal with now?"

In a low, meek voice, Loretta said, "I wanted to surprise you. I thought you'd be thrilled." Her tears had started, and he came over to wipe her face with his handkerchief and kiss her forehead.

"Sweetheart, never in my life has anything made me so happy. I was ready to accept what you'd achieved already as a miracle. At first, you were patient through all that speech therapy, and I worried maybe you'd be discouraged because you wouldn't be able to express yourself. I worried you wouldn't be able to grasp a pair of scissors or read a book. And I worried some life-long disability might make you frustrated and angry. But you've held to your faith more than I have. You've been getting better and better. And now this? It's glorious!"

"Then why are you so upset with me?"

"Not with you," he insisted. "Never with you. But I should have suspected — the dress, the makeup, the coaching. Emilie Shinn put you up to this... performance... didn't she?"

"We both wanted to surprise you. She said everyone would be thrilled. Something memorable for your first service."

Evan started to pace. "What she orchestrated looks like a faith healing. There was no laying on of hands, no invocation. But she's well aware rumors were already flying around town about me. She knew what people would think. She knows I wouldn't go along with staging a stunt — much less, making claims — but now she'll get the media to play it up, and people will think I'm being modest but doing hocus-pocus behind the scenes."

Loretta's tone changed, her voice taking on an edge, when she said, "Is that so bad?"

"My main motivation in taking Shackleton's money was to make sure you had the best possible chance to recover. And, yes, it met our expenses as a family so I could continue in the ministry. The church budget can barely keep the lights on in the old building. But now we're playing on a whole new level. And like they say, nothing fails like success."

"Maybe you should concentrate on serving all those people who came. Isn't your job to make sure they hear the gospel? Can't you consider the possibility that God is using Shackleton to give you a louder voice?"

"My fear has been that Shackleton will use me to sell whatever people will pay him to sell."

"Evan, I've known some salesmen who could make people spend more money than they could ever hope to have. But I know you are the kind of person who can't sell anything you don't believe in. You just can't. And you and I both know there are days when you have your doubts about the messages in your prayers and sermons."

"You know me better than I know myself," he told her. "What do you think I should do?"

"What I want you to do is to be wise enough to know how to use what you've been given."

The knock at the door was Reverend Thurston, who had attended the service seated among the worshippers.

Evan let him in and, realizing they were about to have a full and frank exchange of views, he suggested Loretta ride home with Melissa in the new Navigator. (This one was Pristine White Metallic, courtesy the church's insurance carrier.) She had attended with Luke and Buzz and had just gotten her license.

THURSTON SAT with Evan in the office as the young pastor put on a pot of coffee. It was their ceremonial drink, like a brew of magic mushrooms shared between shamans, signaling they'd be taking their time to reflect.

Evan made sure to let the older man speak first. He didn't want to begin by apologizing.

"Impressive. Didn't look at all staged or contrived," Thurston mused.

Evan handed him a mug, took his own, and sat behind the desk. "If it was staged — and it might have been — it wasn't by me."

"Don't get me wrong. It's a miracle, and we should all be thankful prayers have been answered in abundance. But I can tell by your reaction you know how this will play."

"I do," Evan said. "And you and I have worried all along that Shackleton wants to exploit us. But this is the first time it's looked like show business. His publicist bought the dress for Loretta and helped her get fixed up. She even ordered a brand of makeup you can't get locally. But now I'm sure Loretta was coached, and the result is exactly what they intended."

"Do you still think he has reformed? Repented his evil ways?"

"I never thought that. But I was betting he'd behave himself because the authorities are watching him much closer now."

Thurston seemed worried. "What's next? Do you have any control over what they'll be saying about you?"

"I'm due to go on Nora Gibbons next week. It was supposed to be all about this new building, a preview of plans for the grand one, and no doubt a video tour, including clips of the service today. There was nothing for me to object to in all of that. But now you can bet they'll lead with Loretta, and maybe you can help me think about how to handle it from there."

"Your position all along has been not to say anything you don't believe."

"And I can tell them the real magic was the new ultrasound treatment the medical team at Mizzou used on her brain. More than anything, that's what got her back."

"You know saying that won't do anything to stop the gossip about you. If you're going to continue to go in front of the cameras, you'll have to accept the consequences."

Evan grew thoughtful. "You know, I've been reading Whitley Strieber's book on Jesus."

"I haven't seen it," Thurston said. "You should learn not to go looking under rocks. There are all kinds of crazy theories. It's all right for late-night debates among divinity students, but…"

"When Jesus cured that blind man, he rubbed his own spit into the man's eyes. According to Strieber's research, that was a common medical practice used by the cult of Therapeutae in Alexandria. Some scholars have guessed Jesus spent time studying with them during the lost years. And then there's the story he raised Lazarus from the dead. The old guy could have been out like Loretta was, his heartbeat barely noticeable. It's not like they had any diagnostic tools to know for sure. Premature burial was a thing until as recently as the nineteenth century."

"What are you getting at?"

"Maybe the historical Jesus didn't claim to work miracles. Maybe he used everything he knew how to do to help people who were beyond help. Maybe gossip made *his* rep."

"You're not claiming you're the son of God though."

Evan smiled. "You know you should really expand your reading list. There's a fascinating alternative scripture, *The Aquarian Gospel of Jesus the Christ,* written in 1907. These days they'd say the author channeled it. One of the most remarkable things Jesus says is, 'What I have done all men can do, and what I am all men shall be.' In our doctrine, we're called to be Christlike, but no one ever taught us we would *become* Christ. That strikes me as a message the church as an institution of social control wouldn't have wanted to make popular."

"Is that the kind of thing you plan to say on the air? Sounds like you'll be inviting more trouble. The Convention could disown us, for starters."

"I was upset with Loretta. I wish I had known what Emilie was trying to pull off. It's clear to me now I'll have to confront them on their agenda, even if it means losing their support. But now that the temple's doors are open, he won't dare back out. Loretta was hurt I didn't seem overjoyed, but she says she didn't think about the consequences. Then I asked her what she thought I should do. We're in this together, and she'll have to live with it as much as I will."

"Is she afraid for you? Does she want you to resign?"

"No," Evan said. "She says I'd be a fool not to use what we've been given."

Thurston looked reluctant to speak. "Evan, before you took up the ministry, you did some righteous things, you helped some people, but also — especially when it came to your own health and lifestyle — you made some very bad judgments. I never thought of you as self-centered, but if Shackleton's plans get out of control, you could get a swell head, and your ego might lead you places you should refuse to go."

I wish you didn't have to say it. I know, I know.

35

Nora Gibbons led off where Evan had hoped she would end. "Reverend Wycliff, you insist you can't work miracles, but in your service last Sunday, your wife who had been in a coma for months got up and walked!"

Evan said in measured tones, "Her recovery has been an answer to prayer, certainly. But we owe a lot of her progress to God's hand working through medical science. With funding from the Shackleton Trust, we brought in a team of neurospecialists from University Hospital. They have a new ultrasound treatment that stimulates sleeping brains. It's miraculous, sure, but there's nothing mysterious about what cured her."

She followed with, "You know, some of your critics claim you don't even believe in God. They're saying, at best, you're an agnostic."

"Oh, I believe in God," Evan said. "But some days I worry he's gone fishing."

That drew a smile from her. "So that's how you answer?"

"If you want theology, I'll say this. The scientists are telling us everything began with the Big Bang. Before that — nothing. And that's consistent with Genesis One-One: 'In the beginning, God created the heaven and the Earth.' But think about it. If in the beginning there was nothing, the Creator had to create the Creation out of itself! I've heard preachers say, 'God is all that there is.' And I'd say, I'd have to agree. That's all there can be!"

"God is in the rocks and the trees? And in Muslim terrorists?"

"In all there is, yes."

"I doubt many people believe that, Reverend. Including most Baptists." Then she asked, "If God is in everything, why is this world in such a mess?"

"The world is evolving — just as humans are evolving — from nothing into something glorious. We're intensely focused on the here and now — as we must be — but all of human history is just a tiny sliver in time. We must summon our faith that what we're doing — whatever we're trying to achieve in the limited time we have as mortals — will be worthy in God's eyes."

"It sounds so simple when you say it," Gibbons said. "But do you really believe everything you're telling us?"

Evan grinned. "Someone pointed out to me the other day that I'm nothing more than a salesman. I'm selling the story of salvation. That person — who knows me very well — assured me that I could never hope to sell a product I don't believe in. I have hope that as a community we will set our differences aside and begin to act like we care for the welfare of our neighbors — regardless of what they believe or whom they follow."

"That's sounding vaguely political, Preacher."

"It's not. Believe me, it's not. But if politicians want to take it to heart, God bless 'em."

36

As Loretta recovered her strength and became surefooted, she grew randy as a broodmare. Evan reminded her that, as she lay in the coma, he'd suggested they have a love-child, but now he worried her body wasn't ready.

"Evan, you're not going to break me!"

"I'm kind of out of practice."

"I guess I should be glad to hear that. But it's like riding a bicycle. Jump on and *push off!*"

IT WAS ALMOST a year after the accident, in the spring of the year. Loretta was feeling fit, to say the least. She wasn't slurring her sentences even when she was tired. Daily life in the Wycliff household seemed gloriously normal. As normal as it could be with a rock-star minister who was about to get his own TV show on a national network.

When Evan was home, it seemed he was on the phone constantly except for his self-imposed offline time at sit-down meals with the family. Loretta made him silence his phone when they closed the door to their bedroom at night, and the hypervigilant Luke, who often was awake at odd hours, could hear muffled conversations when their bed wasn't thumping against the common wall.

Caregivers were still very much with them. The house had been reno-vated practically and cleanly, if not lavishly, and Loretta was now preoccupied with interior decoration when she wasn't involved in Loving Embrace activities. (She was understandably reluctant about driving, so Melissa took her most places when Evan couldn't.) A vestibule at the back entrance of the house, which Redwine had used as a mudroom, was converted and outfitted prettily, including a camp bed, along with a heater and swamp cooler, as Leslie's room. And every day except Sundays Cora would come straight to the house from her morning shift at the C'mon, cooking and baking and filling the house with the tantalizing aromas of her roasts and stews and pies and cookies.

Evan had tried to avoid private conversations with Stuart Shackleton. The man's occasional visits to the house were pleasant enough. He seemed genuinely surprised and pleased that Luke had overcome his resentments of his mother and was now seeing her often, if only to play a ridiculous card game that had only one rule. But even now, Luke was suspicious around his father, and the two weren't talking. Melissa was wary around him as well, but Evan thought it unlikely she knew about the man's former connections to the crimes at the casino. Shackleton doted on Baby Buzz, who was just learning to talk and was calling his grandpa alternately "Gappa" and "Shtoo." Whenever Buzz managed to spit these out, it was the only time Evan ever saw the banker laugh without his characteristic sardonic grin.

On one of Shackleton's visits, he'd brought an armful of gifts, one in a plain brown-paper bag which he set aside unopened. After dinner, he grabbed the bag and drew Evan close to say, "I heard you're a bourbon man, so I bought us some fine sippin' whiskey. Care for a snort and a chat, Rev?"

Evan knew the conversation was long overdue. Now would be his chance to confront the banker about his concerns. Their talk would have to be private, and ordinarily Evan would suggest they go out on the porch or take a walk, but as if cued by higher powers, a mighty thunderstorm was rolling in. During dinner, the bulging gray clouds broke open and let go a pounding rain that thudded like angry fists on the roof.

Leslie was busy with Buzz, and Luke and Melissa were with Cora in the kitchen cleaning up. Evan suggested, "There's a little room in the back." And taking a couple of glasses from the sideboard, he led Shackleton into Leslie's room.

Evan sat on the edge of the narrow bed, and Shackleton lowered his lanky frame onto the wooden chair of the girl's modest dressing table. The room was so small their knees almost touched.

The storm raged outside. In a Greek myth, Hephaestus would be throwing thunderbolts to signal his latest fury with these pathetic mortals.

Leslie's table became their bar. Shackleton poured, they sipped, and he eagerly refilled. Evan didn't recognize the label, but he expected this small-batch brand probably cost hundreds of dollars a bottle.

"Thank you, Stuart," Evan said as he drank. "You're right, this used to be one of my major vices, and I'm happy to indulge. It's good stuff."

"We've needed to talk."

"Yes," Evan agreed but didn't want to be the first to say why.

"You're doing a fine job," Shackleton said, taking a shot-sized gulp rather than a sip. "I hope you feel it's worthwhile for you."

"So far, as we've agreed, the message points have been mine. I've been forthright, and it hasn't been uncomfortable."

"Good. And wonderful that Loretta is doing so well."

Here we go!

Evan said reluctantly, "That walk of hers looked staged. I had no idea. I would have objected. She insists she just wanted it to be a sweet surprise, but she admitted Emilie coached her."

"And Nora Gibbons no doubt coached Emilie. Come on, Evan, this is the real world. No matter how it came to public attention, your wife has been cured."

"And I'm deeply grateful, believe me. Without the trust fund and that experimental procedure, I might still be visiting her every day and praying for her to wake up. She got her life back, and so did I, and I'm in your debt."

Shackleton smiled. His face was gaunt, his cheekbones hollow. When he smiled, he couldn't help baring his long front teeth, and it occurred to Evan the look was sardonic regardless of the intention. The banker said, "And you're worried I'm going to start telling you what to say?"

Evan took another drink, more than a sip, and replied, "I know you're a practical man, Stuart. I suppose it can be said that all human interactions are transactional, but I really can't see what you're getting out of all this unless you have a plan you haven't shared with me."

He chuckled. "You know me well enough. I've always had plans, always shopping for opportunities. Some deals work out, some pay off, others I hope I'm smart enough to dump before they go bad." Evan was about to speak when Shackleton hastened to add, "In your case, I will promise you here and now that I will never ask you to say anything you don't completely believe in. As you've been doing."

"I've been telling it the way I see it, and I worry that to some of the faithful my views might seem downright blasphemous. But even though the church has played an active role in politics in recent years, I won't go there. I can't be carrying those messages — for you or for anybody — whether or not I believe them personally to be correct."

"A wise man," Shackleton said. "Evan, now that you're going to have a much wider audience in the media, understand this. Whether you're at the pulpit or on the air, no one will remember for very long what you say. That's why politicians have catchphrases and preachers have favorite Bible verses. Most people not only don't know much about theology but they also don't give it much thought. At weddings and funerals maybe. But what they will always remember is how you make them *feel.* Hollywood actors who can make you cry know this. Would-be autocrats who can make you hate exploit this. As for you, your honesty shines through. What people see in you is not some claim you can work miracles — you claim no such thing. No, what they feel is your sincerity. As a banker, I know how difficult it can be to earn a new client's trust. People trust you. And that's power."

Power to do what? You're still not telling me!

Evan's question wasn't so blunt. "If you don't put words in my mouth, what can I do for you? What stake do you have in building me up?"

I can't imagine what comes next, but I'm already worried about the consequences.

Shackleton gazed at the pastor for a long moment, then said in a low tone to emphasize his sincerity, "Preacher, I'm asking you to baptize me."

37

Evan couldn't sleep that night. When Loretta asked him what had transpired during the huddle in Leslie's room, he'd quoted Shackleton as saying he'd never ask the preacher to lie for him — or even to deliver messages. But Evan didn't share the man's surprising request with her. He assumed she'd simply urge him to do it. How could he refuse?

Shackleton hadn't insisted on an answer right away. He could see he'd made Evan uncomfortable. He'd left the unfinished bottle and slipped out quietly after Buzz had been put to bed.

Evan should have challenged the man there and then, but he was more torn by this request than any decision he'd had to make since his discussions with Dr. Ravi about Loretta's care and treatment.

He knew Thurston was the only one who could guide him, so in the morning he phoned the old pastor and drove straight to the parsonage after a light breakfast of dry toast on a queasy stomach.

He asked Thurston nervously, "Should a minister baptize someone who may not be sincere?"

They were drinking Thurston's instant coffee. Evan broke his habit and added cream because he was feeling nauseous. He'd been tempted to bring what was left of Shackleton's booze to relax himself, but he knew Marcus abstained and might scold him for falling back on his old ways. The older man mused, "We knew he'd come up with a huge ask, but this one is a corker. I'm as suspicious of the man as you are, but are you sure he's not sincere?"

"I really don't know. My gut says no, he's not. But he visits us, has dinner, acts like a family member. Yes, he got the Emmett farm like he wanted, but he made Josh and Linda thrilled with the generosity of the deal, and instead of some clip joint he's put up this church for us. And an even more impressive place on the way."

"Which we're still not sure whether he regards as a commercial enterprise."

"Granted. But before he told me what he wanted, he swore he would never ask me to carry messages for him. And he encouraged me to keep speaking the truth as I see it. I insisted I'm for separation of church and state, and he didn't disagree. He as much as said he didn't care what came out of my mouth as long as I stick to being honest and sincere."

Thurston said, "It isn't all that difficult to understand what he wants to achieve with this request. If people see you as credible — as a man of unquestioned integrity — and you baptize him, he'll be washed clean. If not in the eyes of God, in the opinion of all the people who matter to Shackleton down here."

"And then what does he do?"

Thurston shrugged, "Whatever he wants? Worst case, he acts outwardly righteous but still up to his old tricks."

Evan fretted, "He's really backed me into a corner. What I need to ask you is — doctrinally and morally — and personalities aside — what's my duty in these matters?"

Thurston thought a moment and answered, "In my experience, the question isn't as uncommon as you might think. It comes up every time some youngster comes forward and I'm pretty sure the kid just wants to please the parents. Or worse, feels pressured."

"So what did you do?"

"We used to do the baptisms quarterly, at the beginning of each season, so if one was coming up I'd make a point of rescheduling it. I'd suggest to the parents I do some counseling sessions with the child first. And I'd ask the candidate, 'Do you understand what this is? What's the purpose? Do you know what it means to repent? Do you think your life and your choices will be different now?' And somewhere in there I'd ask casually if anyone had urged them to do it."

"And then you'd go ahead?"

"Sure. None of them ever told me they'd decided not to. As a pastor, you can't be certain about anybody. The genuineness of their conversion isn't up to you. Now, if it was an adult — say, a drunk who will fall right off the wagon or some guy who wants to impress his girlfriend — yeah, I might want to refuse. But I never have. And then of course there are those couples planning to get married and one of them is from another faith. I'll counsel them before I help, but I'm not about to throw a monkey wrench into a lifelong love story before it gets started."

"Are you saying I should do it?"

"Evan, all you can do is have a heart-to-heart with the man. Ask him those questions. Challenge his answers. Remember, there was the malefactor on the cross who as Jesus was dying beside him asked for forgiveness. Who are we to take the measure of Shackleton's soul? Let's fear God — but if we don't expect a miracle, maybe it won't come to pass."

THE SKIES HAD CLEARED since last night's storm. The landscape was littered with tree limbs, and the ground was soaked. But it promised to be a fine, sunny day, a hopeful day, and Evan resolved he'd adjust his mood accordingly.

He phoned Shackleton, who invited him onto his boat dockside at the marina. He'd been living on the boat now, and Evan assumed the banker would be moving into the Taggart place.

When Evan politely challenged Shackleton on his decision, the man insisted he knew the difference between his Catholic christening as an infant and this Baptist ceremony. In the former, the parents and the godparents commit themselves to raising the child in the church and doing everything they can to ensure his or her spiritual development. In professing to the Baptists, a person who is old enough to under-stand the decision not only expresses faith in salvation but also commits to a lifelong effort of Christlike behavior.

Evan agreed he'd perform the baptism on the condition that it be a private ceremony. The sanctuary in the temporary house of worship had not been outfitted with a baptismal font. The usual practice was for the candidate to come forward at the conclusion of a worship service in response to an invitation from the pulpit. In doing so, the person would be making a public decision in front of the congregation.

But the thought of Shackleton walking forward in the new sanctuary in front of thousands and all those cameras made Evan shudder, even if the man was serious. Loretta's performance had taught him to be doubly shy about how those events would be interpreted in the media.

He proposed to Shackleton that they do the baptism in the pond behind the Redwine house, beneath the weeping willow tree. Reverend Thurston, Loretta, Luke, and Melissa would look on as witnesses.

On the day, at dawn on a Saturday morning, Shackleton drove up wearing a pair of jeans, a plain white T-shirt, and a well-worn pair of canvas sneakers. No satin robes for him. His passenger in the car was

Emilie Shinn, who hadn't been invited, but Evan saw no reason to exclude her.

During the ceremony, the witnesses were lined up on shore. Evan waded out to where the water was waist-high, wearing his fishing boots and ceremonial robe.

Evan's back was toward the shore so that Shackleton could face the proud witnesses. Evan made the pronouncement, he covered the man's mouth and nose with a handkerchief, lowered him fully into the water, and lifted him back up.

The preacher failed to notice that Ms. Shinn had captured it all on her iPhone.

And the video went viral.

38

Evan was once again in-studio, on-camera, and live worldwide as Nora Gibbons welcomed him to her show. Before he could say anything more than, "Thank you, Nora, for having me," she'd aired the clip of Shackleton's baptism.

"Reverend, it seems you've performed another miracle!" she enthused.

Evan tried to remain composed when he responded, "Nora, I also perform weddings. And yes, I'm sure you'd agree uniting a couple in love who are committing to a new life *is* a wondrous miracle. But it's nothing *I* do. I officiate. I say the words. I'm just following orders, you might say."

She bore in, not wasting a second after he'd finished speaking. "Stuart Shackleton was an accused murderer. And some say a financial manipulator who was less than honest, associated with some nasty folks. Granted, he has been acquitted of the murder charge, and no other specific crimes have been alleged — but do you honestly think he's a new man?"

If she really wanted to roast me, she'd tell everyone I've accepted his money. But she knows not to go near the subject.

Evan was grateful for Thurston's guidance so he could almost quote the answer, "It's not for me as a pastor or as a fellow mortal to judge what's in Stuart Shackleton's heart — or the state of his soul. Our teaching is that anyone who has faith and desires to repent can accept salvation at any time. Forgiveness is immediate, total, and unconditional — and it matters not at all what you or I may think of the person or his past deeds."

I'm speaking the truth. I'm not lying for him. And yet I might as well be saying the sky is blue when it's a moonless midnight.

She chose not to pursue the question further. Instead, she announced, "And we can now let everyone know that you will be joining me as co-host of 'Religion Matters' next Sunday afternoon. I for one am thrilled to have you on board. What can our viewers expect? Could be you and I won't agree on anything."

"I'm really pleased you've invited me to join you, Nora. We'll be trying a new format. We will have folks on the show — invited guests from among our viewers — who are troubled for whatever reason. We will discuss their questions and concerns on the air. And, for my part, I'll lend my advice based on Bible teachings. You will, of course, offer your point of view — as a journalist? As a humanist?"

She smiled. "Oh, I will have no shortage of opinions, Reverend."

"Also, while our guests are on the air with us, we'll be taking calls, texts, and tweets. And we'll all get a sense of what our viewers think of the issues."

And I'll either be building my platform or digging my grave.

She grinned. "I'm going to put you on notice now, Reverend Wycliff. You've told me you want to stay out of politics, but I'm not going to let you dodge any questions!"

Evan answered humbly, "If you don't know me by now, you will."

∾

EVAN AND LORETTA were getting ready for bed.

"Why did I agree to this?" he asked his wife, as if she knew and he was not expecting an answer.

She was already under the covers, having shucked her baggy flannel pajamas, casting him expectant looks, and wondering why he was taking so long. She suggested, "Because you want to have a voice? Because you want people to know that thinking for themselves with the intelligence God gave them is not a sin?"

"Nora is going to box me in!" Evan fumed. "She's going to push me into a corner and keep on punching until I go down."

"She's clever, but she's not Gloria Allred, darling. You haven't done too bad the times you've appeared with her."

Evan sighed. "The truth is, I care very much about politics. And I see everything going the wrong way. I cringe at the divisiveness and the rancor, but I can't say honestly that I don't have a side. It doesn't take a mind reader to know that all of Shackleton's friends are conservative, reactionary, and probably downright racist. Since when did anyone in power ever willingly give it away?"

Loretta answered, "You've always taken your stand. I've never known you to deliberately mislead anyone. You're a straight shooter, and everyone knows it. And that's what Stuart likes about you. That's who he wants you to be. There will be times, you can bet, he will want you to stand next to him. That's how he intends to use you, and you will have to know when and where to draw the line."

"Billy Graham stood with Nixon," Evan muttered. "The Dalai Lama runs round kissing anyone. Gandhi won the hearts of millions by resisting British taxation and telling everybody they could run down to the sea and make their own salt."

"It's going to be okay," she cooed. "What I want to know is whether that bicycle of yours is a ten-speed. Show me you can pace yourself and go the distance, big guy."

THE DAY before Evan's premiere appearance as co-host of "Religion Matters" was a Saturday on a slow-news weekend.

That was the day Stuart Shackleton's press release went out declaring his candidacy for the United States Senate as a conservative from Missouri.

39

The Easter Egg was overdue for an oil change. Evan had been driving the tires off of it, refusing to consider trading it in for a less remarkable vehicle. Appleton City wasn't exactly overrun with paparazzi, but Evan did wonder whether his newfound celebrity would be attracting unwanted attention. He'd already bought into the idea that erecting the new temple would bring in a wider audience, and the TV show would extend his outreach. He vowed to himself to keep his intentions good and his messages righteous. He was fully aware that proximity to Shackleton was a risk, and some folks inevitably would accuse him of making deals with the devil.

Shackleton's jumping into politics was just what Evan and Thurston had feared, but the move was hardly surprising. And Evan was also acutely aware that it was far more important what an elected official actually did, not what the candidate promised. For now, he resolved to watch and wait, giving the banker the benefit of the doubt.

On the Saturday morning of Shackleton's announcement, Evan pulled his Fiat Cinquecento into the service bay of Zed Motors in Rockville. Besides the oil being low, Evan was also overdue for a chat with Zip Zed, the proprietor and his former employer.

Evan found Zip on the showroom floor, which in this modest store was just large enough to hold two shiny new vehicles — a sport-utility and a pickup truck. When he saw Evan approach, Zip cut off his conversation with Max Alumbaugh, the service manager, and extended his hand. "Preacher! Are you ready to pick out a new set of wheels?" To their warm handshake, Zed added a friendly pat on the back. Lowering his voice, he added, "Real good news about the missus. We've all been prayin', you know."

Evan was still smiling when he said, "Haven't seen you in church, Zip. Was it something I said?"

Zip's winning smile dropped, and by way of answering he said, "Let's step into my office."

What's up? I was teasing. I've never come out and asked him for a donation. And it was Redwine who bought us the Lincoln. I hope he hasn't got some gas-hog he needs to get off his hands. I'm not in the mood.

On their stroll to the backroom, Zed chatted, "You know you can plug that truck into your house to light it up? Thought I'd never live to see it. Now, there's an angle I can sell. I used to think electrics wouldn't sell at all in these parts. Folks would be too afraid they'd get stranded. But, hey, put in solar and thumb your nose at the power company? They can get behind that."

By the end of his speech, they were in his private office, which despite his new love of high-tech was strewn high with bound manuals and paperwork he hadn't had time to misfile.

Evan took a seat, but Zed preferred to shove a stack of paper aside and lean his ample backside against the desk.

"Evan, you've done real good. When you worked for me, you were honest and you were effective — on the days you worked, that is. But other times you were off helping some damsel in distress. You were footloose and single, so what the heck?"

Evan insisted, "I'm just here for an oil change. Max said they'd do it while I wait. I didn't come here to jerk your chain."

"Now that you're here, you'll excuse me if I give yours a gentle tug or two."

"I was only teasing. Are you saying I've offended you somehow?"

"There's a coupla things. And no offense taken. Frankly, you haven't seen me over at that new temple because it's not my idea of church. I'm not the most God-fearing man on the planet, but I used to take the family more or less regular. But in the new place, it's all showbiz. On Sundays, I want to see my neighbors. I want to hang for coffee and cake after, chat them up, and — okay I'll admit it — find out what my customers are saying about each other. Including their choices for transportation and farm equipment — which tastes are changing, as I'm sayin'."

Evan confessed, "I've also worried we'd lose a sense of community. I've been thinking we'll do small doctrinal classes so folks like you who want to meet up can have a group. Maybe even meet Sunday evenings. A little chapel inside the temple."

"I want to hug my neighbors after service, Evan. But in that big place, I don't even know who most of them are!"

"You connect with people better than anybody, Zip. You sound like a little kid on the first day of school — *but I don't know anybody.*"

"You know very well what I'm saying. Community, you're right. Isn't that the main reason you squared off with Shackleton over the Emmett property? It wasn't just to honor Bob Taggart's last wishes. It was also out of fear what the guy would do to the place — what he still wants to do to everything around here. His business model is Branson. Gambling and golf and country music — with water sports not all that far away. Granted, the old days of growing corn and cattle are long gone. Now it's soybeans and more soybeans, and cattle just don't pay. This isn't the place I grew up in, but I'm confounded where I could move."

"The world is changing everywhere we look, Zip. You and me, we're going to grow old as we watch it change, turn it over to the smart-phone crowd, and we probably won't like what we see."

"I'm not sure I'm gonna like Stuart Shackleton with *Senator* in front of his name."

"We have to give him his chance to show us he's a new man. Stranger things have happened."

"Do you know he resigned as Grand Master of the Lodge?"

"I do. He thought he was going to prison, even with all his high-priced legal help. But turns out he didn't do it. I thought he did, but I was wrong. Now, he might have been involved in other crimes, but he's kept his hands clean. Now he claims he will repent. We'll see what he does, judge him by his actions."

"You always think the best of people, Evan. You were good with folks who'd fallen behind through hard luck, but you could never spot a deadbeat."

"Perhaps you're saying I'm in the right job now?"

"I respect what you're doing, but you need to know. People are talking."

"Who and about what?"

"Guys in the Lodge. The wife's friends. Now, nobody's blaming you for sticking by Loretta and not being shy about taking Shackleton's money. And to tell you the truth I'd guess most folks think this new church of yours is a good thing, no matter who put up the dough. But what's got chins waggin' is those teenagers in your house. Living in sin."

"Zip, you know it's kind of an unusual situation. We're going to work it out. But they're committed to each other, I can assure you of that. They're dealing with their disabilities, and they're both more mature than I was at that age."

"Let me put it this way," Zip said. "You get too big for your britches with that new church, there will be people who want to bring you down — no matter how much good you're doin'. And maybe they won't be able to sink you on anything big. But trust a guy who knows a skunk from a polecat. They'll nail you with this petty gossip."

LUKE MUST SOMEHOW HAVE HEARD the same stories, because when Evan got home that afternoon, the boy informed him, "We need a family meeting."

It was a cool evening, unusual for late May, the dampness perhaps a sign more rain would roll in that night. Leslie had gone back to her room, and Clint had already come by to take Cora home.

They sat down in the parlor. Loretta was next to Evan on the couch. Melissa sat in the rocker with Buzz on her lap, and Luke took his place cross-legged on the floor beside her. Murphy stretched out at Luke's side, her paws thrust forward in a Sphinxlike pose.

She's chairing the meeting.

Luke quavered nervously. He wasn't one to preface his speeches. He blurted out, "Are we going to live with you guys forever? I'm almost nineteen."

Evan and Loretta exchanged a look. They'd discussed this, but they'd never come to any decisions, and they'd never talked about it with the young couple. Evan said, "Luke, you know it's been crazy around here, and I hope you'll understand we haven't given it much thought. Things are better now that we have helpers, but we have no plan. But what is it you and Melissa want?"

Melissa answered, "You said you'd do a wedding. You did say that. Do we just keep pretending we're married?"

Evan replied, "It is that time of year. Do you want a June wedding? Luke, your father would have to approve. Melissa, you don't need your sister's permission, but I'm sure she thinks, as I do, you two are made for each other."

Loretta echoed, "You watch out for each other, and that's why you're doing so well. Buzz is happy and healthy. We're so pleased to have you with us."

Luke's mood hadn't changed. He said, "But is this the place for us? Don't we get to make a life on our own?"

Evan told him, "We were taking it a step at a time. I don't think a big wedding at the temple would be the thing to do. Too much attention from people who won't understand. We could do a small ceremony, maybe here, out back."

"I don't care how we do it," Luke insisted.

"Neither do I," Melissa added.

Luke followed right after. "What happens then?"

Evan asked him, "Like I said, what do you two want to happen?"

I still see you both as children, but I can see I'll have to get over it.

"I get a trust fund from my dad, right?" Luke asked.

"There is money set aside for your care. From him, yes," Evan answered. "No one expects either of you to be wage earners. That's why living here seemed to make sense. If we give it some time, I expect you'll find things you want to do."

With help from Walter Engstrom, Luke would be passing his high-school equivalency exams in a few weeks. Even though Melissa might have pursued the same program, she hadn't wanted to take time away from reconnecting with her son. No one urged her to do otherwise.

Luke announced, "It's summer. I'll have my diploma. We don't know what exactly we want to do next, but in some ways staying in the house feels like being locked up in the clinic. Now, I know you think it's not safe for me to drive. But Melissa does just fine." He looked up at them for any hint of disapproval. Then he added, "We want to take a road trip, just the three of us. Oh, and Murphy. Get out there in the world, see what's what."

Evan and Loretta exchanged concerned looks again. Then Evan asked, "For how long?"

Luke shrugged. "Until we decide to come back."

Evan adjourned the meeting with, "Can you give us tonight to think about it? Pray about it?"

Luke cast a look at Melissa before he said, "We're not asking for permission. But you've got all the control. Let us do this."

WHEN THEY WERE ALONE in their bedroom, Loretta told Evan, "I know how they feel, and I suppose it's a sign they think they're… normal… but they have not the faintest clue what the world could do to them."

Evan said, "Your sister is more hard-headed than you are. And you can see Luke is downright stubborn, if not rebellious. If we don't give them some slack, they'll find a way to leave anyway. Then we'll have almost no control, and the risks to them will be even greater."

"Would we report them as runaways?"

"They're not wards of the state anymore. And now that they're both of age, as far as the law is concerned, the burden would be on us to prove they're not competent. I'm not saying we'd do that, but if we did, the process would probably take months, and they could be gone all that time. And if they go on their own, they might not tell us where."

"It's a huge risk," Loretta said, "but we have to do it some way they believe we trust them. Or, you're right, they could take off and we'd never hear. Until something bad happens. How are we going to do it?"

"We give them use of the Navigator. And an ATM card. With our blessings." He thought a moment and added, "And we give them a date. We don't insist they come back here to live, but they must promise to at least come home to check in with us by the first week in September. Maybe by then they'll be tired of living on the road."

Loretta smiled. "Does this mean you and I ride around in the Easter Egg?"

Evan shook his head. "No, I'd like to see you in an armored vehicle, but I'm sure Zip Zed will be tickled to find you something new."

"And what about the wedding?"

Evan replied, "We won't announce. We'll keep it small, and for benefit of the iPhones, you'll discourage her from wearing white."

THE COUPLE WAS MARRIED DISCREETLY under the weeping willow tree, which Evan had come to think of as his favorite ceremonial spot. The rippling water of the pond soothed, and the drooping branches of the tree both wept and consoled.

Although Luke yearned to be in the outside world, he was terrified about venturing out into it. His main worry was whether he'd be able to control his behavior and, if he couldn't, whether anyone would notice. Although Melissa's epilepsy was potentially more controllable with meds than his mood swings, Luke was ever watchful and fiercely protective of her. The clinical care they'd each experienced was not only restrictive but also protective. Their caregivers knew what to do and ddn't judge them. No such understanding could be expected from the people they would meet on the road. Luke's greatest fear was their harsh judgment and possibly their wrath. Both he and his new bride had sometimes been accused of being possessed by devils.

He fretted over her, and she did the same for him. And both of them fretted nonstop about the welfare of Baby Buzz, who was exceptionally even-tempered for his age, except when he was hungry.

Along with the ATM card, Evan promised Luke he'd monitor their expenses — not to track their whereabouts but as a way of making sure they were getting all the things they needed. Luke expressed his worries to Evan about interactions with strangers, and it was Luke who suggested they use social media sparingly. Although he knew it would be difficult for him to control Melissa's addictive use of her phone, Luke warned Evan they wouldn't go crazy taking selfies that, via GPS stamps or location backgrounds, would readily disclose their movements. And they'd use a secure messaging app to exchange text updates. Evan promised to explain the plan to Loretta so she could be careful about her eager and frequent communications with Melissa.

Because Luke and Melissa had set off in the new angel-colored Navigator, Evan bought Loretta a new F-150 pickup from Zed Motors. The only color available on the lot was Rapid Red. When they took delivery on the vehicle, Zip teased Evan again about the distinctive color and diminutive size of the Easter Egg, but the preacher wouldn't allow himself to be talked into trading it.

40

Whenever they rode with each other in the abbey's battered Toyota pickup, Sister Margaret and the Reverend Mother squabbled like jaybirds. Even though she was hard of hearing and prone to fits of drowsiness, Margaret drove because Bernadette insisted on navigating. People seeing them in the supermarket where they had just been might assume they were a cleaning crew. Margaret's denims were spotted with paint, and Bernadette was wearing the overalls she had for gardening. The Carmelite dress code was strict on the wearing of habits, but the nuns' only deference to the rules today was their drab headscarves. Do-it-yourself was the expected operational mode at Sisters of Mercy, and both of them were proud of their self-sufficiency. What's more, when they were running errands — admittedly rare events because they'd buy in bulk and stock up — they didn't want to stand out in a crowd. They'd go to the store for provisions, not to offer counseling or catch up on local gossip.

The truck had no GPS. Bernadette squinted at a paper roadmap while Margaret tried to ignore her superior's fussing and watch the road. Neither of them had a phone, so eventually they had to inquire at the ZipGas station, the same place where Evan had stopped for directions on his visit years ago to see Arthur Redwine.

After following a circuitous route that should have taken half the time, the nuns pulled up at the Redwine farmhouse. Speaking loudly, Margaret asked, "Did you bother to tell them we were coming?"

"Do I have a phone?" Bernadette snapped.

"Rude not to let them know," the other woman muttered as her boots hit the mud of the yard.

"You best wipe your feet," the Reverend Mother scolded as they walked toward the house.

"What? Angels going to clean yours?" Margaret quipped.

Loretta answered the door to their knock. She was dressed in her usual unassuming church-wife dress because within minutes she was intending to leave to attend another meeting of the Loving Embrace committee.

"Oh, my!" Loretta exclaimed simply, unable to recall at the moment just how nuns should be addressed. She hugged each of them in turn and showed them in.

Margaret muttered, "Sorry to pop in. Don't know why we're here, actually."

Bernadette said to Loretta in answer to her colleague, "High time we looked in on our dear Loretta and our darling Melissa!"

Loretta stiffened slightly, but Bernadette might not have noticed. Both visitors made a show of wiping their feet on the entry mat, then removing their shoes without being asked. Loretta was leading them into the kitchen after offering tea, but Margaret went straight for an easy chair in the parlor, plunked herself down, and announced, "I'll just bide a while in here. Bernadette, let me know when it's time to go."

Bernadette shot Loretta an apologetic look, and the two of them proceeded into the kitchen, where Loretta put the kettle on to boil.

"I've got English Breakfast and ginger-lemon," Loretta told her.

Bernadette thought carefully then decided, "Oh, I'd say the black. Can't do milk with the lemon. You do have some milk?"

"Oh, yes," Loretta said. "Sugar or sweetener as well." Then she asked, "Lovely to see you! Is everything okay? I've heard they might close the abbey, and I've been concerned. I should have come to see you before this. Evan speaks so highly of you. He says you offered him comfort at a difficult time."

Sister Margaret could be heard snoring as she slumped in the chair in the parlor.

"As he's done for me," Bernadette said without further explanation. She sat on a kitchen stool as Loretta busied herself with measuring loose black tea into a china teapot. Then, her tone more serious, the Reverend Mother said, "We're doing fine, as well as can be expected. The Lord provides. But frankly, I've been worried about you, my dear."

"Me? I'm fully recovered! It was a miracle!"

"Indeed," Bernadette said soberly. "We all held you in our prayers, and we're all so thankful. But that's not what has me worried. I'm thinking about today. And tomorrow."

"Look around you. My life couldn't be better. Evan loves me. I love him. He's doing wonderful work, and I'm doing everything I can to help."

"You were always a practical girl. A survivor. You saw what needed to be done, and you did it, usually before any of us could advise you. You looked after Melissa. Her welfare was your mission. But it disturbed you deeply that, despite all your efforts, you couldn't save her from the epilepsy. It angered you. I could see it."

"She's on good medication now, and so is Luke. They look after each other better than I ever could. And Buzz is healthy, almost always happy. Except maybe he likes his food a little too much. She's trying not to spoil him."

"May I see her? I've prayed about you both, and I haven't seen either of you in ages."

Loretta hesitated. She didn't owe the Reverend Mother an explanation, and she was sure she couldn't have done otherwise about anything. But there was nothing else to say but the truth. "Melissa isn't living here these days. She and Luke have set off with Buzz on a road trip. They send me pictures on Instagram, and she texts me on WhatsApp. They must be somewhere near Boulder, Colorado now." She added by way of excuse, "They're both of age, and there was no keeping them."

Bernadette was shocked but her face remained placid. "Was that wise? Letting them go?"

Loretta remembered now how she was supposed to address the nun, and her old tone of obedience returned. "Reverend Mother, Evan and I considered it carefully. We prayed about it. But if we hadn't let them go, we were sure they'd have gone anyway." Then she realized she needed to explain. "They're married now. A small, private ceremony. Evan wanted to do it there under the weeping willow. I don't know why. It's also where he baptized Mr. Shackleton." She hesitated again before she said, "I'm sorry. We should have invited you. Melissa so appreciates everything you've done for her — for *us.*"

"My girl, you received good instruction and a decent education. When our curriculum didn't serve, you excelled in the public school. But as for Melissa, we owe her our profound apologies. None of us knew — oh, perhaps Father Coyle knew — the risks of sending her to work over at that resort. But you say she's doing well?"

"Yes, Reverend Mother. Very well."

"Melissa wore her heart on her sleeve. She's an emotional, passionate soul. But you? Before you left us, you pulled out your heart and set it aside. I worried you'd have difficulty finding it again."

"I'm not sure what you mean."

"As I say, you've always been a survivor. Evan is a good man. Do you love him because he's good — or because he's good to you? Understand, I know little of what your life was like when you were working at the casino. I'm sure you worked hard and applied yourself. And I know you sent your sister money — faithfully. You've stepped quickly from that world and its life into a new, difficult mission. People in town may think you have it easy now. But there must be enormous pressures on a minister's wife. And people can be cruel, especially when they're envious."

"There was a chance the accident would wreck our lives. I almost lost mine. But don't you see? Evan's ministry has prospered, and all of us are healthier and happier than ever!"

Bernadette mused, "When I heard Stuart Shackleton had converted, I didn't believe it. I still don't. Were you baptized as well?"

In a low voice, Loretta admitted, "No. Evan said to take my time. He even said if I still feel I'm a Catholic, I don't owe it to anyone to change."

Bernadette stated simply, "Suicide is a mortal sin."

"Yes, Reverend Mother. I know."

"There was that time, right before you left us, I found you with a razor blade. The only place you could have gotten it was Father Coyle's bathroom. I can't imagine how you got in there."

"I wasn't going to hurt myself! I may have been thinking about it—"

"Then there was your accident."

"What are you suggesting? That's ridiculous!"

"Father Coyle often said there are no accidents in God's universe. Every time one of us slipped up and called it an *accident,* he'd insist it was an *on-purpose.*"

They hadn't yet had their tea. Loretta tried to smile when she said, "Look at the time! I'm sorry. I really do have to get going!"

41

Candidate Shackleton had built his campaign messaging around combatting the onrushing tyranny of globalist corporations. In his speeches and press releases, the example he cited most frequently was Green Monster Logistics. He was particularly alarmed because the word on Wall Street was they intended to move into Big Tech by buying CranialAI, a concern that had been particularly effective exploiting the fusion between social media networks and virtual-reality user experience.

"They want to put chips in our brains," the candidate would say repeatedly. "It'll be mind control by the folks who want to do away with individual freedom and personal property."

The primary election in Missouri for congressional seats would take place next month in early August. Shackleton was up against the party incumbent, a senior woman, Claudia Skerritt, who held doctorates in both law and economics. His counter to her long and respectable record was that she was old-guard and insufficiently wary of how limousine liberals in the other party would be abetted by Silicon Valley in pursuing their secret agenda to limit freedoms. She still used the word *bipartisanship,* to which her opponent always smirked knowingly.

And if Shackleton should prevail in the primary, the November contest would be a done deal for him. In the current political climate and because of recent voting restrictions (some would say *reforms*), no one from the left, even a centrist, could possibly win in this state.

EVAN WAS FINDING it difficult to make time for his TV appearances on "Religion Matters." He didn't do much prep for the shows, but the weekly roundtrip drive to the studio in Springfield took time. Nevertheless, he'd resolved to keep up with his ministerial responsibilities — at least with the core congregation that had come from Evangel Baptist. He visited, he officiated, and he composed his weekly sermons. He met with the deacons on policy and administrative concerns, and he conferred regularly with the Sunday-school teachers. The swelling congregation at Shining Waters generated a profusion of prayer requests and counseling sessions. As long as he was going to stick to his former responsibilities, he couldn't handle all of those, and he resolved to recruit an assistant minister. Thurston volunteered to help in the search.

The TV show aired live on Sunday afternoons to permit call-in requests from viewers. Evan liked responding spontaneously. He thought it kept him honest, and it was another reason he didn't have to fret with preparation or advance study.

A phone call from a distressed mother brought the request, "Please, Reverend Wycliff. Pray for my son. His exam is tomorrow morning. Ask God in his infinite mercy to grant my boy a B minus!"

Evan smiled and tried not to chuckle. He replied, "Let me understand this. You want me to pray on your behalf to the creator of the universe to gift your son with a B-minus?"

"Yessir, that's what he needs."

"Why not ask for an A? Or A-plus?"

"B-minus is what he needs!"

Evan insisted, "I still don't understand. If B-minus is what the boy deserves, it's more than likely that's what he'll get — even without divine intervention. It's sounding to me like you're afraid, without heavenly help, your son will probably score lower — perhaps much lower."

The caller said reluctantly, "Yes, Preacher, that's right."

"If he doesn't deserve the B-minus but God miraculously gives it to him, how will that consequence help your son? Will he be likely to study harder in the future? Or perhaps you can give him my phone number so he can call me right before every exam." Evan could hear her begin to sob. He hastened to add, "I'm sorry if I'm sounding mean. I certainly hope your son deserves the grade and gets it. Let's affirm that his performance will surprise him and he will summon skills he didn't know he has. We'll pray here and now that he finds the confidence in himself to meet all the challenges of the test."

"Thank you," she said meekly as if she'd been afraid all along she was asking for the impossible. And she ended the call before Evan could thank her with a blessing.

On set, Nora turned to Evan to say, "Is this tough love, Evan?"

He replied, "It's real-world advice tempered with love, yes. But there's a larger question here, a lesson I preach about often but I fear doesn't get through. God isn't Santa Claus. God not only knows what we need and want before we ask — it's already been given! Our prayers should be thanksgiving. We have everything we need, right here and right now, to satisfy our needs and even to fulfill our fondest wishes. We may not see the results right away — earthly events take time. That's why we must also pray for faith and patience."

Gibbons countered with, "So when a singer wins a Grammy or a quarterback wins the Heisman — and they thank God in their acceptance speech — are they mistaken?"

"Nora, I'd like to think they're thanking God for giving them the talent and the discipline to perfect their performance. The idea that God would favor one competitor over another because the winner is

— what? more righteous? — is simply wrong, I believe. Otherwise, it's the old 'lady or the tiger' question. It's an ancient superstition that humans could devise tests to determine the will of the gods. The Romans used it against Christians in the Colosseum. Behind one door was a reward, behind the other, certain death. The crowd believed the gods would protect the favored and keep them from harm by controlling which door they opened. So when a Christian captive opened a door on a hungry predator or a merciless gladiator, the Romans were sure it was proof the victim's religion was false. Of course, people still believe that God chooses which side wins in sports — and in wars."

"God has no say?"

"On the earth plane — which is governed unerringly by physical laws — I believe only humans have the ability to act. I don't think an angel can so much as lift a teacup. It's all up to us — while we're alive — to do what we believe is right, to do whatever needs doing to feed and clothe ourselves and others, to ease suffering, to advance the causes of peace."

"Did God part the Red Sea?"

"A metaphor, I'd say. I don't think Jonah got swallowed by a whale either. The people of Nineveh started the rumor to exalt this new preacher, probably because one of their legendary gods, Oannes, came from the sea and was part human, part fish — or had an encounter with a mermaid, depending on which story they told. In fact, the names Jonah and Oannes probably came from the same root word."

If they thought I speak for Baptists, they won't now. But I promised myself I'd be honest!

Nora frowned, "So you'd never pray for a new car?"

"Open a savings account. Clean up your credit. And it's up to you to decide whether gas or electric."

∿

Inevitably, Stuart Shackleton was a featured guest on the show. The producers were nameless managers Evan had never met, and according to the network contracts, neither he nor his co-host had approval over guest bookings. Evan might have expected Emilie Shinn would give him a heads-up in advance of the session, but he only knew about it when he saw Shackleton in the green room — and even then the candidate just smiled knowingly and gave him a wink.

He wants them to think we're congenial colleagues and peers, not that he's holding the strings.

On the air, after the introductions, Gibbons led off with, "Our topics on the show cover religion and ethics. My colleague Reverend Wycliff advises we should avoid politics. Mr. Shackleton, we've invited you on today because we understand you hold different views. About the separation of church and state, for example."

"Yes, Nora," Shackleton began, "the Founding Fathers were practicing, churchgoing Christians, most of them married to Christian women. Their intention was to create a republic of freedom-loving citizens, free to worship as they chose. In my view, that means freedom to *choose* a religion — not freedom *from* religion. No one back then thought they were creating a godless society."

Nora Gibbons turned to Evan with a provocative grin, "Evan? Does Mr. Shackleton know his history?"

Evan began with, "I thank the candidate for his appearance today and his eagerness to engage in spirited debate. People should know you are a member and a generous supporter of our church. And you've also made major contributions to the healthcare fund that sustained my wife Loretta through her recent life-threatening crisis. For these things, Stuart, I am greatly in your debt. But, yes, I do beg to differ on the question of separating church and state — and even whether religious leaders should voice opinions about government at all. While most of the founders were avowed Christians, several were criticized at various times for being atheists or agnostics, including Jefferson and Monroe. They owned to being Deists. They believed in God but, like me, they didn't think the Creator micromanages human affairs. Ben

Franklin was a pragmatist, writing often about his doubts, but he did profess his faith at other times. Their intention was to found a secular state, and they were clear about that in their speeches and their writings."

Satisfied Evan had said enough, Nora turned to Shackleton to ask, "Should you be elected to the Senate in November, what reforms will you be pushing for?"

Shackleton's tone was fatherly, almost condescending, when he pronounced, "Nora, for decades now Christians have lost control of the conversation in this country. Spokespersons in the liberal media continually promote all kinds of permissiveness. National pride, moral values, and strong community leadership have suffered. Frankly, the fabric of the family is fraying and won't hold without new, decisive leadership."

Evan jumped in to say, "I'll admit that Christianity is on the decline in the United States. From the last figures I saw, two-thirds of Americans identify as Christian. That's down from as high as eighty-five percent thirty years ago, even higher before that. But I'd say the main reason isn't a lack of faith. We're simply becoming more diverse, more open-minded, as we welcome people from all over the world. We're undergoing a transformation as a country, as a world. I think it's miraculous that humans invented the internet at just the time we need global communication and cooperation to survive as a species. Let's replace warfare with argument and debate! From all sides!"

"The internet! More of a curse than a blessing, I can tell you," Shackleton sneered. "We're becoming an atheist, globalist society. You've made my points, Evan. Our values are getting watered down, and we don't even agree on what it is to be an American anymore!"

Evan asked the candidate, "What's the answer, Stuart?"

Shackleton was sober-faced when he answered, "The government has to impose some discipline, Reverend. The progressives like to say democracy is messy. But when it's become an awful mess, it falls to people who can show some strength to clean it up."

"So, what?" Evan asked, he thought rhetorically. "Are you proposing a temporary Christian dictatorship?"

Shackleton chuckled, "Those are loaded words. But I think you'd agree that all over the world — especially because of swelling populations and competition for resources — public officials who assert authority are gaining ground." He made it sound like a joke when he added, "And temporary? We'll see."

Evan fed him, "Someone needs to take charge?"

Shackleton nodded sagely. "Someone. Right-thinking. Christian. Capitalist. All the virtues that have made this country the greatest in the history of the world."

Evan teased, not without an edge, "It sounds like you wouldn't mind having Julius Caesar back."

Shackleton answered smugly, "When the followers are ready, the leader will emerge."

Nora was quick to ask him, "And that's you?"

Shackleton smiled, "Oh, I'm not the one. Call me John the Baptist."

On Evan's startled look, the segment video faded out.

SHACKLETON'S APPEARANCE on the show had pulled Evan onto shaky terrain. The candidate's views were specific, carefully crafted, and expressed firmly. Evan's positions were less clear and less sure, even to himself. He'd thought being spontaneous and honest was a virtue, but he feared he gave the impression of getting caught unprepared and off-guard.

Then the content of Shackleton's media campaign became deeply disturbing. In his attack on Green Monster, his ads disclosed the details of Loretta's accident, including the trucker's abuse of the drug khat to stay awake. In parallel with his electoral campaign, Shackleton's legal team had initiated a class-action suit against Green Monster alleging gross negligence. And to add pathos to the ads, the video included clips of Loretta lying in coma, along with early speech-therapy sessions during which she'd gag and barely choke out a few words. The ads never showed her as she was today, fully recovered, implying she was still severely impaired as a result of corporatist indifference and greed.

Neither Evan nor Loretta had given permission for those videos, but he did recall signing a blanket release early on, when Shackleton's attorneys were filing the accident insurance claim on their behalf. Evan suspected Emilie Shinn's ubiquitous iPhone. Although the spots infuriated Evan now, he knew he'd look like an ungrateful fool to complain about them publicly.

Perhaps for the first time since Shackleton had offered his financial support, Evan could feel his heart sinking.

42

Loretta was unnerved by Bernadette's visit. Everything had finally seemed to be going so well. She had her health. She had Evan's love, attention, and support. She did have occasional nightmares about the accident, but she felt she could cope. She missed having her sister near her and worried about her condition, but she expected the newlyweds would be returning from their adventure soon enough. She didn't know much about Luke's extrasensory abilities, but she was sure he had them. When he'd informed her he'd visited her "on the other side," it chilled her, and she'd remained suspicious of him. But as long as he took his meds and doted on Melissa and the baby, Loretta wanted to regard him as a lovable eccentric. She'd never seen him in a fit of rage, although Evan had cautioned her such episodes were possible. Apparently, when Luke felt himself losing it, he'd go somewhere no one else could see him.

Loretta felt she couldn't confide in Evan. Not about this. And Melissa, even if she were here, shouldn't have her trust in her older sister shaken.

When it came to full and frank admissions and heart-to-heart confessions, Loretta realized Coralie Angelides was her only friend.

The main topic of the Loving Embrace meeting had been sickbed visitations. The ladies were helping Evan with his rounds. And for the first time since Loretta had served on the committee, a young man, Walter Engstrom, had asked to join. Some of the other members thought it odd, but no one wanted to refuse him. Loretta wondered whether he was gay and closeted. In fact, shy Walter still hadn't mustered the courage to tell Leslie of his crush on her. He had shown up to impress her. Leslie wasn't on the committee, and she wasn't a regular at church, but Walt knew Cora was up on the gossip, and she'd be sure to tell Leslie.

Loretta knew the Baptists weren't generally known to be tolerant on the question of homosexuality, and no one had yet asked Evan to take a position. It would certainly come up sooner or later if a same-sex couple requested marriage in the church, but no one had. Loretta wasn't sure what the letters in LGBTQ stood for, and as far as she knew, people in these parts just assumed those types of folks preferred to live in the big city where certain neighborhoods were proud to welcome them. As with other doctrinal questions, she knew Evan's views would be both liberal and unconventional. And now with the TV show, she hoped he wouldn't embarrass himself. In any of these matters, her worries weren't because she was a believer. In this small town, she dreaded the scorn of her neighbors.

She'd seen Shackleton's TV spots, and they disgusted her as they did her husband. They hadn't yet discussed the matter though. Loretta was more pragmatic than Evan, and she understood the transactional basis of Shackleton's help. She expected one way or another he'd get whatever he was after, and she was in no position to object. And she didn't expect — or require — the guy to have honorable intentions. Except for Evan, she thought most men would behave badly if given the chance.

She knew Shackleton was a snake. His conversion was a sham. And she strongly suspected he'd abetted Churpov's abuse of her sister. And that sin, to her, was unforgivable, no matter how much cleansing water had been poured over him.

If Loretta were honest with herself, she'd admit that she often regarded Evan's kindness as a sign of vulnerability, if not weakness. She worried people would take advantage of him. She worried his opinions were too high of people who might want to hurt him.

How Evan might react to what she had to confess was what she needed to ask Cora.

WHEN LORETTA RETURNED to the house after the committee meeting at church, she found Cora had already let herself in and was busy in the kitchen baking banana bread. The aroma was welcoming and homely, a sweet testimony to Cora's generosity.

Loretta came right out with, "I need to ask you something."

"What is it, hon? Does Evan need some blue pills to fire him up? Ladies at church giving him the wink and the nod? Tell Cora."

Loretta blurted it out. "When I had the accident, it wasn't an accident."

Cora gasped. "That trucker *tried to* hit you?"

"No. I swerved into the path of the truck. Then I lost my nerve, swerved back, and got sideswiped. I should be dead."

"Let's sit down," Cora said softly, and they settled in the parlor. They sat close on the couch, and Cora took Loretta's hands in hers. "I can't believe this," she said. "Oh, dear. Why ever would you?"

"I'd get these moods. Worried I'll never be enough, never find my way out. It didn't make a difference what the problem was. There were so many of them, coming at me from all directions."

Cora gave her friend's hand a comforting pat, saying, "But, sure, you're all better now!"

"I've caused so much trouble! I know I'm going to disappoint Evan. And everybody at church. I've just been faking it, all along."

"Dear, we all feel we can't measure up from time to time. Beating yourself up don't make it better. Take it from me."

"You know, sometimes I think if I hadn't come along, Evan would've married you."

Cora chuckled, "Yeah, and he'd be stuck living in that trailer, chasing deadbeats, and selling his sermons for fifty bucks a pop. Is the Lord working here? Look at the new church! And you and Evan have stepped into a new life. How are we to know what's meant to be?"

"What am I going to do?"

"I want to say there should be no secrets between a husband and a wife. And someday this is bound to come out." She hesitated before she added, "But maybe not now."

"I almost confessed to Reverend Mother Bernadette this morning. She came here, and she acted like she already knew."

Cora sighed. "Get it off your chest some way. Not a bad idea." Then she asked, "What about the insurance? That all settled? No matter whether you decide to tell Evan, you shouldn't go blabbing to anyone else."

"I believe the trucker told the truth, but it was my word against his, and with all the pressure Stuart is putting on the company, everyone thinks the guy is lying, maybe even being told to lie. He *was* driving under the influence. It didn't cause the accident, but it doesn't help their case."

"Don't you fret," Cora advised. "Pray about it yourself, but I suppose you have been. If you weren't already serving on Loving Embrace, I'd tell you to call them for counseling. Maybe you get some pills to buck you up. See a doctor. That way is risky though. Clint can tell you. Every day, he has to deal with people who got a drug habit that way." Cora leaned over to give Loretta a kiss on the cheek, then stood, gently lifting her friend's hand as she suggested, "Why don't we have some tea and cut into my banana bread?"

43

When he'd agreed to do the TV show, Evan had worried Shackleton would eventually tell him what to say. But he'd taken the banker at his word that honesty and sincerity were the only requirement. Even though he knew his comments often departed from church doctrine, Evan never expected the Baptist leadership would object. The denomination's policy was to leave appointment of pastors and ordination matters to local churches and their boards. Evan was confident he had the support of the Evangel Baptist deacons. His detractors had already broken away from the congregation.

But it fell to Thurston to state the hard truth. "They're saying you've strayed way off the reservation, Evan! God didn't part the Red Sea? Jonah's story of the whale is a myth? God *doesn't answer prayer?*"

Misquoted, misunderstood. Marcus knows better, but clearly he's had to answer for me.

"Marcus, you've always known I've never believed in the literal interpretation of scripture. Creation in seven days? The garden and Adam's rib? Maybe you don't hold with science on some things, but you don't believe those stories."

Thurston's tone grew somber, and he asked his friend to sit down. They were in Evan's office in the old church, where he still went when he had a lot on his mind. "Evan, the deacons and I give you a lot of leeway. And I suppose in a small congregation, people can make allowances. The old membership loves you, as I do. But leadership is furious. On that show, the audience will think you're speaking for the denomination. You must respect that. Don't you realize that some of our faithful believe that the astronomy data and the fossil record are creations of Satan? Made to deceive us?"

"You know that's way beyond ridiculous."

"I'm not saying I believe it, but how about all this talk in the scientific community that we're living in some kind of virtual reality? That everything we see and experience is inside some cosmic computer game? Serious scientists are admitting the possibility! If that's the case, those folks of ours who are saying there's only this little planet and nothing else could be right. And eternal life in paradise? Sure, just step out of the game. Explains a lot."

"Don't tell me you believe *that!*"

"I don't, but I was afraid you might."

Evan smirked. "Not this week. We should put you on the show, Marcus. Maybe you want to speak for the rest of them. I thought it was all about frank discussion, sharing different opinions, making people think."

Thurston was trying to understand why Evan would say almost anything he was thinking. He took a dramatic pause before saying, "I got a call from leadership. They'll be asking you to resign, and they want us to revoke your ordination. I doubt our deacons will have the spine to push back."

The old pastor was about to go when he turned back to say, "I've found a good candidate for the assistant minister post. A young woman from Florida Bible College. She's straightforward, inclined toward literal interpretations. Not exactly singing from the same page, but she may be the person we need now. She's inexperienced but sincere and energetic. I'll ask them to consider her for pastor." He was set to go again when he decided to add, "Evan, I don't blame you. You are who you are. I hope you'll forgive us for what we have to do." And he left.

ON THE WAY HOME, Evan turned his phone off. He didn't want to speak to anyone until he knew what to say to them.

What can I say? I should be angry, but I have no desire to fight back, even if that's possible.

He flashed on what he often told families who were grieving over a lost loved one. He would tell them, as he knew psychologists were trained to say, that healing takes time. They will go through the full range of emotions. And all emotions are okay. You have to let them out or you'll burst.

And what I'm feeling now — I hate to admit — is relief!

BY THE TIME he pulled up to the Redwine house, the sun had already set, turning the hills behind it black. As Evan got out of the car, he wondered why there were no lights on in the place. And the Lincoln was gone.

He entered, called out, and got no reply.

He found Cora sitting by herself in the parlor, her head down. When he flipped on a light, he saw her eyes were wet.

"Oh, Evan," she sighed, holding her hands limply in her lap. The body language of this capable woman said helplessness.

"I guess you heard I lost my job," he muttered.

She looked up and her expression changed. "No, no I didn't. I'm so sorry."

She doesn't seem shocked. Maybe it's not the worst news she got today.

He waited for her to continue, but her head nodded back down. He moved to sit beside her and finally had to ask, "What's wrong, Cora?"

She looked up at him again, sniffling. Her face was drawn with exhaustion. She reached over, rested a hand on his knee, and gave it a pat. "She couldn't bring herself to tell you. She said I should."

He felt a sudden jolt of terror. His face flushed. "Has something happened to Luke and Melissa? The baby?"

"No, no," she said. "She packed some things, and Leslie's driving her to the airport in KC. The girl's coming back with your truck. I guess Loretta won't be needing it. Leslie is loyal to her, you know. I told both of them this is all kinds of wrong."

"Who is she going to see? Is somebody sick? She's got no other family."

"She wouldn't say where. Leslie said she had a wad of cash she'd picked up in town today from Western Union. Evan, you'd be in your rights to go looking for her. Or maybe you call the sheriff. She'd be in some kind of trouble, I suppose, if she stayed."

"Cora, I can see you're upset, but you're not making much sense. *Why* did she go?"

"She couldn't bring herself to tell you. She's had it locked up inside her all this time. And all the while, she's acting like the sweetheart of Loving Embrace, smiling and praying and doling out the kind words."

Evan felt like shouting, but urged, "Cora, please!"

He could barely hear her response when she told him, "The poor girl drove herself into that semi. She wanted to be dead, you see, but your love brought her back. Trouble is, she's been carrying around all that guilt. I know she admires you, respects you, maybe even worships you. She didn't say, but the big reason she feels so bad could be she can't manage to love you in the same way you love her."

Are we talking about the same person? I can't believe this!

Evan's voice trembled and he had to admit, "There were times I knew she was uncomfortable being the pastor's wife."

He offered to drive Cora home, but she said Clint was on his way.

Evan didn't turn his phone back on until he'd rehearsed what he was going to say. The call went right to voicemail, so he texted:

I UNDERSTAND. I DON'T BLAME YOU FOR ANYTHING. I'LL WAIT. IF IT MAKES A DIFFERENCE, I'M NOT THE PASTOR ANYMORE. WE CAN FIND OUR WAY TOGETHER.

The reply came:

SOME WOMEN WANT BAD BOYS. I GUESS I'M ONE. YOU'LL DO BETTER IF I'M NOT THERE.

He tried to call back immediately, but the connection dropped right away.

Reading the text a second time, Evan knew where she was going.

PLAGUES COME IN SEVENS. Curses come in threes. Evan was weepy and listless in the empty house. About the time he finally got to sleep that night, a fire broke out in the Shining Waters Temple. No human soul was in the place at the time. The local firefighters weren't equipped to handle an industrial-sized blaze, and even though crews from three counties did respond, the remoteness of the location resulted in a costly delay.

The conflagration was fierce and thorough. The interior furnishings provided enough wood and cloth to keep it going until by morning all that was left was a concrete slab piled with smoking, charred rubble.

Later investigation would disclose that the tilt-up walls had been cast from substandard concrete, which buckled in the heat, causing the walls and the roof to cave in. The timing of the event — in the wee hours when no one was in the place — suggested arson.

A further complication was that the church's fireproof safe was found empty.

44

Sheriff Otis growled, "It won't come as news. Gossip around town likes you for this. You lose your job in the afternoon, then you torch your place of work that night? After cleaning out the safe?"

"You forgot to mention, before I lit the match I'd learned my wife skipped town to shack up with her old boyfriend."

"Mick Heston. A piece of work, that guy. Shiny as a new penny and slick as snot." Otis shook his head morosely. "She had everybody thinking she's a fine woman. No way she'd take up with the likes of him — again, I mean. And now you tell me she drove into that semi deliberately? Get outta here!"

"She didn't actually tell me. She confessed to Cora, and Cora told me. Cora also said Loretta might have told Bernadette, but that's a guess on her part."

"Oh, we could ask the nun, but it's all hearsay and speculation."

"The driver of the semi did say her car was coming straight at him. No one believed him."

"He said, she said! Not evidence either way. There are photos and forensics from the scene, but the road was muddy that day, and there's nothing conclusive. But her car could have gone out of control for whatever reason. It's not like her memory of the accident a year ago would be all that reliable — especially after brain damage and a coma. She feels guilty all kinds of ways, so her mind creates a version of the story where she's at fault. A defense attorney could spin that version of her story real good."

"So, should I lawyer up?"

The sheriff huffed, "Don't leave the state. Make sure your phone works. I doubt the law wants much to do with you, but I hear some church folks are getting the tar and feathers ready."

AFTER HE'D COME from seeing the sheriff, Evan was cleaning out his office in the old church in town when Birch walked in.

"Real sorry, pastor," the man said as he stood reluctantly just inside the doorway. "Real sorry."

Evan was packing up the bookshelves, handed the book of poetry to the sexton, and indicated for him to sit. "You best keep the book, Birch. If I put these in storage, no telling when anyone will see them."

Birch said frankly, "I know you didn't do it."

"The fire? The sheriff says it was arson. The building was insured, but the church hasn't paid the contractor, so the firm could get the payoff."

"There was supposed to be money in the safe," Birch told him.

"How do you know?"

"The collection goes in the safe after service on Sunday. We never had such a fine safe — or reason to have one — here at Evangel. The money stays there overnight, then I pick it up on Monday morning, drive it in here. Alice logs the receipts into her computer, then she takes it over to put it in the bank."

Evan shrugged. "The fire was early Tuesday morning. The safe must've been empty."

"Nossir. I was feeling like the flu on Monday, didn't make the run. No worries, you see, cuz it's in the safe."

"How much was in there?"

"Hundred thousand, maybe two. A lot of it in cash."

"Who else has access to that safe?"

"Reverend Thurston has the combination, but he says he didn't give it to you. He gave it to your wife to give to you."

"Loretta!"

"She was helping with the accounting. Mrs. Olinger is just learning spreadsheets."

"Thank you for telling me, Birch. Have you told all this to Reverend Thurston?"

"He knows the money is gone. That's all. I say you tell him what he needs to know."

"Thank you, Birch. I'm not going anywhere. I hope I see you in town from time to time."

Birch stood, walked over, and gave Evan a hug.

HERE WAS one more potentially incriminating thing to share with the sheriff. So far, Evan had followed through with his promise to be honest — to himself, to his congregation, and to the public. Before he'd taken up the ministry, he'd joked with Thurston that little fibs, white lies, and "useful fictions" didn't count. Then when he started doing visitations, he realized that giving the patient or the family the brutal truth wasn't always kind. These days, doctors had to be straight with patients or they could be sued. But a pastor was there to give comfort, even or especially when medical science offered no hope.

According to Birch, Loretta had the combination to the safe and was helping Alice Olinger, who wasn't about to retire yet, with the accounting. So his wife had the means and the opportunity to steal the funds.

And now that Evan knew she'd gone off to be with Heston, he realized she must've also had the motive.

Circumstantial — and not convincing!

Evan didn't believe she had the skill or the professional accomplices to set the fire. The temple was a large structure, and it was devastated thoroughly. And after he did some concerted data-drilling online, Evan knew enough about the technical challenges to be sure the fire wasn't her doing. Sloppy criminals might douse the place with an accelerant, such as kerosene, which investigators could easily detect. An amateur acting alone might succeed in setting the drapes on fire, but the damage would be limited. It would take a small crew of experienced firebugs to achieve a total burnout and yet leave little or no evidence.

And then there was the question of whether the arson had anything to do with the theft from the safe. Certainly, the fire could obliterate evidence of break-in and tampering. But the safe was found intact, its door swung open. If the arsonists and the thieves were the same crew and they had the combination to the safe, they might also have had keys to the building and the code for the alarm system.

Evan wondered what connection the building contractor had with Shackleton. He'd bought the land dearly and financed the project.

Perhaps Shackleton had learned of Evan's humiliation and the loss of his ministry. Evan's carefully built reputation for honesty and sincerity would be lost. His credibility would be blown and the TV show canceled. And his usefulness to Shackleton would be over. Not only would the fire and the theft recover some of the banker's investment, but also rumors about Evan's role in those crimes — whether proven or not — would help Shackleton distance himself from the preacher and his messages.

For now, Evan chose not to share the tip he'd gotten from Birch with either Reverend Thurston or Sheriff Otis.

He hoped — yes, he prayed — Loretta had already landed safely in New Zealand.

45

The first week in September, as promised, Luke and Melissa returned home in the white Navigator with Buzz and Murphy. Their only notice to Evan was a brief text from Luke to Evan:

Home early 6th. All r well. Will stay if ok w u.

To which Evan replied, expecting he knew the answer so not afraid to ask:

Sure, yes! Welcome. Has Melissa heard from Loretta? Do you know she's left?

Luke replied simply:

Sad 4 u.

Evan fully expected Loretta would have explained her intentions to Melissa before acting on them. He did want to know whether Melissa had begged her to stay.

❧

LUKE HAD GROWN A BEARD. Evan thought it made him look like a college instructor. Luke said Melissa wanted them to have another child. Evan sat him down in the parlor as Melissa and Leslie conversed in hushed tones in the kitchen. Buzz was happily kicking in his high-chair as he ate spoonfuls of cooked cereal. He was probably delighted to have two mothers now, both eager to deliver food to his mouth.

Evan said, "You didn't have to stick to September. You could have come home anytime. You didn't wait on account of your promise, did you?"

Luke shrugged. "We didn't wait, but we didn't want to stay out there either."

"How did it go?"

"It's a helluva country out there. Huge. You don't get that seeing it on TV."

"You drove through Kansas to Colorado?"

"Yeah, and up into Iowa for a ways on the trip out. Dipped down into Arkansas on the way back. Those mountains are something. Out west, we took Buzz for a ride in the old Durango Silverton steam train. We took lots of pictures that day. They blew the whistle a lot, and he was toot-tooting all the way back. It was getting annoying but then he kind of forgot to do it."

Evan encouraged him. "But you decided you don't want to live anywhere but here."

Murphy ambled in from the kitchen and sat dutifully by Luke. Evan sensed their attachment.

Evan asked, "Seems like you came through it okay. Any… challenges?"

"Melissa chilled the whole way. She's the best. Whenever Buzz started to fuss, she knew what to do. The kid thinks she's a god. They're Mary and Jesus, go figure. But me, we're in Arkansas and I almost lost it. Okay, I admit I was driving. Drove the whole way, actually. A guy in a Camaro flips me off. I'm going too slow. You try and you try, and you let the big things slip past you, then something small like this sets you off. I didn't go after him, but I was pretty angry that night, and I yelled at Melissa. I never do that. For the first time in a while, I was actually afraid of myself, what I might do. The next day she has me call some church, and we stop over in that town. We leave Murphy in the car and we go to some support group. I mean, both of us did group all the time before, so we figure we know the drill. And by then I'm cool anyway, but I'm thinking maybe I don't share at all. I figure they're okay with it, being that they're all there for something they're not proud of. I go ahead and tell them I hear voices, and I'm guessing they'll be curious. But then you can see them get all tight-assed, and it was the old story. Here are druggies and alkies who smoke like fiends so they won't do something worse, and they all think I'm some freak. It wasn't what they said, it was the looks. We got outta there quick, hit the highway, and I drove until the next morning. That was two days ago. And, yeah, we might have stayed out longer, but that dose of reality was what brought us back."

"I'm sorry, Luke. Truly sorry. I wish I'd been able to talk to those people, but I guess you're right, you never know when somebody is going to think it's not safe to have you around."

"The night we did the session, I'm curled up with my laptop in the motel. I'm looking for math problems I can do in my head. Relaxes me. I'm online and I find this Hearing Voices Network site in the UK. They're saying a lot more people hear voices or have visions but are afraid to tell anybody about it. And they don't have to be deranged. They're just tuned into some different channel."

"You know very well how your special talents have helped. Melissa wouldn't be with us, and maybe you wouldn't have Buzz. Maybe you helped bring Loretta back from limbo, wherever that was."

Luke smiled and patted the dog. "I'm pretty sure it was Murphy who brought her back."

Evan had to tell him, "I lost my ministry. They asked me to resign because some of the church leaders didn't like what I had to say on TV. And the show was canceled."

"Wow," Luke teased, "and here I'm thinking you were *da man.*"

"I've been thinking, Luke. Who knows when Loretta will be coming back, if ever? Maybe she's got to get something out of her system. I dearly hope she will, but we can't put our lives on hold. Redwine gave this house to me — not to the church — and I want it to be a home for you and Melissa and Buzz and however many more ankle-biters you guys decide to raise."

The boy smiled. "I'd like that. We'd like that. I've been thinking maybe I could lead a support group somewhere. A hearing-voices group." And he laughed. "We'd find out how many other crazies we have around here!" He took a deep breath and then said softly, "Also, I need to see my mom. Card game, you know, to keep her happy."

Evan said, "I hear she's still hanging in there. I had a talk with Walter. He let me know he finally managed to tell Leslie how he feels about her, and of course, she's been on his wavelength all along. I asked him if they want to share this place with you guys, and he insisted they'd pay rent. She'd pay her part by keeping on helping with Buzz and the chores around here. I'm thinking Cora should stay on as well. I'll pay her wages."

"Evan, you still are da man, you know. Thanks. But what about you?"

Evan sighed. "Me, I'd just be in the way. I've got another place not far away, a comfy spot I know quite well."

Luke smiled again when he gazed at Murphy and said, "Buzz needs his shots. You take the dog."

"Oh, I thought you were close?"

"We are," Luke said proudly. "But you two have a lot of catching up to do. Besides, you'll pay her vet bills."

Loretta had taken their only suitcase, so Evan put his clothes in two large trash bags. He was about to carry them out to his car when he was startled by the sound of a motorcycle approaching. It had been almost two years since he'd heard the distinctive noise, but he knew right away who was coming.

Followed by the ever-attentive Murphy, Evan walked out with the bags and stuffed them in the trunk of the Fiat as Stu Shackleton pulled up riding his gleaming black Ducati. As he had appeared to Evan on the fateful day of Father Coyle's death, the lean banker was dressed all in black, from his ebony Tony Lama lizard boots up to his full-face helmet with the dark-smoke screen that totally obscured his face.

He dismounted and pulled off the helmet as he strode vigorously toward the preacher. "I heard the newlyweds are back," he said, catching his breath.

"Back this morning," Evan confirmed. "You must get good intel."

"Can't go anywhere without it," he agreed. "Mind if I stick my head in?"

Murphy sat at attention at Evan's side. The dog was serene, but her stare told Shackleton she'd bite his hand off if he made the slightest threatening move toward her guardian.

"You're the dad," Evan said. "I'm just a caregiver."

Shackleton squinted, "Looks to me like you're packing up."

"Yeah," Evan said. "They're going to stay, and I'm going to get out of their way. They can tell you about their plans."

"What about your plans? Before I go in, why don't we have a sit by the pond? That's where you rescued me from perdition, isn't it?"

"None of my doing," Evan shrugged. "I'm still wondering who the savior is you will be announcing to the world."

He won't answer that one!

As they walked with Murphy following close behind, Shackleton made it clear to Evan that he was up on all the news, including Loretta's leaving, Evan's resignation from the ministry, and the cancellation of "Religion Matters."

He didn't mention the fire at the temple or the theft. So Evan asked him, "The fire was suspicious. Also the missing money. Have you got any clues?"

Instead of answering, the banker asked him, "You and the sheriff are pals. What does he think?"

"You mean, did he warn me I'm a suspect?"

"Are you?"

"He's sure I'm not, but he might be a minority of one. He took an affidavit about my whereabouts. So far no one has come calling."

They'd arrived at Evan's designated spot under the weeping willow. Shackleton actually rested a hand on the preacher's shoulder, saying, "As long as we're friends, they won't."

"People who don't think I had a hand it in might think you did. For the insurance and the cash."

He chuckled. "I'm arms-length from the contractor, and the donation money is small change. There could be interested parties who needed to recover some costs, but you needn't concern yourself. The temple served its purpose, and the permanent structure can wait — until we decide how to develop the area."

"Then again, it could be you had the fire set to make a point. Put a period to the end of my sentence?"

"Oh, Evan. Ye of little faith!"

Evan was beginning to get sore when he came back with, "Stuart, don't you go quoting the Bible to me. I won't be telling people that I question the sincerity of your conversion, but my silence doesn't mean I believe it."

Shackleton seemed amused. "You've heard me say democracy is messy. Let me give you an example of just how messy things are going to get.

Since the Industrial Revolution, the wealth of the western world has been built on ownership and control of fossil fuels. What about the prospect of green energy? Once you get the infrastructure in place for solar, wind, and geothermal, energy will be essentially free. Same holds for nuclear fusion, but the payback will take longer. When energy is free all over the world, my friend, what then will happen to the petrodollar? How will this great nation of ours still dominate world markets? How will we make our influence felt, make sure our interests prevail?"

"Sounds like a job for the Department of Defense. Until we run out of money."

Shackleton nodded and said, "Add the complications of climate change, worldwide pandemics, water shortages, overpopulation, and food insecurity. Do you think our bickering form of government is up to dealing with all that?"

"What's your point, Stuart? Your brand of politics has been no secret."

"Just because you're not a minister anymore doesn't mean you can't have a voice. A loud one."

"I seem to be surrounded by suspicion these days. Depending on whom you talk to, I'm an arsonist or a thief. As well as a shameless blasphemer, which, considering how I got canned, I won't deny."

"I'm going to need a speechwriter. You're the best."

Evan's annoyance returned. "Using Bible verses to justify the rise of the dictatorship?"

"You know your history. It's a new approach that's stood the test of time."

If Evan had more energy and more fight in him, he'd be angry. Instead, he was sad, telling Shackleton, "I took that gig because you said I could stick to being sincere and honest. I don't see how I could respect myself and carry messages for you."

"You can be sincere about wanting a paycheck. Honest about your debts," Shackleton said dismissively, then added, "And staying out of jail. Maybe you'd want a new house. I've got nobody in the Taggart place. You could move in there, then we tear down this old farmhouse and build you a fine new residence. Say, five-thousand square feet?"

Evan bit his tongue. "I have to get going. Why don't you go on inside?"

He didn't seem to need Evan's decision right away. Instead, he asked, "Do you think they'll want to see me?"

"Why not? Did you bring toys for Buzz?"

"I got fudge cookies," he said, patting the pocket of his jacket. "I hope she'll let him have them."

As they walked back toward the house, Evan said, "Luke is saying he wants to visit Ann again. That's a hopeful sign. How about you? Why don't you pay her a visit before she slips away?"

"She's not alive to me, Evan. I told you that. Besides, Edie wants me back." And he muttered, "Nora and I never had a thing, despite what you might've heard."

"Is Edie willing to start over? She was pretty disgusted with you, as I recall."

Shackleton smirked. "Evidently the prospect of playing society hostess in Washington holds some appeal."

46

Evan had packed up, left the house, loaded Murphy into the back seat, and headed north on the state route before he bothered to phone Zip Zed to ask. The preacher wanted use of the broken-down trailer home again, and he needed his old job back. Zip didn't hesitate to agree, but Evan wondered whether it was out of friendship, pity, or moral obligation. Although hardly devout, his former employer had been one of his steadfast supporters at the church. So he was one who might be genuinely sorry to see Evan knocked down. Of course, depending on the rumors and whether there were actually charges brought, Evan figured he might weather the storm and — at some distant future date — be invited back on occasion when the new minister needed someone to sub the Sunday sermon. As Shackleton apparently believed, Evan did have the knack.

Evan suspected the trailer had gone unrented and vacant since he'd moved out two years ago. The place was derelict, but before he'd met Loretta and taken a rocket-ship ride to the giddy heights of responsibility and celebrity, this modest one-room tin shack had been his home. Evan found the key just where he'd posted it, hanging on a nail on a sycamore tree, the spot located at eye level on the opposite side of the tree from the road.

Evan hoped Zip had gone to the trouble of having the place cleaned, but when he popped the door, the funk and the oppressive musty odor told him no one had had any reason to go back in there. At first, Murphy didn't even want to go in. In this first week of September, the summer heat still lingered, so Evan propped the door open and cranked up the swamp cooler to air the place out. Along with his clothes, he'd brought linens and some towels. He might have to replace the mattress and the cushion on the only chair.

In winter, Evan imagined the dog's body heat would be welcome. As it was on this warm day, her unwashed funk would need attention. Evan resolved to borrow a garden hose in the morning from next door to wash her down.

His kitchenware and utensils were still there.

Where else can you get a furnished place with all amenities essentially free?

Housesitting for Zip was one reason he wouldn't have to pay rent, but considering that no one had maintained the place and nothing must have been worth stealing, Evan wondered whether his presence would be adding value. Zip had told him that the newer trailer on the adjacent lot — the one he'd rented to Loretta before she and Evan hooked up — had been rented to a nurse who came down from KC to work in the Covid ICU ward at Oak Hill Memorial.

I hope she's not young and cute. I'm going to hold the slim chance that Loretta will come back to me.

"What do you think, Murphy?" Evan asked the dog. "Is she coming back?"

Murphy stared at him knowingly. Her look told him all would be revealed in the fullness of time.

I expected a more satisfying answer.

It was drawing on toward evening, and as a gentle breeze wafted through his new-old home, Evan popped his laptop, shoved in his earbuds, and hoped to soothe his heartache with a tune. At times when he'd been pining away here in years past, he'd find Roy Orbison on

YouTube and play "Only the Lonely" in a loop. Or, if he was filled with lustful longing, "Pretty Woman." This time he hit upon Kate Melua singing "I Will Be There," a song about a mother's love lasting longer than the grave, and his thoughts turned again to whether he would have been able to cope if Loretta hadn't survived. Now he was thankful she was alive, even if she was with someone else.

Will we ever be together again?

Evan seriously doubted the promise of physical resurrection. But he couldn't discount possibilities such as Thurston's mention of stepping out of the movie into some other dimension or alternate reality. As Thurston had told him, "That would explain a lot."

Ann Shackleton might know. He wished he'd asked her but then he remembered she probably wouldn't have the presence of mind to tell him.

About an hour after sunset — long before Evan was used to turning in — as the music played on, he reached over to close and lock the door, curled up on the mattress, and fell asleep in his clothes, the earbuds still in place. Murphy curled up beside him. Evan didn't relish the extra warmth, but he appreciated the companionship.

He woke briefly in the middle of the night. There was a full moon high above, bathing his living space in a magical, phosphorescent glow.

Murphy's eyes opened, she raised her head up, but she didn't bark. For the briefest moment, Evan thought he saw Naomi sitting there, perched on the barstool at the breakfast counter, staring back at him and smiling wickedly like the watchful witch she was.

Now that I'm cocooning, back in isolation, she'll be back more often. She always insisted on having the last word.

EVAN WAS AWAKENED by the sounds of a car pulling up outside, followed by a gentle knock on the tin of the trailer.

Murphy barked loudly, announcing the arrival of a suspicious stranger.

Shaking his head to clear the grogginess, he opened it to find Special Agent Leon Weiss standing there, looking like the G-man he was, clad in a gray pinstripe suit, obligatory white shirt, and politically correct rep tie. No longer shaggy, his wiry gray hair was close-cropped and military-neat. He was grinning maniacally, but Evan's first impression was that his friend and former cohort had come to arrest him.

Murphy stood at the ready at Evan's side. The intruder would not enter uninvited.

"Evan!" Weiss exulted, stretching out his arms. Evan welcomed the welcome, and they hugged like long-separated brothers.

He could see that Leon had come alone in an unmarked sedan with plates that began with *G*.

Evan demanded, "How did you know where to find me?"

Leon chuckled, "After all we've been through together, you have to ask?"

Evan quipped, "I was kind of hoping for a damsel in distress, and I have to admit, by that standard, you're a disappointment."

Leon's smile dropped and he confided in all seriousness, "As I believe you know, Churpov was allowed to skate. He flew off to Montenegro because he gave our guys the gold seam — and if we want him later, that country won't extradite."

"The money trail? He could be a lying bastard, you know. But I suppose you factored that in."

"Yes. Among the dirt he spilled, his buddies in the Kremlin are financing Shackleton's campaign. As they have most of the prick's business interests for the last dozen years."

"Hoo-boy. Should I say I'm not surprised? Although I am."

The man's body language signaled he didn't expect to be invited in but wanted Evan to join him in the car. His invitation was, "So, are you willing to help? Ready to shove your hands back in the shit?"

"Murphy will have to go with us. She's my guardian," Evan informed him.

Leon smiled, saying, "If you tell me this is a service dog, federal law says she can go anywhere."

Evan answered with a wry smile, "Okay, as it happens, I do have some time on my hands."

LUKE SAT across from his mother and reached to draw the next-to-last card in the deck. In defiance of the odds he had calculated so carefully for Evan, she'd won all of the previous eight games legitimately.

He drew a Jack of Spades.

She drew a Queen of Hearts.

Luke appreciated the miracle when she cackled with joy.

NOW READ THE SEQUEL

PREACHER STALLS THE SECOND COMING - SAMPLE

In the fourth book in the series, a cult leader is planning to fake the Second Coming with advanced virtual-reality technology as he lures disadvantaged people to the End-Times Retreat Center with promises of food. Evan must act when a young woman from his church and her invalid mother disappear inside the internment camp. Fourth in the award-winning series.

Chapter 1

"Reverend Wycliff, much of what you believe in your Christian faith is true, but not for the reasons you believe."

The grizzled old man at my door was muttering in heavily accented English, but his message was unmistakable. It didn't help my perception that I was severely hungover, having spent most of the night alternately guzzling cheap bourbon and praying.

It was a spring morning, only slightly chilly, promising a day that might be perfectly fine. I was clad in my habitual sweatsuit, which might well have reeked, but I'd grown so accustomed to my own stink I wouldn't know. I worried he did, even though his outward appearance was no more respectable than mine. He was dressed in a black business suit, but it wasn't his size and looked rumpled and dirty, as if he'd been sleeping in doorways.

I'd finally managed to drop off to sleep moments before a polite knock on my door, and I was having trouble keeping my eyes open.

"You've made coffee?" he asked with an approving sniff. It wasn't so much a question as an insistent hint. When I had prepared with undue optimism last night to crawl into bed, I'd set the automatic drip machine for precisely this hour.

It seems I have no choice but to invite him in.

I still hadn't greeted him or said a word yet. I simply opened the door to my humble cube-sized trailer home and waved toward its shabby interior.

On the narrow counter where I undertake food preparations often no more complex than opening a can, I could only find one crusty mug. As he jostled behind me and sat in the only chair, I rummaged in the wall-mounted crate that housed dinnerware, condiments, and pharmaceuticals. I was delighted to find a second cup, this one emblazoned with the logo of Twin Dragons Casino. I couldn't remember the last time I'd needed to use it, but it looked reasonably clean.

I filled both cups from the steaming carafe, turned to offer him his, and before I could finally manage to speak to ask his preferences, he blurted what sounded like, "*Kine krim, kine sook.* Trying to quit *zucker.*"

German, I realized. Or perhaps his accent was of some other Eastern European extraction, and he was telling me he'd be more comfortable if I shared his other common language.

I sat down on my cot and blew out a puff of exhaustion, doubly fatigued after my long, dark night of the soul and the presumably unpleasant surprise of this intrusion on my unenviable privacy.

We both sipped, reverently it seemed.

He smacked his lips before he sighed and said, "I took long time finding you. Fortunately, your neighbors are shameless gossips."

I took another restorative sip, cleared my throat, and asked gruffly, "To what do I owe the pleasure, Mister …?"

"Doctor Hans Gropius. Forgive the similarity in name to the famous historical person, but no relation. The surname not my choice, of course. People assume I must be from family of architects." He sipped again, this time long and noisily, then added with a chuckle, "Although I stand in awe of the grand design."

Somehow I caught the hint. My brain was waking up. There had to be a reason this fellow had taken pains to seek *me* out. So I asked, "Design? Physical or spiritual?"

He chuckled again. "Insight, you have! I knew I was in the right place. I simply toss out phrases that suggest scheme of Creation, and you jump on it. Clever fellow. We are going to be friends, I am sure of it."

I cautioned him by displaying the upraised palms of my hands. It occurred to me he might think I was intending to show him stigmata or perhaps pre-Parkinson's tremor, which might seem crazy, but based on his behavior so far I had no reason to expect he was sane either. "When you talk about what I believe, I don't know how you'd know. I will say I'm not an agnostic, although certainly I've been accused of such. I insist I am a man of faith, but faith in what mostly defies definition, depends on the day and my mood."

He smiled, explaining, "I was faithful listener to your broadcasts until you went off the air. The news of your resignation from your ministry was also upsetting."

"I didn't resign. I was kicked out, but the result is the same. I suppose my tumble downhill began when my wife left me. Turns out being a minister's wife is an even heavier cross to bear than being a pastor. And as for my show, I tried to speak truth to power one too many times."

"Do you believe in afterlife?" he asked quietly.

At that moment, I wished the coffee were bourbon and I could stiffen myself with a shot. I began to worry he might be a journalist or some emissary from church leadership sent to chastise me, but I decided I might as well answer as honestly as I could. "I don't believe in resurrection of the body — as a living, breathing, human body. But reincarnation? Transference of consciousness from one being — or state of being — to another? I won't say it's impossible. I worry it's not, but because I have an obsessively curious intellect, I worry a lot."

"My dear Evan," he began then stopped himself to ask, "May I address you so? I feel I know you so well, you see."

His manner was amusing, endearing. "Go ahead," I allowed. "Please tell me more about myself than I know, and I'll gift you another cup of coffee."

He loved this. Grinning broadly, he teased, "You are, of course, aware of virtual reality?"

"Sure," I said, "but can't say I've indulged. Not games for kids anymore, I understand. Frankly, it's scary."

"And you know work of physicist Nick Bostrum?"

"I do," I admitted. "Not in depth, but I believe he's famous for speculating we don't live in what's termed *base reality.*"

"Just so," the visitor said approvingly. "We say now we live in post-information age. Soon we live in post-reality. Dreaming, waking — who can know the difference?"

"What are you trying to tell me, Hans?"

"My dear Evan, you are a man of faith. You believe what you cannot see. We scientists, we say seeing is believing. I'm here to tell you that seeing means nothing anymore."

EXPLORE THE SERIES
(YOU NEEDN'T READ THEM IN SEQUENCE)

Preacher Finds a Corpse (#1)

A lapsed divinity student who is fascinated by astrophysics finds his best friend shot dead in a cornfield. It looks like suicide. Having returned to his farm roots near Lake of the Ozarks, Evan works as a skip tracer for the local car dealer. He learns his friend was involved in a dispute over farmland ownership that goes back two centuries - complicated now by plans to make an old weapons facility a tourist attraction.

Paperback · Kindle · EPUB · Audiobook

Preacher Fakes a Miracle (#2)

Evan often gets dragged into dealing with problems others have given up solving. An orphanage serves young women, and some get placed in part-time work at the lakeside resorts. They're supposed to be working in the laundry, but some get recruited as escorts for favored guests. And then one goes missing. Along with related abuses of the child welfare system, Evan uncovers the teen trafficking ring run out of a luxury casino resort by a Russian oligarch.

Paperback · Kindle · EPUB

Preacher Raises the Dead (#3)

A full-time minister now, Evan visits the hospitals. He attends to near-death experience, late-stage dementia, long-term coma, and consequences of the pandemic. His old nemesis investment banker Stuart Shackleton is back — and claims to be converted. Shackleton's money sustains a critical-care medical breakthrough, the building of a new church, and a career boost for Evan as a celebrity evangelist. Has Evan sold his soul?

Paperback · Kindle · EPUB

This Book - Preacher Stalls the Second Coming (#4)

A crazed scientist knocks on Evan's door with a bizarre warning - the Deep State may be planning to fake the Second Coming of Christ with advanced virtual-reality technology. Meanwhile, a faith-healing evangelist is luring poor and homeless people to a religious retreat with promises of ample food, then exhorting them to prepare for the End Times by starving themselves to death. Evan can't ignore these unbelievable stories when a young woman from his church disappears inside the cult leader's farm.

Paperback · Kindle

ACKNOWLEDGMENTS

In writing the Evan Wycliff Mystery series, I've surprised myself many times over. It will therefore surprise me if readers find anything in the plots predictable. I resolved at the outset to let my subconscious self do most of the work. And after the stage was set and the characters stepped onto it, many times they told me where they wanted to go and said whatever they wanted to say. I haven't always worked like this. Years ago, when I wrote mainly technical and business nonfiction for publishing houses, I wrote to strict outlines, and I sought approval from in-house editors if ever I chose to depart from the agreed plan.

When I set out to write *Preacher Raises the Dead,* I had the notion of describing both near-death experience (NDE) and coma. In the beginning, I didn't know who would be stricken or how those subplots would turn out. Many other plot elements were likewise uncertain right up until the words flowed into the manuscript draft, including Evan's core religious beliefs and consequences of Luke's schizophrenia and Melissa's epilepsy. The reappearance of Stuart Shackleton was a complete surprise until Evan saw him again that fateful day in the courtroom. He and I should have known we weren't done with him yet!

Although these novels are fiction – and perhaps implausible at times – I did inform the narrative with research and fact-checking, especially on its controversial topics. I am indebted to Dennis Hutchison, coproprietor of Afterglow of Sedona, for pointing me to a variety of esoteric books, including memoirs about NDE. Dr. Esther Hennig reviewed the manuscript for medical realism, particularly the treatment of long-term coma. Editorial assistants Jillian Pincus and Emma Graham researched scholarly publications on NDE and coma, along with Missouri law on "right to die" and Southern Baptist ordination policy. Nonetheless, no one should regard anything in this book as reliable advice on any of these issues.

My street-team of professional colleagues generously provided early reviews of drafts to help me recover from goofs, gaffes, and logic gaps. Any errors that remain are entirely my own responsibility. These pros include Roberta Edgar, Ina Hillebrandt, John Rachel, Pamela Jaye Smith, Clyve Rose, Edgar Scott, and Paula Berinstein. All are esteemed published authors themselves. Thanks also to Jason Letts for his careful editorial notes.

Evan's theology is bound to be controversial. The very thought of a practicing minister who is too often an agnostic will raise eyebrows. But do churchpersons have occasional doubts? I don't doubt it. My limited understanding of cosmology and astrophysics has most recently been updated by Brian Greene's brilliant survey, *Until the End of Time.* Much of Evan's theology can be found in the New Thought religious movement and the writings of Ernest Holmes, who was said to have approached guests at parties asking, "Don't you think God is all that there is?" (Spinoza would have agreed.) I applied my father's scholarship on the Jonah story from his book *Searching for Jonah: Clues in Hebrew and Assyrian History.* Thanks also to publicists Desiree Duffy, A. G. Billig, Anna Tjeltveit, and Lu Ann Sodano for their tireless efforts to find Evan a wider audience.

Finally, my wife Georja Umano has sustained, supported, and inspired me. Her work in journalism, environmental sustainability, and wildlife conservation is remarkable and tireless. And her recently released novel, *Terriers in the Jungle,* touches on all of these efforts while being a delightful tale narrated by two endearing little dogs.

Gerald Everett Jones

Santa Monica, California

January 2022

ABOUT THE AUTHOR

GERALD EVERETT JONES is a freelance writer who lives in Santa Monica, California. He has been a longtime board member of the Independent Writers of Southern California (IWOSC) and host of the GetPublished! Radio podcast. He holds a Bachelor of Arts with Honors from the College of Letters, Wesleyan University, where he studied under novelists Peter Boynton *(Stone Island)*, F.D. Reeve *(The Red Machines)*, and Jerzy Kosinski *(The Painted Bird, Being There)*.

Find out more at geraldeverettjones.com, and read his Thinking About Thinking blog posts at geraldeverettjones.substack.com.

ALSO BY GERALD EVERETT JONES

Fiction

Harry Harambee's Kenyan Sundowner: A Novel – Multiple awards in Literary Fiction

Preacher Finds a Corpse (Evan Wycliff #1) – Multiple awards in Mystery

Preacher Fakes a Miracle (Evan Wycliff #2) – NYC Big Book Silver 2020

Preacher Raises the Dead (Evan Wycliff #3) – Multiple awards in Mystery

Preacher Stalls the Second Coming (Evan Wycliff #4)

Mick & Moira & Brad: A Romantic Comedy - Multiple awards in Romantic Comedy

Clifford's Spiral: A Novel – IPA Silver in Literary Fiction 2020

Mr. Ballpoint – Page Turner Award in Fiction Finalist 2022

Christmas Karma – WGA Diversity Award (Screenplay) 2016

Choke Hold: An Eli Wolff Thriller

Bonfire of the Vanderbilts: A Novel / *Bonfire of the Vanderbilts: Scholar's Edition*

My Inflatable Friend (Misadventures of Rollo Hemphill #1)

Rubber Babes (Misadventures of Rollo Hemphill #2)

Farnsworth's Revenge (Misadventures of Rollo Hemphill #3)

Stories and Essay *Boychik Lit*

Nonfiction

How to Lie with Charts - Eric Hoffer Award Finalist in Business 2020

The Death of Hypatia and the End of Fate

The Light in His Soul: Lessons from My Brother's Schizophrenia (with Rebecca Schaper)

Searching for Jonah: Clues in Hebrew and Assyrian History by Don E. Jones (Afterword)

www.ingramcontent.com/pod-product-compliance
Lightning Source LLC
Chambersburg PA
CBHW020236260626
47156CB00002B/701